Kingdoms of Sorcery

OTHER BOOKS BY LIN CARTER

Fiction:

AS THE GREEN STAR RISES
BEYOND THE GATES OF DREAM
BLACK LEGION OF CALLISTO
THE BLACK STAR
BY THE LIGHT OF THE GREEN STAR
CONAN (with Robert E. Howard and L. Sprague de Camp)
CONAN OF CIMMERIA (with Robert E. Howard and L. Sprague de Camp)
CONAN OF THE ISLES (with L. Sprague de Camp)
CONAN THE BUCCANEER (with L. Sprague de Camp)
CONAN THE WANDERER (with Robert E. Howard and L. Sprague de Camp)
DESTINATION: SATURN (with David Grinnell)
THE ENCHANTRESS OF WORLD'S END
FLAME OF IRIDAR
THE GIANT OF WORLD'S END
IN THE GREEN STAR'S SPELL
INVISIBLE DEATH
JANDAR OF CALLISTO
KING KULL (with Robert E. Howard)
LANKAR OF CALLISTO
LOST WORLD OF TIME
MAD EMPRESS OF CALLISTO
THE MAN WHO LOVED MARS

THE MAN WITHOUT A PLANET
MIND WIZARDS OF CALLISTO
THE NEMESIS OF EVIL
OUTWORLDER
THE PURLOINED PLANET
THE QUEST OF KADJI
SKY PIRATES OF CALLISTO
THE STAR MAGICIANS
STAR ROGUE
THE STONE FROM MNAR
THIEF OF THOTH
THONGOR AND THE WIZARD OF LEMURIA
THONGOR AND THE DRAGON CITY
THONGOR AGAINST THE GODS
THONGOR IN THE CITY OF MAGICIANS
THONGOR AT THE END OF TIME
THONGOR FIGHTS THE PIRATES OF TARAKUS
TIME WAR
TOWER AT THE EDGE OF TIME
TOWER OF THE MEDUSA
UNDER THE GREEN STAR
THE VALLEY WHERE TIME STOOD STILL
THE VOLCANO OGRE
THE WARRIOR OF WORLD'S END
WHEN THE GREEN STAR CALLS

Kingdoms
of
Sorcery

Edited by
LIN CARTER

DOUBLEDAY & COMPANY, INC.

GARDEN CITY, NEW YORK

1976

Library of Congress Cataloging in Publication Data
Main entry under title:
Kingdoms of sorcery.
Includes bibliographical references.
CONTENTS: Voltaire. The history of Babouc the
Scythian.—Beckford, W. The palace of subterranean fire.
—Macdonald, G. The witch woman. [etc.]
1. Fantastic fiction, English. 2. Fantastic fiction,
American. I. Carter, Lin.
PZ1.K5824 [PR1309.F3]
ISBN 0-385-09975-4
Library of Congress Catalog Card Number 75-14810

"A Night-Piece on Ambremerine" is from *Mistress of Mistresses* by E. R. Eddison (E. P. Dutton & Co., Inc., 1935), copyright © 1935 by E. P. Dutton & Co., Inc. By arrangement with E. P. Dutton & Co., Inc.

"Dr. Meliboë the Enchanter" is from *The Well of the Unicorn* by George U. Fletcher (pseud. Fletcher Pratt) (William Sloane Associates, 1948), copyright © 1948 by William Sloane Associates. By permission of the Estate of Fletcher Pratt.

"The Two Best Thieves in Lankhmar" is from *Swords Against Wizardry* by Fritz Leiber. (Ace Books, Inc., 1968), copyright © 1968 by Fritz Leiber. By arrangement with Fritz Leiber.

"Fables from the Edge of Night" by Clark Ashton Smith appeared as follows: "Sadastor" in *Weird Tales*, July 1930, copyright © 1930 by The Popular Fiction Publishing Company; "The Passing of Aphrodite" in *The Fantasy Fan*, December 1934; "From the Crypts of Memory" in *Ebony and Crystal*, copyright © 1922 by Clark Ashton Smith. By arrangement with the Estate of Clark Ashton Smith.

"Merlyn vs. Madame Mim" is from *The Sword in the Stone* by T. H. White (G. P. Putnam's Sons, 1939), copyright © 1939 by T. H. White. By permission of G. P. Putnam's Sons.

"The Owl and the Ape" is from *Imagination*, November 1951, copyright © 1951 by *Imagination*. By arrangement with L. Sprague de Camp.

For Philip José Farmer,
whose own "kingdoms of sorcery"
have given me many hours of
marvelous entertainment

CONTENTS

IV. *Fantasy as Anecdote*

V. *Fantasy as Epic*

The Introduction:

MAGIC CASEMENTS

Fantasy is simultaneously the most maligned, ignored, overlooked, ancient and respectable of fictional genre. But you would never know this from a look at the library shelves, where it is either jumbled in with science fiction or relegated to the children's section. As far as the librarians and the teachers are concerned, it either does not exist as a separate school of literature, or belongs somewhere between the fairy tales and the sci-fi.

Those dedicated and solemn scholars who compile our official dictionaries unfortunately agree. I have a typical product of their labors before me on my desk as I write these words (more in anger than in sorrow). Calling itself *The American College Dictionary*, first published in 1947 and last "revised and updated" in 1956, it defines fantasy as:

1. imagination, esp. when unrestrained. 2. the forming of grotesque mental images. 3. a mental image, esp. when grotesque. 4. *Psychol.* an imaginative sequence, fulfilling a psychological need; a daydream. 5. a hallucination. 6. a supposition based on no solid foundation; a visionary idea. 7. caprice; whim. 8. an ingenious or odd thought, design, or invention. Also *phantasy.* —Syn.1. See *fancy.*

So much for the bright boys who compile dictionaries, yet are not even aware of the existence of an entire world of literature which can be dated back through Malory and Spenser, *Orlando Furioso* and *The Faerie Queene* and *Amadis of Gaul,* to the very beginnings of literature itself in the Homeric poems, the Greek myths, the Sumerian epics.

Phrased as succinctly as I can manage it, a fantasy is a story which does not reflect reality as we know it, or, more accurately,

presents us with an *alternate* reality. A reality essentially the same
as the one we live in (and with), but stretched into new contours in
order to accommodate a new element. And that element is that
there really *are* gods and ghosts, demons and dragons; that magic
does *so* work and hence enchanted swords and magicians' spells
and amulets and curses have genuine power.

Once you have reshaped the universe in order to fit in this new
ingredient, obviously you have to redesign the entire world. A
world in which heroes battle with charmed swords would probably
never bother inventing gunpowder; a world where wizards can fly
about on dragonback or in wyvern-drawn chariots has no need for
six-lane highways. For this reason, most of the writers who have
explored the shadowy margins of the fantasy world have preferred
to lay their stories amid invented scenery or in milieus born in the
writer's imagination, and therefore not to be found in history books
or geographies.

The kingdoms of sorcery and realms of wizardry are many and
richly varied. Here I have put together an entire bookful of them
for your entertainment and amusement. And for those among you
who might like to know just a little about how such stories came to
be written, and who wrote them, I have added notes to each tale—
which you may safely skip, if all you want is a good story that en-
tertains you.

Entertainment is a much-maligned quality rare in modern fiction.
Today's writers feel vaguely uncomfortable unless they are striving
to arouse you to the eminent dangers of rampant pollution, world
socialism, depletion of the ozone layer in the upper stratosphere,
the population problem, or some other doubtless worthy but irrele-
vant cause. Fiction has no cause: it exists, or should exist, to entertain you. By entertain, I mean *divert*: to take your mind away from
yourself, your own life, your own problems, to refresh and re-create
you.

School teachers, literary critics, and other good people tend to
class this as *escapism* and to condemn it as being essentially frivolous. This is nonsense, of course; playing chess, listening to Bach
(or rock), working a mathematical problem, or studying the
eclipses of the moons of Jupiter are equally escapist pursuits. *Anything* that takes you out of yourself—philosophy, music, drama, all
literature and poetry—is sheer, unabased escapism. Show me why
reading Tolstoy, Dostoevsky, Kafka or Vonnegut is any less a
wallowing in sheer escapist reading than reading fantasy or science

fiction, and I will swallow my words. (But I'm safe, because you *can't!*)

A story is a window into another person's life experience, virtually another world. A *"charm'd magic casement,"* in that fine phrase of Keats's,

> *opening on the foam*
> *Of perilous seas, in faery lands forlorn.*

—LIN CARTER

Hollis, Long Island, New York

Kingdoms of Sorcery

It is not down on any map;
true places never are.

—Herman Melville/*Moby Dick*

Kingdoms of Sorcery

I.
The Forerunners
of
Modern Fantasy

VOLTAIRE

BECAUSE you must reshape the world or build a new one in writing a fantasy, the genre of the fantastic narrative has appealed to many very different writers for many very different reasons. Voltaire, for instance, used fantasy to satirize the social conditions of his time, to puncture the complacent pomposities of human nature, and to ridicule the shibboleths of the state without getting into any more trouble with the authorities than he had gotten into already. (It's easy to make fun of the policies of the French Government of your time, if, instead of calling the country "France" you call it "Persia"—and make it a neverneverland Persia, to boot.)

Voltaire was a French wit, philosopher, dramatist, playwright, poet and polymath. The Socrates of his day, he, too, was a gadfly, busily stinging the statesmen and clergy of his time as Socrates did in his own. Born François Marie Arouet (1694–1778), he wrote under the pen name of "Voltaire," which in the language and in the orthography of his period could be seen as an anagram for "Arouet,

Jr." By sheer instinct or genius—he had copious amounts of both—
he knew that you could pack a lot of propaganda and preaching
into a tale if only you sugar-coat it with entertainment. Which is
why his fables and romances have lived for three hundred years
while the drearier, more didactic preachments of his contemporaries crumble unread.

He is best known, I suppose, for a rather tiresome and episodic
novella called *Candide,* which I personally find a bore. If you enjoy
the wit and sparkle of the following short fable (never before
anthologized), look up *Zadig,* or *The Princess of Babylon,* or *The
White Bull.* They are among the most delightful fantasies ever written.

THE HISTORY OF BABOUC THE SCYTHIAN

AMONG the genii who preside over the empires of the earth,
Ithuriel held one of the first ranks, and had the department of
Upper Asia. He one morning descended into the abode of Babouc,
the Scythian, who dwelt on the banks of the Oxus, and said to him:

"Babouc, the follies and vices of the Persians have drawn upon
them our indignation. Yesterday an assembly of the genii of Upper
Asia was held, to consider whether we would chastise Persepolis or
destroy it entirely. Go to that city; examine everything; return and
give me a faithful account; and, according to thy report, I will then
determine whether to correct or extirpate the inhabitants."

"But, my lord," said Babouc with great humility, "I have never
been in Persia, nor do I know a single person in that country."

"So much the better," said the angel, "thou wilt be the more im-
partial: thou hast received from heaven the spirit of discernment, to
which I now add the power of inspiring confidence. Go, see, hear,
observe, and fear nothing. Thou shalt everywhere meet with a favorable reception."

Babouc mounted his camel, and set out with his servants. After
having traveled some days, he met, near the plains of Senaar, the
Persian army, which was going to attack the forces of India. He first

addressed himself to a soldier, whom he found at a distance from the main army, and asked him what was the occasion of the war?

"By all the gods," said the soldier, "I know nothing of the matter. It is none of my business. My trade is to kill and to be killed, to get a livelihood. It is of no consequence to me whom I serve. To-morrow, perhaps, I may go over to the Indian camp; for it is said that they give their soldiers nearly half a copper drachma a day more than we have in this cursed service of Persia. If thou desires to know why we fight, speak to my captain."

Babouc, having given the soldier a small present, entered the camp. He soon became acquainted with the captain, and asked him the cause of the war.

"How canst thou imagine that I should know it?" said the captain, "or of what importance is it to me? I live about two hundred leagues from Persepolis: I hear that war is declared: I instantly leave my family, and, having nothing else to do, go, according to our custom, to make my fortune, or to fall by a glorious death."

"But are not thy companions," said Babouc, "a little better informed than thee?"

"No," said the officer, "there are none but our principal satraps that know the true cause of our cutting one another's throats."

Babouc, struck with astonishment, introduced himself to the generals, and soon became familiarly acquainted with them. At last one of them said:

"The cause of this war, which for twenty years past hath desolated Asia, sprang originally from a quarrel between a eunuch belonging to one of the concubines of the great king of Persia, and the clerk of a factory belonging to the great king of India. The dispute was about a claim which amounted nearly to the thirtieth part of a daric. Our first minister, and the representative of India, maintained the rights of their respective masters with becoming dignity. The dispute grew warm. Both parties sent into the field an army of a million of soldiers. This army must be recruited every year with upwards of four hundred thousand men. Massacres, burning of houses, ruin and devastation, are daily multiplied; the universe suffers; and their mutual animosity still continues. The first ministers of the two nations frequently protest that they have nothing in view but the happiness of mankind; and every protestation is attended with the destruction of a town, or the desolation of a province."

Next day, on a report being spread that peace was going to be concluded, the Persian and Indian generals made haste to come to an engagement. The battle was long and bloody. Babouc beheld every crime, and every abomination. He was witness to the arts and stratagems of the principal satraps, who did all that lay in their power to expose their general to the disgrace of a defeat. He saw officers killed by their own troops, and soldiers stabbing their already expiring comrades in order to strip them of a few bloody garments torn and covered with dirt. He entered the hospitals to which they were conveying the wounded, most of whom died through the inhuman negligence of those who were well paid by the king of Persia to assist these unhappy men.

"Are these men," cried Babouc, "or are they wild beasts? Ah! I plainly see that Persepolis will be destroyed."

Full of this thought, he went over to the camp of the Indians, where, according to the prediction of the genii, he was as well received as in that of the Persians; but he saw there the same crimes which had already filled him with horror.

"Oh!" said he to himself, "if the angel Ithuriel should exterminate the Persians, the angel of India must certainly destroy the Indians."

But being afterward more particularly informed of all that passed in both armies, he heard of such acts of generosity, humanity, and greatness of soul, as at once surprised and charmed him:

"Unaccountable mortals! as ye are," cried he, "how can you thus unite so much baseness and so much grandeur, so many virtues and so many vices?"

Meanwhile the peace was proclaimed; and the generals of the two armies, neither of whom had gained a complete victory, but who, for their own private interest, had shed the blood of so many of their fellow-creatures, went to solicit their courts for rewards. The peace was celebrated in public writings which announced the return of virtue and happiness to the earth.

"God be praised," said Babouc, "Persepolis will now be the abode of spotless innocence, and will not be destroyed, as the cruel genii intended. Let us haste without delay to this capital of Asia."

He entered that immense city by the ancient gate, which was entirely barbarous, and offended the eye by its disagreeable rusticity. All that part of the town savored of the time when it was built; for, notwithstanding the obstinacy of men in praising ancient at the expense of modern times, it must be owned that the first essays in every art are rude and unfinished.

Babouc mingled in a crowd of people composed of the most igno-

rant, dirty and deformed of both sexes, who were thronging with a
stupid air into a large and gloomy inclosure. By the constant hum;
by the gestures of the people; by the money which some persons
gave to others for the liberty of sitting down, he imagined that he
was in a market, where chairs were sold; but observing several
women fall down on their knees with an appearance of looking directly before them, while in reality they were leering at the men by
their sides, he was soon convinced that he was in a temple. Shrill,
hoarse, savage and discordant voices made the vault re-echo with ill-
articulated sounds, that produced the same effect as the braying of
asses, when, in the plans of Pictavia, they answer the cornet that
calls them together. He stopped his ears; but he was ready to shut
his mouth and hold his nose, when he saw several laborers enter
into the temple with picks and spades, who removed a large stone,
and threw up the earth on both sides, from whence exhaled a
pestilential vapor. At last some others approached, deposited a
dead body in the opening, and replaced the stone upon it.

"What!" cried Babouc, "do these people bury their dead in the
place where they adore the deity? What! are their temples paved
with carcasses? I am no longer surprised at those pestilential
diseases that frequently depopulate Persepolis. The putrefaction of
the dead, and the infected breath of such numbers of the living,
assembled and crowded together in the same place are sufficient
to poison the whole terrestrial globe. Oh! what an abominable city
is Persepolis! The angels probably intend to destroy it in order to
build a more beautiful one in its place, and to people it with inhabitants who are more virtuous and better singers. Providence may
have its reasons for so doing; to its disposal let us leave all future
events."

Meanwhile the sun approached his meridian height. Babouc was
to dine at the other end of the city with a lady for whom her husband, an officer in the army, had given him some letters: but he
first took several turns in Persepolis, where he saw other temples,
better built and more richly adorned, filled with a polite audience,
and resounding with harmonious music. He beheld public fountains, which, though ill-placed, struck the eye by their beauty;
squares where the best kings that had governed Persia seemed to
breathe in bronze, and others where he heard the people crying
out:

"When shall we see our beloved master?"

He admired the magnificent bridges built over the river; the superb and commodious quay; the palaces raised on both sides; and an immense house, where thousands of old soldiers, covered with scars and crowned with victory, offered their daily praises to the god of armies. At last he entered the house of the lady, who, with a set of fashionable people, waited his company to dinner. The house was neat and elegant; the repast delicious; the lady, young, beautiful, witty, and engaging; and the company worthy of her; and Babouc every moment said to himself:

"The angel Ithuriel has little regard for the world, or he would never think of destroying such a charming city."

In the meantime he observed that the lady, who had begun by tenderly asking news about her husband, spoke more tenderly to a young magi, toward the conclusion of the repast. He saw a magistrate, who, in presence of his wife, paid his court with great vivacity to a widow, while the indulgent widow held out her hand to a young citizen, remarkable for his modesty and graceful appearance.

Babouc then began to fear that the genius Ithuriel had but too much reason for destroying Persepolis. The talent he possessed of gaining confidence let him that same day into all the secrets of the lady. She confessed to him her affection for the young magi, and assured him that in all the houses in Persepolis he would meet with similar examples of attachment. Babouc concluded that such a society could not possibly survive: that jealousy, discord, and vengeance must desolate every house; that tears and blood must be daily shed; and, in fine, that Ithuriel would do well to destroy immediately a city abandoned to continual disasters.

Such were the gloomy ideas that possessed his mind, when a grave man in a black gown appeared at the gate and humbly begged to speak to the young magistrate. This stripling, without rising or taking the least notice of the old gentleman, gave him some papers with a haughty and careless air, and then dismissed him. Babouc asked who this man was. The mistress of the house said to him in a low voice:

"He is one of the best advocates in the city, and hath studied the law these fifty years. The other, who is but twenty-five years of age, and has only been a satrap of the law for two days, hath ordered him to make an extract of a process he is going to determine, though he has not as yet examined it."

"This giddy youth acts wisely," said Babouc, "in asking counsel of an old man. But why is not the old man himself the judge?"

"Thou art surely in jest," said they; "those who have grown old in laborious and inferior posts are never raised to places of dignity. This young man has a great post, because his father is rich; and the right of dispensing justice is purchased here like a farm."

"O unhappy city!" cried Babouc, "this is surely the height of anarchy and confusion. Those who have thus purchased the right of judging will doubtless sell their judgments; nothing do I see here but an abyss of iniquity!"

While he was thus expressing his grief and surprise, a young warrior, who that very day had returned from the army, said to him:

"Why wouldst thou not have seats in the courts of justice offered for sale? I myself purchased the right of braving death at the head of two thousand men who are under my command. It has this year cost me forty darics of gold to lie on the earth thirty nights successively in a red dress, and at last to receive two wounds with an arrow, of which I still feel the smart. If I ruin myself to serve the emperor of Persia, whom I never saw, the satrap of the law may well pay something for enjoying the pleasure of giving audience to pleaders."

Babouc was filled with indignation, and could not help condemning a country, where the highest posts in the army and the law were exposed for sale. He at once concluded that the inhabitants must be entirely ignorant of the art of war, and the laws of equity; and that, though Ithuriel should not destroy them, they must soon be ruined by their detestable administration.

He was still further confirmed in his bad opinion by the arrival of a fat man, who, after saluting all the company with great familiarity, went up to the young officer and said:

"I can only lend thee fifty thousand darics of gold; for indeed the taxes of the empire have this year brought me in but three hundred thousand."

Babouc inquired into the character of this man who complained of having gained so little, and was informed that in Persepolis there were forty plebeian kings who held the empire of Persia by lease, and paid a small tribute to the monarch.

After dinner he went into one of the most superb temples in the city, and seated himself amidst a crowd of men and women, who had come thither to pass away the time. A magi appeared in a machine elevated above the heads of the people, and talked a long time of vice and virtue. He divided into several parts what needed no division at all: he proved methodically what was sufficiently clear, and he taught what everybody knew. He threw himself into a passion with great composure, and went away perspiring and out of breath. The assembly then awoke and imagined they had been present at a very instructive discourse. Babouc said:

"This man had done his best to tire two or three hundred of his fellow-citizens; but his intention was good, and there is nothing in this that should occasion the destruction of Persepolis."

Upon leaving the assembly he was conducted to a public entertainment, which was exhibited every day in the year. It was in a kind of great hall, at the end of which appeared a palace. The most beautiful women of Persepolis and the most considerable satraps were ranged in order, and formed so fine a spectacle that Babouc at first believed that this was all the entertainment. Two or three persons, who seemed to be kings and queens, soon appeared in the vestibule of their palace. Their language was very different from that of their people; it was measured, harmonious, and sublime. Nobody slept. The audience kept a profound silence which was only interrupted by expressions of sensibility and admiration. The duty of kings, the love of virtue, and the dangers arising from unbridled passions, were all described by such lively and affecting strokes, that Babouc shed tears. He doubted not but that these heroes and heroines, these kings and queens whom he had just heard, were the preachers of the empire; he even purposed to engage Ithuriel to come and hear them, being confident that such a spectacle would forever reconcile him to the city.

As soon as the entertainment was finished, he resolved to visit the principal queen, who had recommended such pure and noble morals in the palace. He desired to be introduced to her majesty, and was led up a narrow staircase to an ill-furnished apartment in the second story, where he found a woman in a mean dress, who said to him with a noble and pathetic air:

"This employment does not afford me a sufficient maintenance. I want money, and without money there is no comfort."

Babouc gave her an hundred darics of gold, saying:

"Had there been no other evil in the city but this, Ithuriel would have been to blame for being so much offended."

From thence he went to spend the evening at the house of a tradesman who dealt in magnificent trifles. He was conducted thither by a man of sense, with whom he had contracted an acquaintance. He bought whatever pleased his fancy; and the toy man with great politeness sold him everything for more than it was

worth. On his return home his friends showed him how much he
had been cheated. Babouc set down the name of the tradesman in
his pocketbook, in order to point him out to Ithuriel as an object of
peculiar vengeance on the day when the city should be punished.
As he was writing, he heard somebody knock at the door: this was
the toy man himself, who came to restore him his purse, which he
had left by mistake on the counter.

"How canst thou," cried Babouc, "be so generous and faithful,
when thou hast had the assurance to sell me these trifles for four
times their value?"

"There is not a tradesman," replied the merchant, "of ever so little note in the city, that would not have returned thee thy purse;
but whoever said that I sold thee these trifles for four times their
value is greatly mistaken: I sold them for ten times their value; and
this is so true, that wert thou to sell them again in a month hence,
thou wouldst not get even this tenth part. But nothing is more just.
It is the variable fancies of men that set a value on these baubles; it
is this fancy that maintains an hundred workmen whom I employ;
it is this that gives me a fine house and a handsome chariot and
horses; it is this, in fine, that excites industry, encourages taste,
promotes circulation, and produces abundance.

"I sell the same trifles to the neighboring nation at a much higher
rate than I have sold them to thee, and by these means I am useful
to the empire."

Babouc, after having reflected a moment, erased the tradesman's
name from his tablets.

Babouc, not knowing as yet what to think of Persepolis, resolved
to visit the magi and the men of letters; for, as the one studied wisdom and the other religion, he hoped that they in conjunction
would obtain mercy for the rest of the people. Accordingly, he went
next morning into a college of magi. The archimandrite confessed
to him, that he had an hundred thousand crowns a year for having
taken the vow of poverty, and that he enjoyed a very extensive empire in virtue of his vow of humility; after which he left him with
an inferior brother, who did him the honors of the place.

While the brother was showing him the magnificence of this
house of penitence, a report was spread abroad that Babouc was
come to reform all these houses. He immediately received petitions
from each of them, the substance of which was, "Preserve us and
destroy all the rest." On hearing their apologies, all these societies
were absolutely necessary: on hearing their mutual accusations, they

all deserved to be abolished. He was surprised to find that all the members of these societies were so extremely desirous of edifying the world, that they wished to have it entirely under their dominion.

Soon after a little man appeared, who was a demi-magi, and who said to him:

"I plainly see that the work is going to be accomplished: for Zerdust is returned to earth; and the little girls prophesy, pinching and whipping themselves. We therefore implore thy protection against the great lama."

"What!" said Babouc, "against the royal pontiff, who resides at Tibet?"

"Yes, against him, himself."

"What! you are then making war upon him, and raising armies!"

"No, but he says that man is a free agent, and we deny it. We have written several pamphlets against him, which he never read. Hardly has he heard our name mentioned. He has only condemned us in the same manner as a man orders the trees in his garden to be cleared from caterpillars."

Babouc was incensed at the folly of these men who made profession of wisdom; and at the intrigues of those who had renounced the world; and at the ambition, pride and avarice of such as taught humility and a disinterested spirit: from all which he concluded that Ithuriel had good reason to destroy the whole race.

On his return home, he sent for some new books to alleviate his grief, and in order to exhilarate his spirits, invited some men of letters to dine with him; when, like wasps attracted by a pot of honey, there came twice as many as he desired. These parasites were equally eager to eat and to speak; they praised two sorts of persons, the dead and themselves; but none of their contemporaries, except the master of the house. If any of them happened to drop a smart and witty expression, the rest cast down their eyes and bit their lips out of mere vexation that it had not been said by themselves. They had less dissimulation than the magi, because they had not such grand objects of ambition. Each of them behaved at once with all the meanness of a valet and all the dignity of a great man. They said to each other's face the most insulting things, which they took for strokes of wit. They had some knowledge of the design of Babouc's commission; one of them entreated him in a low voice to extirpate an author who had not praised him sufficiently about five years before; another requested the ruin of a citizen who had never laughed at his comedies; and the third demanded the destruction of the academy because he had not been able to get admitted into it. The repast being ended, each of them departed by himself; for in the whole crowd there were not two men that could endure the company or conversation of each other, except at the houses of the rich, who invited them to their tables. Babouc thought that it would be no great loss to the public if all these vermin were destroyed in the general catastrophe.

Having now got rid of these men of letters, he began to read some new books, where he discovered the true spirit by which his guests had been actuated. He observed with particular indignation those slanderous gazettes, those archives of bad taste, dictated by envy, baseness, and hunger; those ungenerous satires, where the vulture is treated with lenity, and the dove torn in pieces; and those dry and insipid romances, filled with characters of women to whom the author was an utter stranger.

All these detestable writings he committed to the flames, and went to pass the evening in walking. In this excursion he was introduced to an old man possessed of great learning, who had not come to increase the number of his parasites. This man of letters always fled from crowds; he understood human nature, availed himself of his knowledge, and imparted it to others with great discretion. Babouc told him how much he was grieved at what he had seen and read.

"Thou hast read very despicable performances," said the man of letters; "but in all times, in all countries, and in all kinds of literature, the bad swarm and the good are rare. Thou has received into thy house the very dregs of pedantry. In all professions, those who are least worthy of appearing are always sure to present themselves with the greatest impudence. The truly wise live among themselves in retirement and tranquillity; and we have still some men and some books worthy of thy attention."

While he was thus speaking, they were joined by another man of letters; and the conversation became so entertaining and instructive, so elevated above vulgar prejudices, and so conformable to virtue, that Babouc acknowledged he had never heard the like.

"These are men," said he to himself, "whom the angel Ithuriel will not presume to touch, or he must be a merciless being indeed."

Though reconciled to men of letters, he was still enraged against the rest of the nation.

"Thou art a stranger," said the judicious person who was talking to him; "abuses present themselves to thy eyes in crowds, while the good, which lies concealed, and which is even sometimes the result of these very abuses, escapes thy observation."

He then learned that among men of letters there were some who were free from envy; and that even among the magi themselves there were some men of virtue. In fine, he concluded that these great bodies, which by their mutual shocks seemed to threaten their common ruin, were at bottom very salutary institutions; that each society of magi was a check upon its rivals; and that though these rivals might differ in some speculative points, they all taught the same morals, instructed the people, and lived in subjection to the laws; not unlike to those preceptors who watch over the heir of a family while the master of the house watches over them. He conversed with several of these magi, and found them possessed of exalted souls. He likewise learned that even among the fools who pretended to make war on the great lama there had been some men of distinguished merit; and from all these particulars he conjectured that it might be with the manners of Persepolis as it was with the buildings; some of which moved his pity, while others filled him with admiration.

He said to the man of letters:

"I plainly see that these magi, whom I at first imagined to be so dangerous, are in reality extremely useful; especially when a wise government hinders them from rendering themselves too necessary; but thou wilt at least acknowledge that your young magistrates, who purchase the office of a judge as soon as they can mount a horse, must display in their tribunals the most ridiculous impertinence and the most iniquitous perverseness. It would doubtless be better to give these places gratuitously to those old civilians who have spent their lives in the study of the law."

The man of letters replied:

"Thou hast seen our army before thy arrival at Persepolis; thou knowest that our young officers fight with great bravery, though they buy their posts; perhaps thou wilt find that our young magistrates do not give wrong decisions, though they purchase the right of dispensing justice."

He led him next day to the grand tribunal, where an affair of great importance was to be decided. The cause was known to all the world. All the old advocates that spoke on the subject were wavering and unsettled in their opinions. They quoted an hundred laws, none of which were applicable to the question. They considered the matter in a hundred different lights, but never in its true point of view. The judges were more quick in their decisions than the advocates in raising doubts. They were unanimous in their sentiments. They decided justly, because they followed the light of reason. The others reasoned falsely because they only consulted their books.

Babouc concluded that the best things frequently arose from abuses. He saw the same day that the riches of the receivers of the public revenue, at which he had been so much offended, were capable of producing an excellent effect; for the emperor having occasion for money, he found in an hour by their means what he could not have procured in six months by the ordinary methods. He saw that those great clouds, swelled with the dews of the earth, restored in plentiful showers what they had thence derived. Besides, the children of these new gentlemen, who were frequently better educated than those of the most ancient families, were sometimes more useful members of society; for he whose father hath been a good accountant may easily become a good judge, a brave warrior, and an able statesman.

Babouc was insensibly brought to excuse the avarice of the farmer of the revenues, who in reality was not more avaricious than other men, and besides was extremely necessary. He overlooked the folly of those who ruined themselves in order to obtain a post in the law or army; a folly that produces great magistrates and heroes. He forgave the envy of men of letters, among whom there were some that enlightened the world; and he was reconciled to the ambitious and intriguing magi, who were possessed of more great virtues than little vices. But he had still many causes of complaint. The gallantries of the ladies especially, and the fatal effects which these must necessarily produce, filled him with fear and terror.

As he was desirous of prying into the characters of men of every condition, he went to wait on a minister of state; but trembled all the way, lest some wife should be assassinated by her husband in his presence. Having arrived at the statesman's, he was obliged to remain two hours in the ante-chamber before his name was sent in, and two hours more after that was done. In this interval, he resolved to recommend to the angel Ithuriel both the minister and his insolent porters. The ante-chamber was filled with ladies of every rank, magi of all colors, judges, merchants, officers, and pedants; and all of them complained of the minister. The miser and the usurer said:

"Doubtless this man plunders the provinces."

The capricious reproached him with fickleness; the voluptuary said:

"He thinks of nothing but his pleasure."

The factious hoped to see him soon ruined by a cabal; and the women flattered themselves that they should soon have a younger minister.

Babouc heard their conversation, and could not help saying:

"This is surely a happy man; he hath all his enemies in his ante-chamber; he crushes with his power those that envy his grandeur; he beholds those who detest him groveling at his feet."

At length he was admitted into the presence-chamber, where he saw a little old man bending under the weight of years and business, but still lively and full of spirits.

The minister was pleased with Babouc, and to Babouc he appeared a man of great merit. The conversation became interesting. The minister confessed that he was very unhappy; that he passed for rich, while in reality he was poor; that he was believed to be all-powerful, and yet was constantly contradicted; that he had obliged none but a parcel of ungrateful wretches; and that, in the course of forty years labor, he had hardly enjoyed a moment's rest. Babouc was moved with his misfortunes; and thought that if this man had been guilty of some faults, and Ithuriel had a mind to banish him, he ought not to cut him off, but to leave him in possession of his place.

While Babouc was talking to the minister, the beautiful lady with whom he had dined entered hastily, her eyes and countenance showing all the symptoms of grief and indignation. She burst into reproaches against the statesman; she shed tears; she complained bitterly that her husband had been refused a place to which his birth allowed him to aspire, and which he had fully merited by his wounds and his service. She expressed herself with such force; she uttered her complaints with such a graceful air; she overthrew objections with so much address, and enforced her arguments with so much eloquence, that she did not leave the chamber till she had made her husband's fortune.

Babouc gave her his hand, and said: "Is it possible, madam, that thou canst take so much pains to serve a man whom thou dost not love, and from whom thou hast everything to fear?"

"A man whom I do not love!" cried she; "know, sir, that my husband is the best friend I have in the world; and there is nothing I would not sacrifice for him, except my own inclinations."

The lady conducted Babouc to her own house. The husband, who had at last arrived overwhelmed with grief, received his wife with transports of joy and gratitude. He embraced by turns his wife, the little magi, and Babouc. Wit, harmony, cheerfulness, and all the graces, embellished the repast.

Babouc, though a Scythian, and sent by a geni, found that should he continue much longer in Persepolis, he would forget even the angel Ithuriel. He began to grow fond of a city, the inhabitants of which were polite, affable, and beneficent, though fickle, slanderous, and vain. He was much afraid that Persepolis would be condemned. He was even afraid to give in his account.

This, however, he did in the following manner. He caused a little statue, composed of different metals, of earth, and stones, the most precious and the most vile, to be cast by one of the best founders in the city, and carried it to Ithuriel.

"Wilt thou break," said he, "this pretty statue, because it is not wholly composed of gold and diamonds?"

Ithuriel immediately understood his meaning, and resolved to think no more of punishing Persepolis, but to leave "The world as it goes."

"For," said he, "if all is not well, all is passable."

Thus Persepolis was suffered to remain; nor did Babouc complain like Jonas, who, [according to the scriptures], was highly incensed at the preservation of Nineveh.

WILLIAM BECKFORD

THE fantasy as satire, of course, goes back far before Voltaire—at least as far back as Aristophanes. But did you notice how skillfully Voltaire spun his yarn out of the Fabulous East, probably the East as envisioned by the Greek storytellers such as Herodotus? Voltaire was heavily influenced by the Greek and Roman romancers, encyclopedists, and so-called historians. But he found the Orient a more fertile field than the sober Classical world for his fantasies.

Another early writer who was even more caught up in the color and mystery and glamour of the Orient was the Englishman William Beckford (1760–1844), who was eighteen when Voltaire died. He had by that time already inherited a staggering fortune which made him the wealthiest commoner in England: he lived magnificently, playing with life in a manner and to a degree most of us can only dream about.

For example, lots of rich boys have had private music lessons—but Beckford's tutor was Mozart. And lots of wealthy men build fine country homes—but Beckford built one on what might truly be called the Grand Scale. (The wall around it was twelve feet high—and eight miles long; one of the rooms was three hundred feet long; the front door stood thirty-five feet high, and the *hinges alone* weighed more than a ton.) That's what I call a *house*.

Beckford did everything lavishly, and he did *everything*. At the age of twenty-two, having done a little of everything, he decided to write a novel. To make it more interesting, he composed it in French, and just for a lark he wrote it in three days. Called *Vathek*, it remains the most gorgeously entertaining Arabian Nights fantasy since Scheherazade herself was in her prime. Published in 1785, and now one hundred and ninety years old, it shows absolutely no sign of aging or of becoming "dated." As if a great fantasy could ever become worn out!

And a great fantasy it is: Beckford's flow of imagination is so delicious and sparkling, his language so fluent and nimble, his sense of gusto and color so enchanting, that the book remains a perennially fresh confection. Into it he poured the rich gleanings of a dilettante's study of Islamic lore and legend, and, alas, being Beckford, having once written the novel, he never bothered to write another.

But at least we have *Vathek*. It tells of the long, leisurely honeymoon trip of the Caliph Vathek of Baghdad and his sweetheart, the nubile Nouronihar, for the weird palace of Eblis, the demon prince, who resides within the fabulous Mountain of Kaf and at the world's very edge. I have included here for your pleasure one of its most imaginative scenes, never before anthologized.

THE PALACE OF
SUBTERRANEAN FIRE

AFTER two days of devotion to the pleasures of the Rocnabad, the expedition proceeded, leaving Shiraz on the right, and verging towards a large plain, whence were discernible on the edge of the horizon the dark summits of the mountains of Istakhar. At this prospect the Caliph and Nouronihar were unable to repress their transports. They bounded from their litter to the ground, and broke forth into such wild exclamations as amazed all within hearing. Interrogating each other they shouted, "Are we not approaching the radiant Palace of Light or gardens more delightful than those of Sheddad?" Infatuated mortals! They thus indulged delusive conjecture, unable to fathom the decrees of the Most High!

The good Genie, who had not totally relinquished the superintendence of Vathek, repairing to Mahomet in the seventh heaven, said:

"Merciful Prophet! Stretch forth thy propitious arm towards thy Vicegerent, who is ready to fall irretrievably into the snare which his enemies the Divas have prepared to destroy him. The Giaour is awaiting his arrival in the abominable Palace of Fire, where if he once set his foot his perdition will be inevitable."

Mahomet answered with an air of indignation:

"He hath too well deserved to be resigned to himself, but I permit you to try if one effort more will be effectual to divert him from pursuing his ruin."

One of these beneficent Genii, assuming without delay the exterior of a shepherd more renowned for his piety than all the Dervishes and Santons of the region, took his station near a flock of white sheep on the slope of a hill and began to pour forth from his flute such airs of pathetic melody as subdued the very soul and awakening remorse drove far from it every frivolous fancy. At these energetic sounds the sun hid himself beneath a gloomy cloud, and the waters of two little lakes that were naturally clearer than crystal became of a colour like blood. The whole of this superb assembly was involuntarily drawn towards the declivity of the hill. With downcast eyes they all stood abashed, each upbraiding himself with the evil he had done; the heart of Dilara palpitated, and the chief of the eunuchs with a sigh of contrition implored pardon of the women, whom for his own satisfaction he had so often tormented.

Vathek and Nouronihar turned pale in their litter, and regarding each other with haggard looks reproached themselves—the one with a thousand of the blackest crimes, a thousand projects of impious ambition—the other with the desolation of her family and the perdition of the amiable Gulchenrouz. Nouronihar persuaded herself that she heard in the fatal music the groans of her dying father, and Vathek the sobs of the fifty children he had sacrificed to the Giaour. Amidst these complicated pangs of anguish they perceived themselves impelled towards the shepherd, whose countenance was so commanding that Vathek for the first time felt overawed, whilst Nouronihar concealed her face with her hands.

The music paused, and the Genie, addressing the Caliph, said:

"Deluded Prince, to whom Providence hath confided the care of innumerable subjects, is it thus that thou fulfillest thy mission? Thy crimes are already completed, and art thou now hastening towards thy punishment? Thou knowest that beyond these mountains Eblis and his accursed Divas hold their infernal empire; and seduced by a malignant phantom thou art proceeding to surrender thyself to them! This moment is the last of grace allowed thee; abandon thy atrocious purpose; return; give back Nouronihar to her father, who still retains a few sparks of life; destroy thy tower with all its abominations; drive Carathis from thy councils; be just to thy subjects; respect the ministers of the Prophet; compensate for thy impieties by an exemplary life; and instead of squandering thy days in voluptuous indulgence lament thy crimes on the sepulchres of thy ancestors. Thou beholdest the clouds that obscure the sun; at the instant he recovers his splendour, if thy heart be not changed, the time of mercy assigned thee will be past for ever."

Vathek, depressed with fear, was on the point of prostrating himself at the feet of the shepherd, whom he perceived to be of a nature superior to man; but his pride prevailing, he audaciously lifted his head, and, glancing at him one of his terrible looks said:

"Whoever thou art, withhold thy useless admonitions; thou wouldst either delude me or art thyself deceived. If what I have done be so criminal as thou pretendest there remains not for me a moment of grace. I have traversed a sea of blood to acquire a power which will make thy equals tremble; deem not that I shall retire when in view of the port or that I will relinquish her who is dearer to me than either my life or thy mercy. Let the sun appear! Let him illumine my career! It matters not where it may end."

On uttering these words, which made even the Genie shudder, Vathek threw himself into the arms of Nouronihar and commanded that his horses should be forced back to the road.

There was no difficulty in obeying these orders, for the attraction had ceased. The sun shone forth in all his glory, and the shepherd vanished with a lamentable scream.

The fatal impression of the music of the Genie remained notwithstanding in the heart of Vathek's attendants. They viewed each other with looks of consternation. At the approach of night almost all of them escaped, and of this numerous assemblage there only remained the chief of the eunuchs, some idolatrous slaves, Dilara and a few other women, who like herself were votaries of the religion of the Magi.

The Caliph, fired with the ambition of prescribing laws to the Intelligences of Darkness, was but little embarrassed at this dereliction; the impetuosity of his blood prevented him from sleeping, nor did he encamp any more as before. Nouronihar, whose impatience if possible exceeded his own, importuned him to hasten his march and lavished on him a thousand caresses to beguile all reflection. She fancied herself already more potent than Balkis, and pictured to her imagination the Genii falling prostrate at the foot of her throne. In this manner they advanced by moonlight till they came within view of the two towering rocks that form a kind of portal to the valley, at whose extremity rose the vast ruins of Istakhar. Aloft on the mountain glimmered the fronts of various royal mausoleums, the horror of which was deepened by the shadows of night. They passed through two villages almost deserted, the only inhabitants remaining being a few feeble old men who at the sight of horses and litters fell upon their knees and cried out:

"O heaven! Is it then by these phantoms that we have been for six months tormented? Alas! it was from the terror of these spectres and the noise beneath the mountains that our people have fled and left us at the mercy of maleficent spirits!"

The Caliph, to whom these complaints were but unpromising auguries, drove over the bodies of these wretched old men and at length arrived at the foot of the terrace of black marble. There he descended from his litter, handing down Nouronihar. Both with beating hearts stared wildly around them and expected with an apprehensive shudder the approach of the Giaour; but nothing as yet announced his appearance.

A deathlike stillness reigned over the mountain and through the air; the moon dilated on a vast platform the shades of the lofty columns which reached from the terrace almost to the clouds; the gloomy watch-towers, whose numbers could not be counted, were veiled by no roof, and their capitals, of an architecture unknown in the records of the earth, served as an asylum for the birds of darkness which, alarmed at the approach of such visitants, fled away croaking.

The chief of the eunuchs, trembling with fear, besought Vathek that a fire might be kindled.

"No!" replied he. "There is no time left to think of such trifles. Abide where thou art, and expect my commands."

Having thus spoken he presented his hand to Nouronihar, and ascending the steps of a vast staircase reached the terrace, which was flagged with squares of marble and resembled a smooth expanse of water upon whose surface not a leaf ever dared to vegetate. On the right rose the watch-towers, ranged before the ruins of an immense palace whose walls were embossed with various figures. In front stood forth the colossal forms of four creatures, composed of the leopard and the griffin, and though but of stone inspired emotions of terror. Near these were distinguished by the splendour of the moon which streamed full on the place characters like those on the sabres of the Giaour, that possessed the same virtue of changing every moment. These, after vacillating for some time, at last fixed in Arabic letters, and prescribed to the Caliph the following words:

"Vathek, thou has violated the conditions of my parchment and deservest to be sent back; but in favour to thy companion, and as the meed for what thou has done to obtain it, EBLIS permitteth that the portal of his palace shall be opened, and the subterranean fire will receive thee into the number of its adorers."

He scarcely had read these words before the mountain against which the terrace was reared trembled, and the watch-towers were ready to topple headlong upon them. The rock yawned and disclosed within it a staircase of polished marble that seemed to approach the abyss. Upon each stair were planted two large torches, like those Nouronihar had seen in her vision, the camphorated vapour ascending from which gathered into a cloud under the hollow of the vault.

This appearance instead of terrifying gave new courage to the daughter of Fakreddin. Scarcely deigning to bid adieu to the moon and the firmament she abandoned without hesitation the pure atmosphere to plunge into these infernal exhalations. The gait of those impious personages was haughty and determined. As they descended by the effulgence of the torches they gazed on each other with mutual admiration, and both appeared so resplendent that they already esteemed themselves spiritual Intelligences; the only circumstance that perplexed them was their not arriving at the bottom of the stairs. On hastening their descent with an ardent impetuosity they felt their steps accelerated to such a degree that they seemed not walking but falling from a precipice. Their progress, however, was at length impeded by a vast portal of ebony, which the Caliph without difficulty recognised. Here the Giaour awaited them with the key in his hand.

"Ye are welcome," said he to them, with a ghastly smile, "in spite of Mahomet and all his dependents. I will now admit you into that palace where you have so highly merited a place."

Whilst he was uttering these words he touched the enamelled lock with his key, and the doors at once expanded with a noise still louder than the thunder of mountains, and as suddenly recoiled the moment they had entered.

The Caliph and Nouronihar beheld each other with amazement at finding themselves in a place which though roofed with a vaulted ceiling was so spacious and lofty that at first they took it for an immeasurable plain. But their eyes at length growing familiar with the grandeur of the objects at hand they extended their view to those at a distance and discovered rows of columns and arcades, which gradually diminished till they terminated in a point, radiant as the sun when he darts his last beams athwart the ocean. The pavement, strewed over with gold dust and saffron, exhaled so subtle an odour as almost overpowered them. They, however, went on and observed an infinity of censers in which ambergris and the wood of aloes were continually burning. Between the several columns were placed tables, each spread with a profusion of viands and wines of every species sparkling in vases of crystal. A throng of Genii and other fantastic spirits of each sex danced lasciviously in troops at the sound of music which issued from beneath.

In the midst of this immense hall a vast multitude was incessantly passing, who severally kept their right hands on their hearts without once regarding anything around them. They had all the livid paleness of death; their eyes, deep sunk in their sockets, resembled those phosphoric meteors that glimmer by night in places of interment. Some stalked slowly on, absorbed in profound reverie; some, shrieking with agony, ran furiously about, like tigers wounded with poisoned arrows; whilst others, grinding their teeth in rage, foamed along, more frantic than the wildest maniac. They all avoided each other, and though surrounded by a multitude that no one could number each wandered at random, unheeded of the rest, as if alone on a desert which no foot had trodden.

Vathek and Nouronihar, frozen with terror at a sight so baleful, demanded of the Giaour what these appearances might mean, and why these ambulating spectres never withdrew their hands from their hearts.

"Perplex not yourselves," replied he bluntly, "with so much at once; you will soon be acquainted with all; let us haste and present you to EBLIS."

They continued their way through the multitude; but notwithstanding their confidence at first they were not sufficiently composed to examine with attention the various perspectives of halls and of galleries that opened on the right hand and left, which were all illuminated by torches and braziers whose flames rose in pyramids to the centre of the vault. At length they came to a place where long curtains brocaded with crimson and gold fell from all parts in striking confusion; here the choirs and dances were heard no longer, the light which glimmered came from afar.

After some time Vathek and Nouronihar perceived a gleam brightening through the drapery, and entered a vast tabernacle carpeted with the skins of leopards. An infinity of elders with streaming beards and Afrits in complete armour had prostrated themselves before the ascent of a lofty eminence, on the top of which, upon a globe of fire, sat the formidable Eblis. His person was that of a young man whose noble and regular features seemed to have been tarnished by malignant vapours; in his large eyes appeared both pride and despair; his flowing hair retained some resemblance to that of an angel of light; in his hand, which thunder had blasted, he swayed the iron sceptre that causes the monster Ouranabad, the Afrits, and all the powers of the abyss to tremble. At his presence the heart of the Caliph sunk within him, and for the first time he fell prostrate on his face. Nouronihar, however, though greatly dis-

mayed could not help admiring the person of Eblis, for she expected
to have seen some stupendous Giant. Eblis, with a voice more mild
than might be imagined but such as transfused through the soul
the deepest melancholy, said:

"Creatures of clay, I receive you into mine empire; ye are numbered amongst my adorers; enjoy whatever this palace affords: the
treasures of the pre-Adamite Sultans, their bickering sabres and
those talismans that compel the Divas to open the subterranean ex-
panses of the mountain of Kaf, which communicate with these;
there, insatiable as your curiosity may be, shall you find sufficient to
gratify it; you shall possess the exclusive privilege of entering the
fortress of Ahriman and the halls of Argenk, where are portrayed
all creatures endowed with intelligence and the various animals
that inhabited the earth prior to the creation of the contemptible
being whom ye denominate the Father of Mankind."

Vathek and Nouronihar, feeling themselves revived and en-
couraged by this harangue, eagerly said to the Giaour:

"Bring us instantly to the place which contains these precious talismans."

"Come!" answered this wicked Diva, with his malignant grin.
"Come, and possess all that my Sovereign hath promised, and
more."

He then conducted them into a long aisle adjoining the tabernacle, preceding them with hasty steps and followed by his disci-
ples with the utmost alacrity. They reached at length a hall of great
extent and covered with a lofty dome, around which appeared fifty
portals of bronze, secured with as many fastenings of iron. A
funereal gloom prevailed over the whole scene; here upon two beds
of incorruptible cedar lay recumbent the fleshless forms of the pre-
Adamite Kings who had been monarchs of the whole earth. They
still possessed enough of life to be conscious of their deplorable
condition; their eyes retained a melancholy motion; they regarded
each other with looks of the deepest dejection; each holding his
right hand motionless on his heart; at their feet were inscribed the
events of their several reigns, their power, their pride, and their
crimes. Soliman Raad, Soliman Daki, and Soliman Di Djinn ben
Djinn, who after having chained up the Divas in the dark caverns
of Kaf became so presumptuous as to doubt of the Supreme Power;
all these maintained great state, though not to be compared with
the eminence of Soliman Ben Daoud.

This king, so renowned for his wisdom, was on the loftiest elevation and placed immediately under the dome. He appeared to possess more animation than the rest, though from time to time he laboured with profound sighs and, like his companions, kept his right hand on his heart; yet his countenance was more composed, and he seemed to be listening to the sullen roar of a vast cataract, visible in part through the grated portals. This was the only sound that intruded on the silence of these doleful mansions. A range of brazen vases surrounded the elevation.

"Remove the covers from these cabalistic depositories," said the Giaour to Vathek, "and avail thyself of the talismans, which will break asunder all these gates of bronze; and not only render thee master of the treasures contained within them but also of the spirits by which they are guarded."

The Caliph, whom this ominous preliminary had entirely disconcerted, approached the vases with faltering footsteps and was ready to sink with terror when he heard the groans of Soliman. As he proceeded a voice from the livid lips of the Prophet articulated these words:

"In my lifetime I filled a magnificent throne, having on my right hand twelve thousand seats of gold where the patriarchs and the prophets heard my doctrines; on my left the sages and doctors, upon as many thrones of silver, were present at all my decisions.

"Whilst I thus administered justice to innumerable multitudes the birds of the air librating over me served as a canopy from the rays of the sun; my people flourished and my palace rose to the clouds.

"I erected a temple to the Most High, which was the wonder of the universe; but I basely suffered myself to be seduced by the love of women and a curiosity that could not be restrained by sublunary things. I listened to the counsels of Ahriman and the daughter of Pharaoh, and adored fire and the hosts of heaven. I forsook the holy city and commanded the Genii to rear the stupendous palace of Istakhar and the terrace of the watch-towers, each of which was consecrated to a star.

"There for a while I enjoyed myself in the zenith of glory and pleasure; not only men but supernatural existences were subject also to my will.

"I began to think, as these unhappy monarchs around had already thought, that the vengeance of Heaven was asleep, when at once the thunder burst my structures asunder and precipitated me hither; where, however, I do not remain, like the other inhabitants, totally destitute of hope, for an angel of light hath revealed that in consideration of the piety of my early youth my woes shall come to an end when this cataract shall for ever cease to flow; till then I am in torments, ineffable torments! An unrelenting fire preys on my heart."

Having uttered this exclamation Soliman raised his hands towards Heaven in token of supplication, and the Caliph discerned through his bosom, which was transparent as crystal, his heart enveloped in flames.

At a sight so full of horror Nouronihar fell back like one petrified into the arms of Vathek, who cried out with a convulsive sob:

"O Giaour, whither hast thou brought us? Allow us to depart and I will relinquish all thou hast promised. O Mahomet, remains there no more mercy?"

"None! none!" replied the malicious Diva. "Know, miserable Prince, thou art now in the abode of vengeance and despair. Thy heart also will be kindled like those of the other votaries of Eblis. A few days are allotted thee previous to this fatal period. Employ them as thou wilt; recline on these heaps of gold; command the Infernal Potentates; range at thy pleasure through these immense subterranean domains; no barrier shall be shut against thee. As for me I have fulfilled my mission; I now leave thee to thyself."

At these words he vanished.

GEORGE MACDONALD

WHILE Voltaire was influenced by the Classical fabulists, and William Beckford by the Oriental romances, another "founding father" of modern fantasy was more strongly shaped by the fairy tale itself. Not—I hasten to add—the cutesy-poo made-up stories of Hans Christian Andersen and that sort, but the bleak, dark, cruel and scary folk tales collected by the Grimm Brothers; stark, often gruesome, sometimes nightmarish myths born in the blacker recesses of the Teutonic imagination.

These stories are memorable and lasting, precisely because of

their heavy strain of mythic meaning. They disturb your imagination, roil it up, touch sensitive places deep in the psyche. Therefore
they last, while many a pretty, made-up fairy tale (such as those
concocted at the French court by the less-talented imitators of
Charles Perrault and Madame d'Aulnoy) have vanished into
deserved oblivion.

From such materials as the Teutonic folk tale, the brilliant Scots
poet and preacher-turned-novelist George MacDonald (1824–1905)
elaborated a new kind of story: a dreamy, darkling allegorical narrative whose shadows contain frightening depths of Kafkaesque symbolism and Freudian power. Indeed, you might describe his two
great "faerie romances," *Lilith* and *Phantastes*, as *Alice in Won-
derland* as Kafka might have written it after studying Freudian
symbolism and the Jungian archetypes. Here is a sampling from the
strangely disturbing, darkly powerful dream epics of George
MacDonald, never before anthologized.

THE WITCH WOMAN

I went walking on, still facing the moon, who, not yet high, was
staring straight into the forest. I did not know what ailed her, but
she was dark and dented, like a battered disc of old copper, and
looked dispirited and weary. Not a cloud was nigh to keep her company, and the stars were too bright for her. "Is this going to last for
ever?" she seemed to say. She was going one way and I was going
the other, yet through the wood we went a long way together. We
did not commune much, for my eyes were on the ground; but her
disconsolate look was fixed on me: I felt without seeing it. A long
time we were together, I and the moon, walking side by side, she
the dull shine, and I the live shadow.

Something on the ground, under a spreading tree, caught my eye
with its whiteness, and I turned toward it. Vague as it was in the
shadow of the foliage, it suggested, as I drew nearer, a human
body. "Another skeleton!" I said to myself, kneeling and laying my
hand upon it. A body it was, however, and no skeleton, though as

nearly one as body could well be. It lay on its side, and was very cold—not cold like a stone, but cold like that which was once alive, and is alive no more. The closer I looked at it, the oftener I touched it, the less it seemed possible it should be other than dead. For one bewildered moment, I fancied it one of the wild dancers, a ghostly Cinderella, perhaps, that had lost her way home, and perished in the strange night of an out-of-door world. It was quite naked, and so worn that, even in the shadow, I could, peering close, have counted, without touching them, every rib in its side. All its bones, indeed, were as visible as if tight-covered with only a thin elastic leather. Its beautiful yet terrible teeth, unseemly disclosed by the retracted lips, gleamed ghastly through the dark. Its hair was longer than itself, thick and very fine to the touch, and black as night.

It was the body of a tall, probably graceful woman.—How had she come there? Not of herself, and already in such wasted condition, surely! Her strength must have failed her; she had fallen, and lain there until she died of hunger. But how, even so, could she be thus emaciated? And how came she to be naked? Where were the savages to strip and leave her? or what wild beasts would have taken her garments? That her body should have been left was not wonderful!

I rose to my feet, stood, and considered. I must not, could not let her lie exposed and forsaken! Natural reverence forbade it. Even the garment of a woman claims respect; her body it were impossible to leave uncovered. Irreverent eyes might look on it, brutal claws might toss it about, years would pass before the friendly rains washed it into the soil—but the ground was hard, almost solid with interlacing roots, and I had but my bare hands.

At first it seemed plain that she had not long been dead: there was not a sign of decay about her! But then what had the slow wasting of life left of her to decay?

Could she be still alive? Might she not? What if she were? Things went very strangely in this strange world! Even then there would be little chance of bringing her back, but I must know she was dead before I buried her.

As I left the forest-hall, I had spied in the doorway a bunch of ripe grapes, and brought it with me, eating as I came: a few were yet left on the stalk, and their juice might possibly revive her! Anyhow it was all I had with which to attempt her rescue! The mouth was happily a little open; but the head was in such an awkward position that, to move the body, I passed my arm under the shoulder on which it lay, when I found the pine-needles beneath it warm: she could not have been any time dead, and *might* still be alive, though I could discern no motion of the heart or any indication that she breathed! One of her hands was clenched hard, apparently enclosing something small. I squeezed a grape into her mouth, but no swallowing followed.

To do for her all I could, I spread a thick layer of pine-needles and dry leaves, laid one of my garments over it, warm from my body, lifted her upon it, and covered her with my clothes and a great heap of leaves: I would save the little warmth left in her, hoping an increase to it when the sun came back. Then I tried another grape, but could perceive no slightest movement of mouth or throat.

"Doubt," I said to myself, "may be a poor encouragement to do anything, but it is a bad reason for doing nothing." So tight was the skin upon her bones that I dared not use friction.

I crept into the heap of leaves, got as close to her as I could, and took her in my arms. I had not much heat left in me, but what I had I would share with her. Thus I spent what remained of the night, sleepless, and longing for the sun. Her cold seemed to radiate into me, but no heat to pass from me to her.

Had I fled from the beautiful sleepers, I thought, each on her "dim, straight" silver couch, to lie alone with such a bed-fellow? I had refused a lovely privilege: I was given over to an awful duty. Beneath the sad, slow-setting moon, I lay with the dead, and watched for the dawn.

The darkness had given way, and the eastern horizon was growing dimly clearer, when I caught sight of a motion rather than of anything that moved—not far from me, and close to the ground. It was the low undulating of a large snake, which passed me in an unswerving line. Presently appeared, making as it seemed for the same point, what I took for a roebuck-doe and her calf. Again a while, and two creatures like bear-cubs came, with three or four smaller ones behind them. The light was now growing so rapidly that when, a few minutes after, a troop of horses went trotting past, I could see that, although the largest of them were no bigger than the smallest Shetland pony, they must yet be full-grown, so perfect were they in form, and so much had they all the ways and action of great horses. They were of many breeds. Some seemed models of cart-horses, others of chargers, hunters, racers. Dwarf cattle and small elephants followed.

"Why are the children not here?" I said to myself. "The moment I am free of this poor woman, I must go back and fetch them."

Where were the creatures going? What drew them? Was this an exodus, or a morning habit? I must wait for the sun; till he came I must not leave the woman!

I laid my hand on the body, and could not help thinking it felt a trifle warmer. It might have gained a little of the heat I had lost, it could hardly have generated any. What reason for hope there was had not grown less.

The forehead of the day began to glow, and soon the sun came peering up, as if to see for the first time what all this stir of a new world was about. At sight of his great innocent splendor, I rose full of life, strong against death. Removing the handkerchief I had put to protect the mouth and eyes from the pine-needles, I looked anxiously to see whether I had found a priceless jewel, or but its empty case.

The body lay motionless as when I found it. Then first, in the morning light, I saw how drawn and hollow was the face, how sharp were the bones under the skin, how every tooth shaped itself through the lips. The human garment was indeed worn to its threads, but the bird of heaven might yet be nestling within, might yet awake to motion and song.

But the sun was shining on her face. I re-arranged the handkerchief, laid a few leaves lightly over it, and set out to follow the creatures. Their main track was well beaten, and must have long been used—likewise many of the tracks that, joining it from both sides, merged in, and broadened it. The trees retreated as I went, and the grass grew thicker. Presently the forest was gone, and a wide expanse of loveliest green stretched away to the horizon. Through it, along the edge of the forest, flowed a small river, and to this the track led. At sight of the water a new though undefined hope sprang up in me. The stream looked everywhere deep, and was full to the brim, but nowhere more than a few yards wide. A bluish mist rose from it, vanishing as it rose. On the opposite side, in the plentiful grass, many small animals were feeding. Apparently they slept in the forest, and in the morning sought the plain, swimming the river to reach it. I knelt and would have drunk, but the water was hot, and had a strange metallic taste.

I leapt to my feet: here was the warmth I sought—the first necessity of life! I sped back to my helpless charge.

Without well considering my solitude, no one will understand what seemed to lie for me in the redemption of this woman from death. "Prove what she may," I thought with myself, "I shall at least be lonely no more." I had found myself such poor company that now first I seemed to know what hope was. This blessed water would expel the cold death, and drown my desolation.

I bore her to the stream. Tall as she was, I found her marvelously light, her bones were so delicate, and so little covered them. I grew yet more hopeful when I found her so far from stiff that I could carry her on one arm, like a sleeping child, leaning against my shoulder. I went softly, dreading even the wind of my motion, and glad there was no other.

The water was too hot to lay her at once in it: the shock might scare from her the yet fluttering life. I laid her on the bank, and dipping one of my garments, began to bathe the pitiful form. So wasted was it that, save from the plentifulness and blackness of the hair, it was impossible even to conjecture whether she was young or old. Her eyelids were just not shut, which made her look dead the more: there was a crack in the clouds of her night, at which no sun shone through.

The longer I went on bathing the poor bones, the less grew my hope that they would ever again be clothed with strength, that ever those eyelids would lift, and a soul look out; still I kept bathing continuously, allowing no part time to grow cold while I bathed another; and gradually the body became so much warmer, that at last I ventured to submerge it: I got into the stream and drew it in, holding the face above the water, and letting the swift, steady current flow all about the rest. I noted, but was able to conclude nothing from the fact, that, for all the heat, the shut hand never relaxed its hold.

After about ten minutes, I lifted it out and laid it again on the bank, dried it, and covered it as well as I could, then ran to the forest for leaves.

The grass and soil were dry and warm; and when I returned I thought it had scarcely lost any of the heat the water had given it. I spread the leaves upon it, and ran for more—then for a third and a fourth freight.

I could now leave it and go to explore, in the hope of discovering some shelter. I ran up the stream toward some rocky hills I saw in that direction, which were not far off.

When I reached them, I found the river issuing full grown from a rock at the bottom of one of them. To my fancy it seemed to have run down a stair inside, an eager cataract, at every landing wild to get out, but only at the foot finding a door of escape.

It did not fill the opening whence it rushed, and I crept through into a little cave, where I learned that, instead of hurrying tumultuously down a stair, it rose quietly from the ground at the back, like the base of a large column, and ran along one side, nearly filling a deep, rather narrow channel. I considered the place, and saw that, if I could find a few fallen boughs long enough to lie across the channel, and large enough to bear a little weight without bending much, I might, with smaller branches and plenty of leaves, make upon them a comfortable couch, which the stream under would keep constantly warm. Then I ran back to see how my charge fared.

She was lying as I had left her. The heat had not brought her to life, but neither had it developed anything to check farther hope. I got a few boulders out of the channel, and arranged them at her feet and on both sides of her.

Running again to the wood, I had not to search long before I found some small boughs fit for my purpose—mostly of beech, their dry yellow leaves yet clinging to them. With these I had soon laid the floor of a bridge-bed over the torrent. I crossed the boughs with smaller branches, interlaced these with twigs, and buried all deep in leaves and dry moss.

When thus at length, after not a few journeys to the forest, I had completed a warm, dry, soft couch, I took the body once more, and set out with it for the cave. It was so light that now and then as I went I almost feared lest, when I laid it down, I should find it a skeleton after all; and when at last I did lay it gently on the pathless bridge, it was a greater relief to part with that fancy than with the weight. Once more I covered the body with a thick layer of leaves; and trying again to feed her with a grape, found to my joy that I could open the mouth a little farther. The grape, indeed, lay in it unheeded, but I hoped some of the juice might find its way down.

After an hour or two on the couch, she was no longer cold. The warmth of the brook had interpenetrated her frame—truly it was a frame!—and she was warm to the touch;—not, probably, with the warmth of life, but with a warmth which rendered it more possible, if she were alive, that she might live. I had read of one in a trance lying motionless for weeks!

In that cave, day after day, night after night, seven long days and nights, I sat or lay, now waking now sleeping, but always watching. Every morning I went out and bathed in the hot stream, and every morning felt thereupon as if I had eaten and drunk—which experience gave me courage to lay her in it also every day. Once as I did so, a shadow of discoloration on her left side gave me a terrible shock, but the next morning it had vanished, and I continued the treatment—every morning, after her bath, putting a fresh grape in her mouth.

I too ate of the grapes and other berries I found in the forest; but I believed that, with my daily bath in that river, I could have done very well without eating at all.

Every time I slept, I dreamed of finding a wounded angel, who, unable to fly, remained with me until at last she loved me and would not leave me; and every time I woke, it was to see, instead of an angel-visage with lustrous eyes, the white, motionless, wasted face upon the couch. But Adam himself, when first he saw her asleep, could not have looked more anxiously for Eve's awaking than I watched for this woman's. Adam knew nothing of himself, perhaps nothing of his need of another self; I, an alien from my fellows, had learned to love what I had lost. Were this one wasted shred of womanhood to disappear, I should have nothing in me but a consuming hunger after life. I forgot even the Little Ones: things were not amiss with them! Here lay what might wake and be a woman, might actually open eyes, and look out of them upon me.

Now first I knew what solitude meant—now that I gazed on one who neither saw nor heard, neither moved nor spoke. I saw now that a man alone is but a being that may become a man—that he is but a need, and therefore a possibility. To be enough for himself, a being must be an eternal, self-existent worm. So superbly constituted, so simply complicated is man; he rises from and stands upon such a pedestal of lower physical organisms and spiritual structures, that no atmosphere will comfort or nourish his life, less divine than that offered by other souls; nowhere but in other lives can he breathe. Only by the reflex of other lives can he ripen his specialty, develop the idea of himself, the individuality that distinguishes him from every other. Were all men alike, each would still have an individuality, secured by his personal consciousness, but there would be small reason why there should be more than two or three such;

while, for the development of the differences which make a large
and lofty unity possible, and which alone can make millions into a
church, an endless and measureless influence and reaction are indispensable. A man to be perfect—complete, that is, in having reached
the spiritual condition of persistent and universal growth, which is
the mode wherein he inherits the infinitude of his Father—must
have the education of a world of fellow-men. Save for the hope of
the dawn of life in the form beside me, I should have fled for
fellowship to the beasts that grazed and did not speak. Better to go
about with them—infinitely better—than to live alone. But with the
faintest prospect of a woman to be my friend, I, poorest of creatures, was yet a possible man.

I woke one morning from a profound sleep, with one of my hands
very painful. The back of it was much swollen, and in the center of
the swelling was a triangular wound, like the bite of a leech. As the
day went on, the swelling subsided, and by the evening the hurt
was all but healed. I searched the cave, turning over every stone of
any size, but discovered nothing I could imagine capable of injur-
ing me.

Slowly the days passed, and still the body never moved, never
opened its eyes. It could not be dead, for assuredly it manifested no
sign of decay, and the air about it was quite pure. Moreover, I
could imagine that the sharpest angles of the bones had begun to
disappear, that the form was everywhere a little rounder, and that
the skin had less of the parchment look: if such change was indeed
there, life must be there; the tide which had ebbed so far toward
the infinite, must have begun again to flow. Oh joy to me, if the rising ripples of life's ocean were indeed burying under lovely shape
the bones it had all but foresaken! Twenty times a day I looked for
evidence of progress, and twenty times a day I doubted—sometimes even despaired; but the moment I recalled the mental picture
of her as I found her, hope revived.

Several weeks had passed thus, when one night, after lying a long
time awake, I rose, thinking to go out and breathe the cooler air;
for, although from the running of the stream it was always fresh in
the cave, the heat was not seldom a little oppressive. The moon outside was full, the air within shadowy clear, and naturally I cast a
lingering look on my treasure ere I went. "Bliss eternal!" I cried
aloud, "do I see her eyes?" Great orbs, dark as if cut from the
sphere of a starless night, and luminous by excess of darkness,

seemed to shine amid the glimmering whiteness of her face. I stole nearer, my heart beating so that I feared the noise of it startling her. I bent over her. Alas, her eyelids were close shut. Hope and Imagination had wrought mutual illusion, my heart's desire would never be! I turned away, threw myself on the floor of the cave, and wept. Then I bethought me that her eyes had been a little open, and that now the awful chink out of which nothingness had peered, was gone: it might be that she had opened them for a moment, and was again asleep—it might be she was awake and holding them close! In neither case, life, less or more, must have shut them! I was comforted, and fell fast asleep.

That night I was again bitten, and awoke with a burning thirst.

In the morning I searched yet more thoroughly, but again in vain. The wound was of the same character, and, as before, was nearly well by the evening. I concluded that some large creature of the leech kind came occasionally from the hot stream. "But, if blood be its object," I said to myself, "so long as I am there, I need hardly fear for my treasure."

That same morning, when, having peeled a grape as usual and taken away the seeds, I put it in her mouth, her lips made a slight movement of reception, and I *knew* she lived.

My hope was now so much stronger that I began to think of some attire for her: she must be able to rise the moment she wished. I betook myself therefore to the forest, to investigate what material it might afford, and had hardly begun to look when fibrous skeletons, like those of the leaves of the prickly pear, suggested themselves as fit for the purpose. I gathered a stock of them, laid them to dry in the sun, pulled apart the reticulated layers, and of these had soon begun to fashion two loose garments, one to hang from her waist, the other from her shoulders. With the stiletto-point of an aloe-leaf and various filaments, I sewed together three thicknesses of the tissue.

During the week that followed, there was no farther sign except that she more evidently took the grapes. But indeed all the signs became surer: plainly she was growing plumper, and her skin fairer. Still she did not open her eyes; and the horrid fear would at times invade me, that her growth was of some hideous fungoid nature, the few grapes being nowise sufficient to account for it.

Again I was bitten; and now the thing, whatever it was, began to pay me regular visits at intervals of three days. It now generally bit me in the neck or the arm, invariably with but one bite, always while I slept, and never, even when I slept, in the daytime. Hour after hour would I lie awake on the watch, but never heard it coming, or saw sign of its approach. Neither, I believe, did I ever feel it bite me. At length I became so hopeless of catching it, that I no longer troubled myself either to look for it by day, or lie in wait for it at night. I knew from my growing weakness that I was losing blood at a dangerous rate, but I cared little for that: in sight of my eyes death was yielding to life; a soul was gathering strength to save me from loneliness; we would go away together, and I should speedily recover.

The garments were at length finished, and, contemplating my handiwork with no small satisfaction, I proceeded to mat layers of the fibre into sandals.

One night I woke suddenly, breathless and faint, and longing after air, and had risen to crawl from the cave, when a slight rustle in the leaves of the couch set me listening motionless.

"I caught the vile thing," said a feeble voice, in my mother-tongue; "I caught it in the very act!"

She was alive! she spoke! I dared not yield to my transport lest I should terrify her.

"What creature?" I breathed, rather than said.

"The creature," she answered, "that was biting you."

"What was it?"

"A great white leech."

"How big?" I pursued, forcing myself to be calm.

"Not far from six feet long, I should think," she answered.

"You have saved my life, perhaps—But how could you touch the horrid thing? How brave of you!" I cried.

"I did," was all her answer, and I thought she shuddered.

"Where is it? What could you do with such a monster?"

"I threw it in the river."

"Then it will come again, I fear."

"I do not think I could have killed it, even had I known how—I heard you moaning, and got up to see what disturbed you; saw the frightful thing at your neck, and pulled it away. But I could not hold it, and was hardly able to throw it from me. I only heard it splash in the water."

"We'll kill it next time," I said; but with that I turned faint, sought the open air, but fell.

When I came to myself the sun was up. The lady stood a little way off, looking, even in the clumsy attire I had fashioned for her, at once grand and graceful. I *had* seen those glorious eyes! Through the night they had shone! Dark as the darkness primeval, they now outshone the day. She stood erect as a column, regarding me. Her pale cheek indicated no emotion, only question. I rose.

"We must be going," I said. "The white leech——"

I stopped: a strange smile had flickered over her beautiful face.

"Did you find me there?" she asked, pointing to the cave.

"No; I brought you there," I replied.

"You brought me?"

"Yes."

"From where?"

"From the forest."

"What have you done with my clothes—and my jewels?"

"You had none when I found you."

"Then why did you not leave me?"

"Because I hoped you were not dead."

"Why should you have cared?"

"Because I was very lonely, and wanted you to live."

"You would have kept me enchanted for my beauty," she said, with proud scorn.

Her words and her look roused my indignation.

"There was no beauty left in you," I said.

"Why, then, again, did you not let me alone?"

"Because you were of my own kind."

"Of *your* kind?" she cried, in a tone of utter contempt.

"I thought so, but find I was mistaken."

"Doubtless you pitied me!"

"Never had woman more claim on pity, or less on any other feeling."

With an expression of pain, mortification, and anger unutterable, she turned from me and stood silent. Starless night lay profound in the gulfs of her eyes: hate of him who brought it back had slain their splendor. The light of life was gone from them.

"Had you failed to rouse me, what would you have done?" she asked suddenly without moving.

"I would have buried it."

"It! What?—You would have buried *this*?" she exclaimed, flashing round upon me in a white fury, her arms thrown out, and her eyes darting forks of cold lightning.

"Nay; that I saw not! That, weary weeks of watching and tending have brought back to you," I answered—for with such a woman I must be plain. "Had I seen the smallest sign of decay, I would at once have buried you."

"Dog of a fool!" she cried, "I was but in a trance!—Samoil! what a fate!—Go and fetch the she-savage from whom you borrowed this hideous disguise."

"I made it for you. It is hideous, but I did my best."

She drew herself up to her tall height.

"How long have I been insensible?" she demanded. "A woman could not have made that dress in a day."

"Not in twenty days," I rejoined, "hardly in thirty."

"Ha! How long do you pretend I have lain unconscious?—Answer me at once."

"I cannot tell how long you had lain when I found you, but there was nothing left of you save skin and bone: that is more than three months ago.—Your hair was beautiful, nothing else! I have done for it what I could."

"My poor hair!" she said, and brought a great armful of it round from behind her; "—it will be more than a three-months' care to bring *you* to life again!—I suppose I must thank you, although I cannot say I am grateful."

"There is no need, madam: I would have done the same for any woman—yes, or for any man either."

"How is it my hair is not tangled?" she said, fondling it.

"It always drifted in the current."

"How?—What do you mean?"

"I could not have brought you to life but by bathing you in the hot river every morning."

She gave a shudder of disgust, and stood for a time with her gaze fixed on the hurrying water. Then she turned to me:

"We must understand each other," she said. "—you have done me the two worst of wrongs—compelled me to live, and put me to shame: neither of them can I pardon."

She raised her left hand, and flung it out as if repelling me. Something ice-cold struck me on the forehead. When I came to myself, I was on the ground, wet and shivering.

And she was gone.

II.
Fantasy
as
Saga

WILLIAM MORRIS

SUCH early fantasy writers as Beckford and Macdonald were before their time, and the new directions in fiction which they pioneered proved to be dead ends. Modern fantastic literature properly begins with an extraordinary Welsh writer named William Morris (1834–96). A man of prodigious energy and protean talents, Morris came down from Oxford with a sheaf of poems stuffed in his pocket, a love for Medieval craftsmanship burning in his heart, and a passion for Gothic architecture he had caught from Ruskin. A burly, bush-bearded wild man from the Severn marches, he came charging into the genteel society of Victorian England like the proverbial bull in the china shop. In no time he had set society on its ear and profoundly altered the taste of his generation.

His accomplishments are fascinating and innumerable. He led the pre-Raphaelite movement and changed Europe's taste in ornament and decoration. A Victorian gentleman's living room simply was not to be lived in without a William Morris wallpaper on its walls. With the poet Rosetti and the painter Burne-Jones, he organized Morris & Company, and redecorated Europe with Morris-designed-and-handcrafted furniture, tapestries, paintings, textiles, jewelry; later, he translated the Icelandic sagas, introducing his countrymen to an entire literature. Almost as an afterthought, in his final years, he invented modern fantasy by authoring a prodigious shelf-full of prose romances in the Malory manner—*The House of the Wolfings* (1889), *The Roots of the Mountain* (1889), *The Glittering Plain* (1891), *The Wood Beyond the World* (1894), *The Water of the Wondrous Isles* (1895), *The Well at the World's End* (1896), *The Sundering Flood* (1896). The last pages of *The Sundering Flood* had to be dictated to a friend, for he was too weak to hold any longer the pen he had wielded so staunchly. He died twenty-five days after the last words were written.

What makes Morris so important and central a figure in the history of fantasy is not so much the value and vigor of his epic romances, although they are powerful literary works and one of them, at least, *The Well at the World's End,* is the greatest epic fantasy written before *The Lord of the Rings.* No, it is the innovation which Morris brought to the crafting of the fantastic narrative. For where earlier writers like Voltaire and Beckford had been content to write romances laid in Persia or Baghdad, however transmogrified, still recognizable—Morris was the first to realize the proper way to go about the task is to *make up the entire world of your story.* He was the first to realize this, and the first to do it; therefore we remember him and venerate his memory as "The Man Who Invented Fantasy."

In selecting something from Morris for this book I had to go far afield, for, happily, virtually all of his fantasies have enjoyed a recent renaissance and are currently in print in paperback. But at last I found this story, which would seem to be the fragment of an unfinished romance, one he did not live to write. It appears here in an anthology for the first time.

THE FOLK OF THE MOUNTAIN DOOR

OF old time, in the days of the kings, there was a king of folk, a mighty man in battle, a man deemed lucky by the wise, who ruled over a folk that begrudged not his kingship, whereas they knew of his valour and wisdom and saw how by his means they prevailed over other folks, so that their land was wealthy and at peace save about its uttermost borders. And his folk was called The Folk of the Mountain Door, or, more shortly, of the Door. Strong of body was this king, tall and goodly to look upon, so that the hearts of women fluttered with desire when he passed them by. In the prime and flower of his age he wedded a wife, a seemly mate, a woman of the Earl-kin, tall and white-skinned, golden-haired and grey-eyed; healthy, sweet-breathed, and soft-spoken, courteous of manners, wise of heart, kind to all folk, well-beloved of little children. In early spring-tide was the wedding, and a little after Yule was she brought to bed of a man-child of whom the midwives said they had never seen a fairer. He was sprinkled with water and was named Host-lord after the name of his kindred of old. Great was the feast of his Name-day, and much people came thereto, the barons of the land, and the lords of the neighboring folk who would fain stand well with the king; and merchants and craftsmen and sages and bards; and the king took them with both hands and gave them gifts, and hearkened to their talk and their tales, as if he were their very earthly fellow; for as fierce as he was afield with the sword in his fist, even so meek and kind he was in the hall amongst his folk and the strangers that sought him.

Now amongst the guests that ate and drank in the hall on the even of the Name-day, the king as he walked amidst the tables beheld an old man as tall as any champion of the king's host, but far taller had he been, but that he was bowed with age. He was clad so that he had on him a kirtle of lambs wool undyed and snow-white, and a white cloak, lined with ermine and welted with gold; a golden fillet set with gems was on his head, and a gold-

hilted sword by his side; and the king deemed as he looked on him
that he had never seen any man more like to the Kings of the Ancient World than this man. By his side sat a woman old and very
old, but great of stature, and noble of visage, clad, she also, in
white wool raiment embroidered about with strange signs of worms
and fire-drakes, and the sun and the moon and the host of heaven.

So the king stayed his feet by them, for already he had noted that
at the table whereat they sat there had been this long time at
whiles greater laughter and more joyous than anywhere else in the
hall, and whiles the hush of folk that hearken to what delights the
inmost of their hearts. So now he greeted those ancients and said to
them: "Is it well with you, neighbors?" And the old carle hailed the
king, and said, "There is little lack in this house today."

"What lack at all do ye find therein?" said the king. Then there
came a word into the carle's mouth and he sang in a great voice:

> Erst was the earth
> Fulfilled of mirth:
> Our swords were sheen
> In the summer green;
> And we rode and ran
> Through winter wan,
> And long and wide
> Was the feast-hall's side.
> And the sun was sunken
> Long under the wold
> Hung ere we were drunken
> High over the gold;
> And as Fowl in the bushes
> Of summertide sing
> So glad as the thrushes
> Sang earl-folk and king.
> Though the wild wind might splinter
> The oak-tree of Thor,
> The hand of mid-winter
> But beat on the door.

"Yea," said the king, "and dost thou say that winter hath come
into my hall on the Name-day of my first-born?" "Not so," said the
carle.

"What is amiss then?" said the king. Then the carle sang again:

> Were many men
> In the feast-hall then,
> And the worst on bench
> Ne'er thought to blench
> When the storm arose
> In the war-god's close;
> And for Tyr's high-seat,
> Were the best full meet:
> And who but the singer
> Was leader and lord,
> I steel-god, I flinger
> Of adder-watched hoard?
> Aloft was I sitting
> Amidst of the place
> And watched men a-flitting
> All under my face.
> And hushed for mere wonder
> Were great men and small
> As my voice in rhyme-thunder
> Went over the hall.

"Yea," said the king, "thou hast been a mighty lord in days gone past, I thought no less when first I set eyes on thee. And now I bid thee stand up and sit on the high-seat beside me, thou and thy mate. Is she not thy very speech-friend?"

Therewith a smile lit up the ancient man's face, and the woman turned to him and he sang:

> Spring came of old
> In the days of gold,
> In the thousandth year
> Of the thousands dear,
> When we twain met
> And the mead was wet
> With the happy tears
> Of the best of the years.
> But no cloud hung over
> The eyes of the sun

> That looked down on the lover
> Ere eve was begun.
> Oft, oft came greeting
> Of spring and her bliss
> To the mead of our meeting,
> The field of our kiss.
> Is spring growing older?
> Is earth on the wane
> As the bold and the bolder
> That come not again?

"O king of a happy land," said the ancient man, "I will take thy bidding, and sit beside thee this night that thy wisdom may wax and the days that are to come may be better for thee than the days that are."

So he spake and rose to his feet, and the ancient woman with him and they went with the king up to the high-seat, and all men in the feast-hall rose up and stood to behold them, and they deemed them wonderful and their coming a great thing.

But now when they were set down on the right hand and the left hand of the king, he turned to the ancient man and said to him: "O Lord of the days gone past, and of the battles that have been, wilt thou now tell me of thy name, and the name of thy mate, that I may call a health for thee first of all great healths that shall be drunk tonight."

But the old man said and sang:

> King, hast thou thought
> How nipped and nought
> Is last year's rose
> Of the snow-filled close?
> Or dost thou find
> Last winter's wind
> Will yet avail
> For thy hall-glee's tale?
> E'en such and no other
> If spoken tonight
> Were the name of the brother
> Of war-gods of might.

Yea the word that hath shaken
The walls of the house
When the warriors half waken
To battle would rouse
Ye should drowse if ye heard it
Nor turn in the chair.
O long long since they feared it
Those foeman of fear!
Unhelpful, unmeaning
Its letters are left;
For the name overweening
Of manhood is reft.

This word the king hearkened, and found no word in his mouth to answer: but he sat pondering heavy things, and sorrowful with the thought of the lapse of years, and the waning of the blossom of his youth. And all the many guests of the great feast-hall sat hushed, and the hall-glee died out amongst them.

But the old man raised his head and smiled, and he stood on his feet, and took the cup in his hand and cried out aloud: "What is this my masters, are ye drowsy with meat and drink in this first hour of the feast? Or have tidings of woe without words been borne amongst you, that ye sit like men given over to wanness awaiting coming of the doom that none may gainsay, and the foe that none may overcome? Nay then, nay; but if ye be speechless I will speak; and if ye be joyless I will rejoice and bid the good wine welcome. But first will I call a health over the cup:

Pour, white-armed ones,
As the Rhine flood runs!
And O thanes in hall
I bid you all
Rise up, and stand
With the horn in hand,
And hearken and hear
The old name and the dear.
To HOST-LORD the health is
Who guarded of old
The House where the wealth is

> The Home of the gold.
> And again the Tree bloometh
> Though winter it be
> And no heart of man gloometh
> From mountain to sea.
> Come thou Lord, the rightwise,
> Come Host-lord once more
> To thy Hall-fellows, fightwise
> The Folk of the Door!

Huge then was the sudden clamour in the hall, and the shouts of men and clatter of horns and clashing of weapons as all folk old and young, great and little, carle and quean, stood up on the Night of the Name-day. And once again there was nought but joy in the hall of the Folk of the Door.

But amidst the clamour the inner doors of the hall were thrown open, and there came in women clad most meetly in coloured raiment, and amidst them a tall woman in scarlet, bearing in her arms the babe new born clad in fine linen and wrapped in a golden cloth, and she bore him up thus toward the high-seat, while all men shouted even more if it were possible, and set down cup and horn from their lips, and took up sword and shield and raised the shield-roar in the hall.

But the king rose up with a joyful countenance, and got him from out of his chair, and stood thereby: and the women stayed at the foot of the dais all but the nurse, who bore up the child to the king, and gave it into his arms; and he looked fondly on the youngling for a short space, and then raised him aloft so that all men in the hall might see him, and so laid him on the board before them and took his great spear from the wall behind him and drew the point thereof across and across the boy's face so that it well nigh grazed his flesh: at the first and at the last did verily graze it as little as might be, but so that the blood started; and while the babe wailed and cried, as was to be looked for, the king cried aloud with a great voice:

"Here mark I thee to Odin even as were all thy kin marked from of old from the time that the Gods were first upon the earth."

Then he took the child up in his arms and laid him in his own chair, and cried out: "This is Host-lord the son of Host-Lord King and Duke of the Folk of the Door, who sitteth in his father's chair and shall do when I am gone to Odin, unless any of the Folk gainsay it."

When he had spoken there came a man in at the door of the hall clad in all his war-gear with a great spear in his hand, and girt with a sword, and he strode clashing through the hall up to the high-seat, and stood by the chair of the king and lifted up his helm a little and cried out:

"Where are now the gainsayers, or where is the champion of the gainsayers? Here stand I Host-rock of the Falcons of the Folk of the Door, ready to greet the gainsayers."

And he let his helm fall down again so that his face was hidden. And a man one-eyed and huge rose up from the lower benches and cried out in a loud voice: "O champion, hast thou hitherto foregone thy meat and drink to sing so idle a song over the hall-glee? Come down amongst us, man, and put off thine armour and eat and drink and be merry; for of thine hunger and thirst am I full certain. Here be no gainsayers, but brethren all, the sons of one Mother and one Father, though they be grown somewhat old by now."

Then was there a clamour again, joyous with laughter and many good words. And some men say, that when this man had spoken, the carle and quean ancient of days who sat beside the king's chair, were all changed and seemed to men's eyes as if they were in the flower of their days, mighty, and lovely and merry of countenance: and it is told that no man knew that big-voiced speaker, nor whence he came, and that presently when men looked for him he was gone from the hall, and they knew not how.

Be this as it may, the two ancient ones each stooped down over the chair whereas lay the little one and kissed him; and the old man took his cup and wetted the lips of the babe with red wine, and the old woman took a necklace from her neck of amber and silver and gold and did it on the youngling's neck and spake; and her voice was very sweet though she were old; and many heard the speech of her:

"O Host-lord of this even, Live long and hale! Many a woman shall look on thee and few that see thee shall forebear to love thee."

Then the nurse took up the babe again and bore him out to the bower where lay his mother, and the folk were as glad as glad might be, and no man hath told of mirth greater and better than the hall-glee of that even. And the old carle sat yet beside the king and was blithe with him and of many words, and told him tales that he had never known before; and these were of the valiant deeds and the lives of his fathers before him, and strange stories of the Folk of the Door and what they had done, and the griefs which they had borne and the joys which they had won from the earth and the heavens and the girdling waters of the world. And the king waxed exceeding glad as he heard it all, and thought he would try to bear it in mind as long as he lived; for it seemed to him that when he had parted from those two ancient ones, that night, he should never see them again.

So wore the time and the night was so late, that had it been summer-tide, it had been no night but early day. And the king looked up from the board and those two old folk, and beheld the hall, that there were few folk therein, save those that lay along by the walls of the aisles, so swiftly had the night gone and all folk were departed or asleep. Then was he like a man newly awakened from a dream, and he turned about to the two ancients almost looking to see their places empty. But they abode there yet beside him on the right hand and on the left; so he said: "Guests, I give you all thanks for your company and the good words and noble tales wherewith ye have beguiled this night of winter and surely tomorrow shall I rise up wiser than I was yesterday. And now meseemeth ye are old and doubtless weary with the travel and the noisy mirth of the feast-hall, nor may I ask you to abide bedless any longer, though it be great joy to me to hearken to your speech. Come then to the bower aloft and I will show you the best of beds and the soft and king place to abide the uprising of tomorrow's sun; and late will he arise, for this is now the very midwinter, and the darkest of all days of the year."

Then answered the old man: "I thank thee, O son of the Kindred; but so it is that we have further to wend than thou mightest deem;

yea, back to the land whence we came many a week of years ago and before the building of houses in the land, between the mountain and the sea. Wherefore if thou wouldest do aught to honor us, come thou a little way on the road and see us off in the open country without the walls of thy Burg: then shall we depart in such wise that we shall be dear friends as long as we live, thou and thine, and I and mine."

"This is not so great an asking," said the king, "but that I would do more for thee; yet let it be as thou wilt."

And he arose from table and they with him, and they went down the hall amidst the sleeping folk and the benches that had erst been so noisy and merry, and out a-doors they went all three and into the street of the Burg. Open were the Burg-gates and none watched there, for there was none to break the Yule-peace; so the king went forth clad in his feasting raiment, and those twain went, one on either side of him. The midwinter frost was hard upon the earth, so that few waters were running, and all the face of the world was laid under snow: high was the moon and great and round in a cloudless sky, so that the stars looked but little.

The king set his face toward the mountains and strode with great strides over the white highway betwixt the hidden fruitfulness of the acres, and he was as one wending on an errand which he may not forego; but at last he said: "Whither wend we and how far?" Then spake the old man: "Whither should we wend save to the Mountain Door, and the entrance to the land whence the folk came forth, when great were its warriors and little was the tale of them."

Then the king spake no more, but it seemed to him as if his feet sped on faster than their wont was, and as if those twain bore him up so that his feet were but light on the face of the earth.

Thuswise they passed the plain and the white-clad ridges at the mountain feet in lo long while, and were come before the yawning gap and strait way into the heart of the mountains, and there was no other way thereinto save this; for otherwhere, the cliffs rose like a wall from the plain-country. Grim was that pass, and high were the sides of it beneath the snow, which lay heaped up high, so now there were smooth white slopes on either side of the narrow road of the pass; while the wind had whistled the said road in most places

well nigh clear of snow, which even now went whirling and drifting
about beneath the broad moon. For the wind yet blew though the
night was old, and the sound of it in the clefts of the rocks and the
windings of the pass was like the rolling of the summer thunder.

Up the pass they went till it widened, and there was a widespace
before them, the going up whereto was as by stairs, and also the
going up from it to the higher pass; and all around it the rocks were
high and sheer, so that there was no way over them save for the
fowl flying; and were it not winter there had been a trickling
stream running round about the eastern side of the cliff wall which
lost itself in the hollow places of the rocks at the lower end of that
round hall of the mountain, unroofed and unpillared. Amidmost
the place the snow was piled on high; for there in summer was a
grassy mound amidst of a little round meadow of sweet grass,
treeless, bestrewn here and there with blocks that had been borne
down thitherward by the waters from the upper mountain; and for
ages beyond what the memory of men might tell of this had been
the Holy place and Motestead of the Folk of the Door.

Now all three went up on to the snow-covered mound, and those
two turned about and faced the king and he saw their faces clearly,
so bright as the moon was, and now it was so that they were no
more wrinkled and hollow-cheeked and sunken-eyed, though scarce
might a man say that they looked young, but exceeding fair they
were, and they looked on him with eyes of love, and the carle said:
"Lord of the Folk of the Door, father of the son new born whom
the Folk this night have taken for their father, and the image of
those that have been, we have brought thee to the Holy Place that
we might say a word to thee and give thee a warning of the days to
come, so that if it may be thou mightest eschew the evil and ensue
the good. For thou art our dear son, and thy son is yet dearer to us,
since his days shall be longer if weird will so have it. Hearken to
this by the token that under the grass, beneath this snow, lieth the
first of the Folk of the Door of those that come on the earth and go
thence; and this was my very son begotten on this woman that here
standeth. For wot thou that I am Host-lord of the Ancient Days,
and from me is all the blood of you come; and dear is the blood of
my sons and my name even as that which I have seen spilt on field
and in fold, on grass and in grange, without the walls of the
watches and about the lone wells of the desert places. Hearken

then, Host-lord the Father of Host-lord, for we have looked into the life of thy son; and this we say is the weird of him; childless shall he be unless he wed as his will is; for of all his kindred none is will-fuller than he. Who then shall he wed, and where is the House that is lawful to him that thou hast not heard of? For as to wedding with his will in the House whereof thou wottest, and the Line of the Sea-dwellers, look not for it. Where then is the House of his wedding, lest the Folk of the Door lose their Chieftain and become the servants of those that are worser than they? I may not tell thee; and if I did, it would help thee nought. But this I will tell thee, when thy fair son is of fifteen winters, until the time that he is twenty winters and two, evil waylayeth on him: evil of the draught, evil of the cave, evil of the wave. O Son and father of my son, heed my word and let him be so watched that while as none hath been watched and warded of all thy kindred who have gone before, lest when his time come and he depart from this land and he wander about the further side of the bridge that goeth to the Hall of the Gods, for very fear of shaming amongst the bold warriors and begotters of kindred and fathers of the sons that I love, that shall one day sit and play at the golden tables in the Plains of Ida."

So he spake, but the king spake: "O Host-lord of the Ancients I had a deeming of what thou wert, and that thou hadst a word for me. Wilt thou now tell me one thing more? In what wise shall I ward our son from the evil till his soul is strengthened, and the Wise-wights and the Ancients are become his friends, and the life of the warrior is in his hands and the days of a chieftain of our folk?"

Then the carle smiled on him and sang:

> Wide is the land
> Where the houses stand,
> There bale and bane
> Ye scarce shall chain;
> There the sword is ground
> And wounds abound;
> And women fair
> Weave the love-nets there.
>
> Merry hearts in the Mountain
> Dales shepherd-men keep,
> And about the Fair Fountain

Need more than their sheep . . .
Of the Dale of the Tower
Where springeth the well
In the sun-slaying hour
They talk and they tell;
And often they wonder
Whence cometh the name
And what tale lies thereunder
For honour or shame.
For beside the fount welling
No castle now is;
Yet seldom foretelling
Of weird wends amiss.

Quote the king, "I have heard tell of the Fair Fountain and the Dale of the Tower; though I have never set eyes thereon, and I deem it will be hard to find. But dost thou mean that our son who is born the Father of the Folk shall dwell there during that while of peril?"

Again sang the carle:

Good man and true,
They deal and do
In the grassy dales
Of that land of the tales;
Where dale and down
Yet wears the crown
Of the flower and fruit
From our kinship's root.
There little man sweateth
In trouble and toil,
And in joy he forgetteth
The feud and the foil.
The weapon he wendeth
Achasing the deer,
And in peace the moon endureth
That endeth the year.
Yet there dwell our brothers,
And should they but know
They thy stem of all others
Were planted to grow

> Beside the Fair Fountain,
> How fain were those men
> Of the God of the Mountain
> So come back again.

Then the king said: "Shall I fulfill the weird and build a Tower in the Dale for our Son? And deemest thou he shall dwell there happily til the time of peril is overpast?"

But the carle cried out, "Look, look! Who is the shining one who cometh up the pass?"

And the king turned hastily and drew his sword, but beheld neither man nor mare in the mountain, and when he turned back again to those twain, lo! they were clean gone, and there was nought in the pass save the snow and the wind, and the long shadows cast by the sinking moon. So he turned again about and went down the pass; and by then he was come into the first of the plain-country once more, the moon was down and the stars shone bright and big; but even in the dead midwinter there was a scent abroad of the coming of dawn. So went the king as speedily as he might back to Burg and his High House; and he was glad in his inmost heart that he had seen the God and the Father of Folk.

E. R. EDDISON

WITH such tales as "The Folk of the Mountain Door" and his epic prose romances, William Morris founded a tradition. Thereafter, most fantasy writers, following his example, invented out of whole cloth the worldscapes in which they set the scene of their stories. And more than a few of them were fascinated by the stark power and narrative richness of the saga literature which Morris had been the first to introduce to modern readers.

An example of this is Eric Rucker Eddison (1882–1945), an Eng-

lish civil servant who retired to produce some of the most gorgeously written and complex and philosophically intriguing of all
fantastic romances in what we call the "imaginary world" tradition.
Eddison translated the sagas as Morris had done, and his first
novel, *Styrbiorn the Strong* was, actually, a novelization of the story
of one of the old saga heroes (one, incidentally, whose saga Morris
had earlier translated—the *Eyrbyggja saga*). But Eddison's major
work was more richly complex, deriving as much from the Homeric
epics and the lusty Tudor and Elizabethan prose masters as from
the Icelandic.

The first and greatest of these books is *The Worm Ouroboros,*
which many fantasy connoisseurs and authorities (myself among
them) consider the single finest fantastic romance ever written. It is
a ringing and glorious story, filled with heroic chivalry, fluttering
banners, clashing swords, villainous magicians, seductive enchant-
resses, wars, sieges, expeditions, sea battles, monsters and marvels.
Published in 1922, it was followed by what we call the "Zimiamvia
Trilogy," which is composed of *Mistress of Mistresses* (1935), *A
Fish Dinner in Memison* (1941), and a posthumous work constructed out of notes and drafts, *The Mezentian Gate* (1958).

Eddison took Morris' great idea—the imaginary world setting—
and elaborated upon it, fleshing out its illusion of historical and
geographical reality by means of detailed and authentic-looking
maps and chronological tables. Instead of writing the sort of gold
filigree prose Morris had borrowed from Malory, Eddison ham-
mered out strong and beautiful language of his own, all bronze and
iron; rather than employ unmotivated characters out of Medieval
romance and the sort of dialogue that should, in James Blish's
phrase, be "intoned through the nose," he peopled his world with
brawling, surging, tumultuous throngs of real-life men and women
that would have been at home in the pages of Chaucer, if not
Shakespeare. You really have to read Eddison to believe that such
stirring and noble works of heroic literature could actually be
penned by a modern writer.

I have selected for your enjoyment one of the most serene and
perfect scenes in all his books, one that has stayed fresh and
exquisite in my memory for all the twenty years that have passed
since I first read it. It has never been anthologized until now.

A NIGHT-PIECE ON AMBREMERINE

PEACE seemed to have laid her lily over all the earth when, that evening, eight gondolas that carried the Duke and his company put out from the water-gate under the western tower and steered into the sunset. In the open water they spread into line abreast, making a shallow crescent, horns in advance, and so passed on their way, spacing themselves by intervals of some fifty paces to be within hail but not to the overhearing of talk within the gondolas. Three or four hundred paces ahead of them went a little caravel, bearing aboard of her the Duke's bodyguard and the last and most delicate wines and meats. Her sweeps were out, for in that windless air her russet-coloured silken sails flapped the masts. From her poop floated over the water the music of old love-ditties, waked in the throb of silver lute-strings, the wail of hautboys, and the flattering soft singing of viols.

North and north-eastward, fainter and fainter in the distance, the foot-hills took on purple hues, like the bloom on grapes. High beyond the furthest hills, lit with a rosy light, the great mountains reared themselves that shut in the habited lands on the northward: outlying sentinels of the Hyperborean snows. So high they stood, that it might have been clouds in the upper air; save that they swam not as clouds, but persisted, and that their architecture was not cloud-like, but steadfast, as of buildings of the ancient earth, wide founded, bastion upon huger bastion, buttress soaring to battlement, wall standing back upon wall, roof-ridge and gable and turret and airy spire; and yet all as if of no gross substance, but rather the thin spirit of these, and their grandeur not the grandeur of clouds that pass, but of frozen and unalterable repose, as of Gods reclining on heaven's brink. Astern, Acrozayana faced the warm light. On the starboard quarter, half a mile to the north, on a beach at the end of the low wooded promontory that stretches far out into the lake there towards Zayana town, two women were bathing. The sunset out of that serene and cloudless sky suffused their limbs and bodies, their reflections in the water, the woods behind them, with a glory that made them seem no women of mortal kind, but dryads or oreads of the hills come down to show their beauties to the opening eyes of night and, with the calm lake for their mirror, braid their hair.

In the outermost gondola on the northern horn was Lessingham, his soul and senses lapped in a lotus-like contentment. For beside him reclined Madam Campaspe, a young lady in whose sprightly discourse he savoured, and in the sleepy little noises of the water under the prow, a delectable present that wandered towards a yet more delectable to come.

'The seven seas,' he said, answering her: 'ever since I was fifteen year old.'

'And you are now—fifty?'

'Six times that,' answered Lessingham gravely; 'reckoned in months.'

'With me,' she said, 'reckonings go always askew.'

'Let's give over reckonings, then,' said he, 'and do it by example. I am credibly informed that I am pat of an age with your Duke.'

'O, so old indeed? Twenty-five? No marvel you are so staid and serious.'

'And you, madam?' said Lessingham. 'How far in the decline?'

'Nay, 'tis me to ask questions,' said she: 'you to answer.'

Idly Lessingham was looking at her hand which rested on the cushion beside him, gloved with a black scented gauntlet with falling cuff of open-work and flower-work of yellow zircons. 'I am all expectation,' he said.

Campaspe stole a glance at him. Her eyes were beady, like some shy creature's of the fields or woods. Her features, considered coldly one by one, had recalled strange deformities as of frogs or spiders; yet were they by those eyes welded to a kind of beauty. So might a queen of Elfland look, of an unfair, unhuman, yet most taking comeliness. 'Well,' said she: 'how many straws go to goose-nest?'

'None, for lack of feet.'

'O, unkind! You knew it afore. That cometh of this so much faring 'twixt land and land: maketh men too knowing.' After a little, she said, 'Tell me, is it not better here than in your northlands?'

'‘Tis at least much hotter,' said Lessingham.

'And which liketh you better, my lord, hot or cold?'

'Must I answer of airs, or of ladies' hearts?'

'You must keep order: answer of that you spoke on.'

'Nay,' said Lessingham, ''tis holiday. Let me be impertinent, and answer of that I set most store by.'

'Then, to be courtly, you must say cold is best,' said she. 'For our fashion here is cold hearts, as the easier changed.'

'Ah,' he said: 'I see there is something, madam, you are yet to learn.'

'How, my lord? i' the fashion?'

'O no. Because I am a soldier, yet have I not such nummed and so clumsy hands for't as tell a lady she's out of fashion. I meant 'tis warm hearts, not cold, are most apt to change: fire at each fresh kindling.'

'Here's fine doctrine,' said she. 'Do you rest it, pray, upon experience?'

He smiled. ''Tis a first point of wisdom', he replied, 'to affirm nought upon hearsay.'

Campaspe sat suddenly forward, with a little murmur of pleasure: 'O, my friend!' addressed, as Lessingham perceived, not to him but to a lady-duck with her seven young swimming close by in column ahead. For a fleeting instant, as she leaned eagerly across to watch them, her hand, put out to steady her, touched Lessingham's knee: a touch that, sylph-like and immaterial as a dream, sent a thousand serpents through his veins. The duck and her children took fright at the gondola, and, with a scutter of feet and wings, left a little wake of troubled water which showed the better, as a foil sets off a diamond, the placid smoothness of that lake.

'And how many foolish ladies ere now,' said Campaspe, very demurely, 'have you found to give open ear to these schoolings?'

'There, madam,' said he, 'you put me to a stand. They come and go, I suppose, with the changing of the moon.'

'I was a fine fool,' said she, 'to come into this boat with you, my lord.'

Lessingham smiled. 'I think,' he said, 'I know an argument, when we come to it, shall satisfy you to the contrary.' His eyes, half veiled under their long lashes, surveyed her now with a slow and disturbing gaze. It was as if the spirit that sat in them tasted, in a profound luxurious apprehension beyond the magic of mortal vintages, the wine of its own power: tasted it doubly, in her veins as in his own, attuning blood to blood. Then, turning his gaze from her to the back of his own hand, he looked at that awhile in silence as if there were there some comic engaging matter. 'Howe'er that be,' he said lightly at last, 'you must remember, 'tis the same moon. That were a quaint folly, for love of last month's moon at the full, to have done with moonlight for ever.'

'O, you can a game beside tennis, my lord, there's ne'er a doubt,' she said.

'I have beat the Duke ere now at tennis,' said Lessingham.

'That is hard,' said she. 'But 'tis harder to beat him at this.'

' 'Tis but another prime article of wisdom,' said Lessingham, 'ne'er to let past memories blunt the fine point of present pleasures. I am skilled,' he said, 'to read a lady's heart from her hand. Let me try.' Campaspe, laughing, struggled against him as he would have drawn off her glove. 'Moist palms argue warm hearts,' he said in her ear. 'Is that why you wear gloves, madam?'

'Nay, but I will not. Fie, shall the gondolier see us?'

'I am discretion itself,' said Lessingham.

'You must learn, my lord,' she said, putting away his hands, 'if you would have me to spread your table, to fall to it nicely, not swallow it like flapdragons.'

Lessingham said close at her ear, 'I'll be your scholar. Only but promise.'

But Campaspe said, 'No promises in Zayana: the Duke hath banned them. As for performance, why, respectful service, my lord, hath its payment here as in other lands.'

Her voice had taken on a new delicacy: the voice of willow-trees beside still water when the falling wind stirs them. The great flattened ball of the sun touched the western hills. Lessingham took her under the chin with his hand and turned her face towards his. 'I like little water-rats,' he said. Her eyes grew big and frightened, like some little fieldish thing's that sees a hawk. For a minute she abode motionless. Then, as if with a sudden resolution, she pulled off her glove: offered her bare hand, palm upwards, to his lips. The gondola lurched sideways. The lady laughed, half smothered: 'Nay, no more, my lord. Nay, and you will not have patience, you shall have nought, then.'

'Jenny wrens: water-rats: willow-leaves sharp against the moon like little feet. Why is your laugh like a night breeze among willows? Do I not descry you? behind your mask of lady of presence: you and your "friend." Are you not these? Tell me: Are you not?'

Each soft stroke of the gondolier's paddle at the stern came like one more drop in the cup of enchantment, which still brimmed and still did not run over. 'It is not time, my lord. O yes, these, and other besides. But see, we shall land upon the instant. I pray you, have patience. In this isle of Ambremerine is bosky glades removed, flowery headlands; in two hours the moon will ride high; and she, you know—'

'And she,' said Lessingham, 'is an ancient sweet suggester of ingenious pleasures.' He kissed the hand again. 'Let us turn the cat in the pan: say, If I have patience I shall have all, then?'

In Campaspe's beady eyes he read his passport.

Their landing was near about the south-east point of that isle, in a little natural harbour, half-moon shaped and with a beach of fine white sand. The sun had gone down, and dusk gathered on the lake; eastward, pale blue smoke hung here and there over Zayana and the citadel; the walls and the roofs and towers were grown shadowy and dim; their lamps came out like stars. In the north, the great peaks still held some light. A wide glade went up into the isle from that harbour in gently sloping lawns, shut in on all but the water side by groves of cypress-trees: pillar-like boles and dense spires so tangled, drenched, and impregnate with thick darkness that not mid-day itself might pierce nor black night deepen their elemental gloom. In the midst of that glade, on a level lawn where in their thousands daisies and little yellow cinquefoils were but now newly folded up and gone to sleep, tables were set for the feast. The main table faced south to the harbour, where the gondolas and the caravel, with their lofty stems and stern-posts and their lights, some red some green, floated graceful over their graceful images in the water. Two shorter tables ran down from that table's either end: the one faced Zayana and the night, and the other westward to the leavings of the sunset, above which the evening star, high in a pellucid heaven of pale chrysolite, burned like a diamond from Aphrodite's neck.

The tables were spread with damask, and set forth with a fish dinner: oysters and lobsters, crayfish both great and small, trout, tunny, salmon, sturgeon, lampreys and caviare, all in fair golden dishes, with mushrooms besides and sparrow-grass, cockscombs and truffles, and store of all manner of delicious fruits, and wines of all kind in great bowls and beakers of crystal and silver and gold: dry and ancient wines golden and tawny, good to sharpen the stomach and to whet the edge of wit; and red wines the heavy sweetness whereof, full of the colour of old sunsets and clinging to the goblet like blood, is able to mellow thought and steady the senses to a quiet where the inner voices may be heard; and wines the foam whereof whispers of that eternal sea and of that eternal spring-time towards which all memories return and all hearts' desires for ever. Fifty little boys, yellow-haired, clothed all in green, planted and tended torches behind the tables to give light to the feasters. Steady with the burning of those torches in the still summer air, with ever a little movement of their light, like the fall and swell of a girl's bosom; and the scent of their burning mingled in wafts with the flower scents and wood scents and the dew-laden breath of evening.

So now they made merry and supped under the sky. Scarcely was the sunset's last ember burned out westward, and night scarce well awake in the eastern heavens behind Zayana town, when from that quarter a bower of light began to spread upward, into which stepped at length, like a queen to lead night's pageant, the lady moon, and trailed her golden train across those sleeping waters. At that, their talk was stilled for a minute. Barganax, sitting in the midst of the cross table with Lessingham on his right, looked at Fiorinda, beside him on his left, as she looked at the moon. 'Your looking-glass,' he said, under his breath. Her face altered and she smiled, saying, with a lazy shrug of the shoulders, 'One of!'

'My Lord Lessingham,' said Campaspe: 'imagine me potent in art magic, able to give you the thing you would. Whether would you then choose pleasure or power?'

'That question,' answered he, 'in such company and on such a night, and most of all by moonrise, I can but answer in the words of the poet:

'My pleasure is my power to please my mistress:
    My power is my pleasure in that power.'

'A roundabout answer,' said the Duke: 'full of wiles and guiles. Mistrust it, madam.'

'Can your grace better it then?' said Campaspe.

'Most easily. And in one word: pleasure.'

Fiorinda smiled.

'Your ladyship will second me,' said the Duke. 'What's power but for the procuring of wise, powerful and glorious pleasures? What else availeth my dukedom? 'Las, I should make very light account thereof, as being a thing of very small and base value, save that it is a mean unto that rich and sunny diamond that outlustreth all else.'

'Philosophic disputation,' said Fiorinda, 'do still use to awake strange longings in me.'

'Longings?' said the Duke. 'You are mistress of our revels to-night. Breathe but the whisper of a half-shapen wish; lightning shall be slow to our suddenness to perform it.'

'For the present need,' said that lady, 'a little fruit would serve.'

'Framboises?' said the Duke, offering them in a golden dish.

'No,' she said, looking upon them daintily: 'they have too many twiddles in them: like my Lord Lessingham's distich.'

'Will your ladyship eat a peach?' said Melates.

'I could,' she said. 'And yet, no. Clingstone, 'tis too great trouble: freestone, I like them not. Your grace shall give me a summer poppering.'

The Duke sent his boy to fetch them from the end of the table. 'You shall peel it for me,' she said, choosing one.

Barganax, as drunk with some sudden exhalation of her beauty, the lazy voice, the lovely pausing betwixt torchlight and moonlight of fastidious jewelled fingers above the dish of pears was taken with a trembling that shook the dish in his hand. Mastering which, 'I had forgot,' he said with a grave courtesy, 'that you do favour this beyond all fruits else.'

'Forgot? Is it then so long ago your grace and I reviewed these matters? And indeed I had little fault to find with your partialities, nor you I think with mine.'

Lessingham, looking on at this little by-play, tasted in it a fine and curious delight; such delight as, more imponderable than the dew-sparkles on grass about sunrise or the wayward airs that lift the gossamer-spiders' threads, dances with fairy feet, beauty fitted to beauty, *allegretto scherzando,* in some great master's music. Only for the whim to set such divisions a-trip again, he spoke and said: 'If your ladyship will judge between us, I shall justify myself against the Duke that, would pleasure's self have had me, I should a refused to wed her. For there be pleasures base, illiberal, nasty, and merely hoggish. How then shall you choose pleasure *per se?*'

'By the same argument, how power *per se?*' replied the Duke. 'What of the gardener's dog, that could not eat the cabbages in the garden and would suffer none else to do so? Call you that power good? I think I have there strook you into the hazard, my lord. Or at least, 'tis change sides and play for the chase.'

'The chase is mine, then,' said Lessingham. 'For if power be but sometimes good, even so is pleasure. It must be noble pleasure, and the noblest pleasure is power.'

Fiorinda daintily bit a piece out of her pear.

'Pray you honour us, madam, to be our umpire,' said Lessingham.

She smiled, saying, 'It is not my way to sit in judgement. Only to listen.'

Barganax said, 'But will you listen to folly?'

'O yes,' answered she. 'There was often more good matter in one grain of folly than in a peck of wisdom.'

'Ha! that hath touched you, Vandermast,' said the Duke.

That aged man, sitting at the outer end of the eastern table betwixt Anthea and the young Countess Rosalura, laughed in his beard. The Lady Fiorinda lifted her eyebrows with a questioning look first upon him, then upon the Duke, then upon Lessingham. 'Is he wise?' she said. 'I had thought he was a philosopher. Truly, I could listen to him a whole summer's night and ne'er tire of his preposterous nonsense.'

'An old fool,' said Vandermast, 'that is yet wise enough to serve your ladyship.'

'Does that need wisdom?' she said, and looked at the moon. Lessingham, watching her face, thought of that deadly Scythian queen who gave Cyrus his last deep drink of blood. Yet, even so thinking, he was the more deeply aware, in the caressing charm of her voice, of a mind that savoured the world delicately and simply, with a quaint, amused humour; so might some demure and graceful bird gracefully explore this way and that, accepting or rejecting with an equable enjoyment. 'Does that need wisdom?' she said again. And now it was as if from that lady's lips some unheard song, some unseen beauty, had stolen abroad and taking to itself wings, mounted far from earth, far above the columnar shapes of those cypresses that, huge and erect, stood round that dim garden; until the vast canopy of night was all filled as with an impending flowering of unimagined wonder.

'There is no other wisdom than that: not in heaven or earth or under the earth, in the world phenomenal or the world noumenal, *sub specie temporali* or *sub specie æternitatis*. There is no other,' said Vandermast, in a voice so low that none well heard him, save only the Countess close by on his right. And she, hearing, yet not understanding, yet apprehending in her very bowels the tenour of his words, as a reed bending before the wind might apprehend dimly somewhat of what betided in the wind-ridden spaces without to bend and to compel it, sought Medor's hand and held it fast.

There was silence. Then Medor said, 'What of love?'

Vandermast said, as to himself, but the Countess Rosalura heard it: 'There is no other power.'

'Love,' said Lessingham, cool and at ease again after the passing of that sudden light, 'shall aptly point my argument. Here, as otherwhere, power ruleth. For what is a lover without power to win his mistress? or she without power to hold her lover?' His hand, as he spoke, tightened unseen about Campaspe's yielding waist. His eyes, carelessly roving, as he spoke, from face to face of that company, came to a stop, meeting Anthea's where she sat beside the learned doctor. The tawny wealth of her deep hair was to the cold beauty of her face as a double curtain of fulvid glory. Her eyes caught and held his gaze with a fascination, hard, bold, and inscrutable.

'I have been told that Love,' said Fiorinda, 'is a more intricate game than tennis; or than soldiership; or than politicians' games, my Lord Lessingham.'

Anthea, with a little laugh, bared her lynx-like teeth. 'I was remembered of a saying of your ladyship's,' she said.

Fiorinda lifted an eyebrow, gently pushing her wine-cup towards the Duke for him to fill it.

'That a lover who should think to win his mistress by power,' said Anthea, 'is like an old dried-up dotard who would be young again by false hair, false teeth, and skilful painting of his face: thus, and with a good stoup of wine, but one thing he lacketh, and that the one thing needful.'

'Did I say so indeed?' said Fiorinda, 'I had forgot it. In truth, this is strange talk, of power and pleasure in love,' she said. 'There is a garden, there is a tree in the garden, there is a rose upon the tree. Can a woman not keep her lover without she study always to please him with pleasure? Pew! then let her give up the game. Or shall my lover think with pleasing of me to win me indeed? Faugh! he payeth me then; doth he think I am for hire?'

Barganax sitting beside her, not looking at her, his shoulder towards her, his elbow on the table, his fingers in an arrested stillness touching his mustachios, gazed still before him as though all his senses listened to the last scarce-heard cadence of the music of that lady's voice.

Fiorinda, in that pause, looked across to Doctor Vandermast. Obedient to her look, he stood up now and raised a hand twice and thrice above his head as in sign to somewhat to come out of the shadows that stirred beyond the torchlight. The moon rode high now over Zayana, and out of torchbeam and moonbeam and star-beam was a veil woven that confounded earth and sky and water into an immateriality of uncertain shade and misty light. At Van-dermast's so standing up, the very night seemed to slip down into some deeper pool of stillness, like the silent slipping of an otter down from the bank into the black waters. Only the purr of a night-jar came from the edge of the woods. And now on the sudden they at the tables were ware of somewhat quick, that stood in the con-fines of the torchlight and the shadowy region without; of man-like form, but little of stature, scarce reaching with its head to the elbow of a grown man; with shaggy hairy legs and goat's feet, and with a sprouting of horns like a young goat's upon its head; and there was in its eyes the appearance as of red coals burning. Piercing were the glances of those eyes, as they darted in swift suc-cession from face to face (save that before Fiorinda's it dropped its gaze as if in worship), and piercing was the music of the song it sang: the song that lovers and great poets have ravished their hearts to hear since the world began: a night-song, bitter-sweet, that shakes the heart of darkness with longings and questionings too tumultuous for speech to fit or follow; and in that song the listener hears echoing up the abysses of eternity voices of men and women unborn answering the voices of the dead.

Surely, hearkening to that singing, all they sat like as amazed or startled out of sleep. Lover clung to lover: Amaury to velvet-eyed Violante, Myrrha to Zapheles, Bellafront to Barrian. Lessingham's encircling arm drew closer about his Campaspe: her breast beneath the silk under his hand was a tremulous dove: her black eyes rested as though in soft accustomed contemplation upon the singer. Pantasilea, with heavy lids and heavy curled lips half closed, as in half eclipse of the outward sense, lay back sideways on Melates's shoulder. Medor held gathered to him like a child his sweet young Countess. Beyond them, in the outermost place of the eastern table, Anthea sat upright and listening, her hair touching with some stray tendrils of its glory the sleeve of old Vandermast's gaberdine where he stood motionless beside her.

Only the Lady Fiorinda seemed to listen fancy-free to that singing, even as the cold moon, mistress of the tides, has yet no part in their restless ebb and flow, but, taking her course serene far above the cloudy region of the air, surveys these and all earthly things with equal eye, divine and passionless. The Duke, sitting back, had this while watched her from the side from under his faun-like eyebrows, his hand moving as if with chalk or brush. He leaned nearer now, giving over that painting motion: his right elbow on the table, his left arm resting, but not to touch her, on the back of her chair. The voice of the singer, that was become as the echoes of a distant music borne on the breeze from behind a hill, now made a thin obbligato to the extreme passionate love that spoke in the Duke's accents like the roll of muffled thunder as, low in her ear, he began to say:

> O forest of dark beasts about the base
>   Of some white peak that dreams in the Empyrean:
> O hare's child sleeping by a queen's palace,
>   'Mid lily-meadows of some isle Lethean:
> Barbaric, beastly, virginal, divine:
>   Fierce feral loveliness: sweet secret fire:
> Last rest and bourne of every lovely line:
>   —All these Thou art, that art the World's Desire.

The deep tones of the Duke's voice, so speaking, were hushed to the quivering superficies of silence, beneath which the darkness stirred as with a rushing of arpeggios upon muted strings. In the corner of that lady's mouth, as she listened, the minor diabolus, dainty and seductive, seemed to turn and stretch in its sleep. Lessingham, not minded to listen, yet heard. Darkly he tasted in his own flesh Barganax's secret mind: in what fashion this Duke lived in that seeming woman's life far sweetlier that in his own. He leaned back to look upon her, over the Duke's shoulder. He saw now that she had glow-worms in her hair. But when he would have beheld her face, it was as if spears of many-coloured light, such light as, like the halo about the moon, is near akin to darkness, swept in an endless shower outward from his vision's centre; and now when he would have looked upon her he saw but these outrushings, and in the fair line of vision not darkness indeed but the void: a solution of continuity: nothing.

As a man that turns from the halcyon vision to safe verities, he turned to his Campaspe. Her lips invited sweetly: he bent to them.

With a little ripple of laughter, they eluded him, and under his hand, with soft arched back warm and trembling, was the water-rat in very deed.

About the north-western point of that island there was a garden shadowed with oaks ten generations old and star-proof cedars and delicate-limbed close-turfed strawberry-trees. Out of its leafy darknesses nightingale answered nightingale, and nightflowers, sweet-mouthed like brides in their first sleep, mixed their sweetness with the breath of the dews of night. It was now upon the last hour before midnight. From the harbour to the southward rose the long slumbrous notes of a horn, swelling, drawing their heavy sweetness across the face of the night sky. Anthea stood up, slender as a moonbeam in those silent woods. 'The Duke's horn,' she said. 'We must go back; unless you are minded to lodge in this isle to-night, my Lord Lessingham.'

Lessingham stood up and kissed her hand. For a minute she regarded him in silence from under her brow, her eyes burning steadily, her chin drawn down a little: an unsmiling lip-licking look. Then giving him her arm she said, as they turned to be gone, 'There is discontent in your eyes. You are dreaming on somewhat without me and beyond.'

'Incomparable lady,' answered he, 'call it a surfeit. If I am discontented, it is with the time, that draweth me from these high pleasures to where, as cinders raked up in ashes,—'

'O no nice excuses,' she said. 'I and Campaspe are not womankind. Truly, 'tis but at Her bidding we durst not disobey we thus have dallied with such as you, my lord.'

His mustachios stirred.

'You think that a lie?' she said. 'The unfathomed pride of mortals!'

Lessingham said, 'My memories are too fiery clear.'

They walked now under the obscurity of crowding cypresses. 'It is true,' said Anthea, 'that you and Barganax are not altogether as the common rout of men. This world is yours, yours and his, did you but know it. And did you know it, such is the folly of mortals, you would straight be out of conceit with it and desire another. But you are well made, not to know these things. See, I tell it you, yet you believe it not. And though I should tell you from now till dawn, yet you would not believe.' She laughed.

'You are pleasantly plain with me,' said Lessingham after a pause.

'You can be fierce. So can I. I do love your fierceness, your bites and scratches, madam. Shall I be plain too?' He looked down; her face, level with his shoulder, wore a singular look of benign tranquillity. 'You,' he said, '(and I must not omit Mistress Campaspe), have let me taste this night such pleasures as the heroes in Elysium, I well think, taste nought sweeter. Yet would I have more; yet, what more, I know not.'

Without looking at him, she made a little mow. 'In your erudite conversation, my lord, I have tasted this night such pleasures as I am by nature accustomed to. I desire no more. I am, even as always I am, contented.'

'As always?' said he.

'Is "always" a squeeze of crab-orange in your cup, my lord? 'Tis wholesome truth, howsoe'er. And now, in our sober voyaging back to Zayana, with the learn'd doctor conducting of us, I do look for no less bliss than—: but this you will think ungracious?'

She looked up, with a little pressure of her arm on his. His eyes, when he turned his face to hers, were blurred and unseeing.

The path came into the open now, as they crossed the low backbone of the island. They walked into a flood of moonlight; on their left, immeasurably far away, the great snow ranges stood like spirits in the moon-drenched air. Anthea said, 'Behold that mountain, my lord, falling away to the west in saw-toothed ridges a handbreadth leftward of the sycamore-tree. That is Ramosh Arkab; and I say to you, I have dwelt there 'twixt wood and snowfield ten million years.'

They were now come down to the harbour. The cypress-shadowed glade lay empty: the tables taken up where their banquet had been: the torches and the feasters gone. Far away on the water the lights of the gondolas showed where they took their course homeward to Zayana. Under an utter silence and loneliness of moonlight the lawns sloped gently to the lake. One gondola only lay by the landing-stage. Beside it waited that aged man. With a grave obeisance he greeted Lessingham; they went aboard all three, loosed, and put out. There was no gondolier. Doctor Vandermast would have taken the paddle, but Lessingham made him sit beside Anthea in the seat of honour, and himself, sitting on the fore-deck with his feet in the boat's bottom, paddled her stern-foremost. So they had passage over those waters that were full of drowned stars and secret unsounded deeps of darkness. Something broke the smoothness on the starboard bow; Lessingham saw, as they neared it, that it was the round head of an otter, swimming towards Ambremerine. It looked at them with its little face and hissed. In a minute it was out of eyeshot astern.

'My beard was black once,' said Vandermast. 'Black as yours, my lord.' Lessingham saw that the face of that old man was blanched in the moonlight, and his eyes hidden as in ocean caves or deep archways of some prison-house, so that only with looking upon him a man might not have known for sure whether there were eyes in truth within those shadows or but void eye-sockets and eclipsing darkness. Anthea sat beside him in a languorous grace. She trailed a finger in the water, making a little rippling noise, pleasant to the ear. Her face, too, was white under the moon, her hair a charmed labyrinth of moonbeams, her eyes pits of fire.

'Dryads,' said Vandermast, after a little, 'are in two kinds, whereof the one is more nearly consanguineous with the more madefied and waterish natures, naiads namely and nerieds; but the other kind, having their habitation nearer to the meteoric houses and the cold upper borders of woods appropinquate to the snows and the gelid ice-streams of the heights, do derive therefrom some qualities of the oreads or mountain nymphs. I have indulged my self-complacency as far as to entertain hopes, my lord, that, by supplying for your entertainment one of either sort, and discoursing so by turns two musics to your ear, *andante piacevole e lussurioso* and then *allegro appassionato,* I may have opened a more easier way to your lordship's perfect satisfaction and profitable enjoyment of this night's revelries.'

That old man's talk, droning slow, made curious harmonies with the drowsy body of night; the dip and swirl and dip again of Lessingham's paddle; the drip of water from the blade between the strokes.

'Where did your lordship forsake my little water-rat?' he asked in a while.

'She was turned willow-wren at the last,' answered Lessingham.

'Such natures,' said Vandermast, 'do commonly suck much gratification out of change and the variety of perceptible form and corporeity. But I doubt not your lordship, with your more settled preferences and trained appetites, found her most acceptable in form and guise of a woman?'

'She did me the courtesy,' answered Lessingham, 'to maintain that shape for the more part of our time together.

They proceeded in silence. Vandermast spoke again. 'You find satisfaction, then, in women, my lord?'

'I find in their society,' Lessingham answered, 'a pleasurable interlude.'

'That,' said that learned man, 'agreeth with the conclusion whereunto, by process of ratiocination, I was led upon consideration of that stave or versicule recited by your lordship about one hour since, and composed, if I mistake not, by your lordship. Went it not thus?—

> 'Anthea, wooed with flatteries,
> To please her lover's fantasies,
> Unlocks her bosom's treasuries.—
> Ah! silver apples like to these
> Ne'er grew, save on those holy trees
> Tended by nymphs Hesperides.'

'What's this?' said Lessingham, and there was danger in his voice.

'You must not take it ill,' said Vandermast, 'that this trifle, spoke for her ear only and the jealous ear of night, was known to me without o'erhearing. Yourself are witness that neither you nor she did tell it me, and indeed I was half a mile away, so scarce could a heard it. A little cold: a little detached, methought, for a love-poem. But indeed I do think your lordship is a man of deeds. Do you find satisfaction, then, in deeds?'

'Yes,' answered he.

'Power,' said that learned doctor: 'power; which maketh change. Yea, but have you considered the power that is in Time, young man? to change the black hairs of your beard to blanched hairs, like as mine: and the last change of Death? that, but with waiting and expecting and standing still, overcometh all by drawing of all to its own likeness. Dare your power face that power, to go like a bridegroom to annihilation's bed? Let me look at your eyes.'

Lessingham, whose eyes had all this while been fixed upon Vandermast's, said, 'Look then.'

The face of the night was altered now. A cool drizzle of rain dimmed the moon: the gondola seemed to drift a-beam, cut off from all the world else upon desolate waters. Vandermast's voice came like the soughing of a distant wind: 'The hairless, bloodless, juiceless, power of silence,' he said, 'that consumeth and abateth and swalloweth up lordship and subjection, favour and foulness, lust and satiety, youth and eld, into the dark and slubbery mess of nothingness.' Lessingham saw that the face of that old man was become now a shrivelled death's-head, and his eyes but windows opening inwards upon the horror of an empty skull. And that lynx-eyed mountain nymph, fiercely glaring, crouching sleek and spotted beside him, was become now a lynx indeed, with her tufted slender ears erect and the whiskers moving nervously right and left of her snarling mouth. And Vandermast spake loud and hoarse, crying out and saying, 'You shall die young, my Lord Lessingham. Two years, a year, may be, and you shall die. And then what help shall it be that you with your high gifts of nature did o'ersway great ones upon earth (as here but to-day you did in Acrozayana), and did ride the great Vicar of Rerek, your curst and untamed horse, till he did fling you to break your neck, and die at the last? What is fame to the deaf dust that shall then be your delicate ear, my lord? What shall it avail you then that you had fair women? What shall it matter though they contented you never? seeing there is no discontent whither you go down, my lord, neither yet content, but the empty belly of darkness enclosing eternity upon eternity. Or what shall even that vision beyond the veil profit you (if you saw it indeed to-night, then ere folk rose from table), since that is but impossibility, fiction and vanity, and shall then be less than vanity itself: less than the dust of you in the worm's blind mouth? For all departeth, all breaketh and perisheth away, all is hollowness and nothing worth ere it sink to very nothing at last.'

'I saw nought,' said Lessingham. 'What is that Lady Fiorinda then?' His voice was level; only the strokes of his paddle came with a more steadier resolution, may be, of settled strength as that old man spoke.

The gondola lurched sideways. Lessingham turned swiftly from his outstaring of that aged man to bring her safe through a sudden turmoil of the waters that rose now and opened downward again to bottomless engulfings. Pale cliffs superimpended in the mist and the darkness, and fires burned there, with the semblance as of corpse-fires. And above those cliffs was the semblance of icy mountains, and streams that rolled burning down them of lava, making a sizzling in the water that was heard high above the voice of the waves; and Lessingham beheld walking shrouded upon the cliffs faceless figures, beyond the stature of human kind, that seemed to despair and lament, lifting up skinny hands to the earless heaven. And while he beheld these things, there was torn a ragged rift in the clouds, and there fled there a bearded star, baleful in the abyss of night. And now there was thunder, and the noise as of a desolate sea roaring upon the coasts of death. Then, as a thought steps over the threshold of oblivion, all was gone; the cloudless summer night held its breath in the presence of its own inward blessedness: the waters purred in their sleep under the touch of Anthea's idly trailing finger.

Lessingham laid down his paddle and clapped his right hand to his hip; but they had gone unweaponed to that feast. Without more ado he with an easy swiftness, scarcely to rock the boat, had gotten in his left hand the two wrists of Vandermast: his right hand slid up beneath the long white beard, and fumbled the doctor's skinny throat. 'Scritch-owl,' he said, 'you would unman me, ha? with your sickly bodings? You have done it, I think: but you shall die for't.' The iron strength of his fingers toyed delicately about that old man's weasand.

Very still sat Doctor Vandermast. He said, 'Suffer me yet to speak.'

'Speak and be sudden,' said Lessingham.

Surely that old man's eyes looked now into his with a brightness that was as the lifting up of day. 'My Lord Lessingham,' he said, '*per realitatem et perfectionem idem intelligo:* in my conceit, reality and perfection are one. If therefore your lordship have suffered an inconvenience, you are not to revenge it upon me: your disorder proceedeth but from partial apprehension.'

'Ha! but did not you frame and present me with fantasticoes? did not you spit your poison?' said Lessingham. 'Do not mistake me: I am not afeared of my death. But I do feel within me somewhat, such as I ne'er did meet with its like aforrow, and I know not what it is, if it be not some despair. Wherefore, teach me to apprehend fully, you were best, and that presently. Or like a filthy fly I'll finger you off to hell.' Upon which very word, he strangely took his fingers from the lean weasand of that old man and let go the lean wrists.

Vandermast said, as if to himself, '*Cum mens suam impotentiam imaginatur, eo ipso contristatur:* when the mind imagineth its own impotence, it by that only circumstance falleth into a deep sadness. My lord,' he said, raising his head to look Lessingham in the face, 'I did think you had seen. Had you so seen, these later sights I did present you, and these prognostications of decay, could not have cankered so your mind: they had been then but as fumadoes, hot and burning spices, to awake your appetite the more and prepare you for that cup whereof he that drinketh shall for ever thirst and for ever be satisfied; yea, and without it there is no power but destroyeth and murdereth itself at last, nor no pleasure but disgusteth in the end, like the stench of the dead.'

'Words,' said Lessingham. 'The mouth jangleth, as lewd as a lamp that no light is in. I tell you, I saw nought: nought but outrushing lights and dazzles. And now, I feel my hand upon a latch, and you, in some manner I understand not, by some damned sleight, withholding me. Teach me, as you said but now, to apprehend fully. But if not, whether you be devil or demigod or old drivelling disard as I am apt to think you: by the blessed Gods, I will tear you into pieces.'

Anthea widened her lips and laughed. 'Now you are in a good vein, my lord. Shall I bite his throat out?' She seemed to slaver at the mouth. 'You are a lynx, go,' said Lessingham. It was as if the passion of his anger was burnt out, like a fire of dead leaves kindled upon a bed of snow.

Vandermast's lean hands twisted and unclasped their fingers together in his lap. 'I had thought,' he said, to himself aloud, in the manner of old men, 'her ladyship would have told me. O inexorable folly to think so! Innumerable laughter of the sea: ever changing: shall I never learn?'

'What is that lady?' said Lessingham.

Vandermast said, 'You did command me, my lord, to learn you to apprehend fully. But here, *in limine demonstrationis,* upon the very threshold, appeareth a difficulty beyond solution, in that your lordship is instructed already in things contingent and apparent, *affectiones, actiones,* phenomenal actualities *rei politiæ et militaris,* the council chamber and the camp, *puella-puellæ* and matters conducive thereunto. But in things substantial I find you less well grounded, and here it is beyond my art to carry you further seeing my art is the doctor's practice of reason; because things substantial are not known by reason but by perception: *perceptio per solam suam essentiam;* and *omnis substantia est necessario infinita:* all substance, in its essence, infinite.'

'Leave this discourse,' said Lessingham, 'which, did I understand its drift, should make me, I doubt not, as wise as a capon. Answer me: of what *substantia* or *essentia* is that lady?'

Doctor Vandermast lowered his eyes. 'She is my Mistress,' he said.

'That, to use your gibberish, old sir, is *per accidens*,' said Lessingham. 'I had supposed her the Duke's mistress: the Devil's mistress too, belike. But *per* essence, what is she? Why did my eyes dazzle when I would have looked upon her but at that moment tonight? since many a time ere then I easily enough beheld her. And why should aught lie on it, that they did so dazzle? Come, we have dealt with seeming women to-night that be nymphs of the lakes and mountains, taking at their will bird-like shapes and beastly. What is she? Is she such an one? Tell me, for I will know.'

'No,' said Vandermast, shaking his head. 'She is not such as these.'

Eastward, ahead, Lessingham saw how, with the dancings of summer lightnings, the sky was opened on a sudden behind the towers and rampires of Acrozayana. For that instant it was as if a veil had been torn to show where, built of starbeams and empyreal light, waited, over all, the house of heart's desire.

That learned man was searching now beneath the folds of his gaberdine, and now he drew forth a little somewhat and, holding it carefully in his fingers, scanned it this way and that and raised it to view its shape against the moon. Then, giving it carefully to Lessingham, 'My lord,' she said, 'take this, and tender it as you would a precious stone; for indeed albeit but a little withered leaf, there be few jewels so hard to come by or of such curious virtue. Because I have unwittingly done your lordship an ill service to-night, and because not wisdom itself could conduct you to that apprehension you do stand in need of, I would every deal I may to serve and further you. And because I know (both of my own judgement and by certain weightier confirmations of my art) the proud integrity of your lordship's mind and certain conditions of your inward being, whereby I may, without harm to my own fealty, trust you thus, albeit tomorrow again our enemy: therefore, my Lord Lessingham, behold a thing for your peace. For the name of this leaf is called *sferra cavallo*, and this virtue it hath, to break and open all locks of steel and iron. Take it then to your bed, my lord, now in the fair guest-chamber prepared for you in Acrozayana. And if, for the things you saw and for the things you saw not to-night, your heart shall be troubled, and sleep stand iron-eyed willing not to lie down with you and fold her plumes about your eyelids, then if you will, my lord, taking this leaf, you may rise and seek. What I may, that do I, my lord, giving you this. There shall, at least, no door be shut against you. But when night is done and day cometh you must by all means, (and this lieth upon your honour), burn the leaf. It is to do you good I give it unto you, and for your peace. Not for a weapon against my own sovereign lord.'

Lessingham took it and examined it well in the light of the moon. Then, with a noble look to Vandermast, he put it away like a jewel in his bosom.

FLETCHER PRATT

ONE of the strongest threads that is woven through the complex tapestry of fantastic literature is a strand spun from the Icelandic sagas. Morris began it and Eddison followed it for a time. Our next author, Fletcher Pratt (1897–1956), read and admired both of these writers and, when he came to create his own imaginary worlds, he worked in their tradition.

Pratt was a historian essentially, and most of his books are on naval history or the Civil War. But a fondness for "the Northern thing" illuminated his inner vision as it had that of Morris and Eddison before him, and C. S. Lewis during his own time. His work in the fantasy genre was very brief; outside of several lighthearted magazine stories written with his friend L. Sprague de Camp, he authored only two fantasy novels. But they are memorable novels, both of them: very different in style and form, but inimitable.

I refer to *The Well of the Unicorn* (1948), a rather straightforward heroic saga, and *The Blue Star* (1952), something very different. Whereas *Well* is set in a raw, brawling, sort of Viking world, with a hero properly heroic, the *Star* is laid in a tawdry, tinsel worldscape rather reminiscent of the Austrian Empire of the eighteenth century—say, about the reign of Maria Theresa—and the story is otherwise noteworthy in its use of an anti-hero for the viewpoint character. To put it bluntly, the fellow is a shameless cad.

But *Well* is not just another gold and "gold and crimson and purple" world of pulp-age heroica: Pratt was too keen and intelligent a man for *that* fluffery. He put together a world the way worlds really are put together, peopled it with noble-hearted and chivalrous kings *as well as* ignorant boorish bumpkins and sniveling gutter-snipes. A world full of gorgeous palaces and magnificent scenery, sure, but with squalid hovels and streets full of stinking mud. In other words: a *world*—warts and all.

His hero is a raw, awkward country bumpkin who does not aspire to greatness, but who accepts the burden when greatness is thrust upon him—to somewhat mangle Shakespeare's encomium on Malvolio—and who grows and matures beneath the burden. Much as a certain Frodo was to grow and mature beneath another burden in a book which was not published until five years after *The Well of the Unicorn.*

And, as *lagniappe*, he gave us one of the most delightful of the magicians in this literature. His Dr. Meliboë, a shameless, silver-tongued old con man, is the most interesting wizard in fantasy between Eddison's Dr. Vandermast and Tolkien's irascible and can-tankerous Gandalf.

Let me introduce you to him in the episode which follows here, and which has never before appeared in an anthology.

DOCTOR MELIBOË THE ENCHANTER

1

AIRAR could hear the horses before they reached the corner of the hedge where the big plane tree was. They were six in number, not talking—an oldish man in dirty blue with a twist-beard, who would be the bailiff; three archers, one of them a dark-skinned Micton man with his bow already strung; and damned Fabrizius in the middle, with his broad flat face and nose held high, well muffled in a fur-lined jacket and followed by a servant on a horse that stumbled.

Airar stood up with the wintry southering sun striking through branches across his face as one of the archers helped his lordship the bailiff to descend, the row of seals across his belly tinkling against each other like cracked pans. He had a parchment in his sleeve.

"I have a mission in the Count's name with Alvar Airarson."

"He is not here. I am Airar Alvarson."

Beyond, Airar could see Fabrizius shake his head—with that expression of decent regret that always covered his baseness.

"Then you stand deputy in his name as the heir of the house?" asked the bailiff, more with statement than question. "In accordance with the statute of the fourth year of Count Vulk, fourteenth of the name, relating to real properties, confirmed by the Emperor Auraris, I make demand on this estate for two years' arrears of the wall tax; and moreover for repayment of certain sums loaned to the estate by one Leonce Fabrizius, the said loan having been duly registered with the chancery of Vastmanstad and attest by the mark of Alvar Airarson."

Airar swallowed and took half a step, but the bailiff surveyed him with the impassive eye of a fish while the Micton archer tittered and nocked a shaft. "I do not have the money," said he.

"Then in the name of the law and the Count, I do declare this stead called Trangsted forfeit to the Empire. Yet as it is provided in the statute of the realm that no stead shall be forfeit without price, but acquired by purchase only, I do offer you the sum of one gold aura therefor out of the Count's generosity, and those present shall be witness. Wherewith you stand quit of all claims against you and go free." He fumbled the piece from the scrip at his side, bored manner of a formula of many repetitions. For a moment Airar seemed like to strike it from his hand; then seeing the Micton's covetous eye fall toward it, reached instead.

"So now this land and house are the property of our Count. I call on you to leave it, bearing not more than you carry on your back without setting the bundle down for five thousand paces." He turned from Airar, business with him done, to look expectant at Fabrizius; but the latter beckoned to Alvarson, who stood a moment with hand on pack, mouth set in a line of mutiny, yet well enough bred to hear what even the Prince of Hell had to say for himself.

"A moment, son of Alvar," said he while Airar noted how the little tuft of fur over his ear wagged as the broad mouth opened. "You have not been altogether well treated, and though you may not believe it, I hold a high regard for you. For as our Count has said, we must all live together, Dalecarles and Vulkings, each giving his best to make one people in this land. So I have made a place for you where you can do better than well. If you will go to Naaros by the dock and tell your name to the master of the cog *Unicorn*, he will make you of his company for a voyage of sure profit. Come, my boy, your hand."

"No hand," said Airar shortly, and swinging his pack up started resolutely down between the hedges wondering whether he ought not to throw a spell, but no, they would have protection. Fabrizius shrugged and turned to the bailiff, but now it was the latter's turn to be busy, signing to the tall archer, the one who had remained mounted, to go with the young man—perhaps fearing some trick of violence like a return along the shadow of the hedge and a flung knife, though Airar carried no other weapon.

As he turned down the road where the hedge fell low, an old brown horse beginning to turn grey at the edges lifted his head and stepped slowly toward the roadside. His name was Pil. Airar looked past him, not meeting his eye, past the house where now no smoke came from the chimney, across the long brown fells rising like waves with crests of brush here and there, till they went up into the rounded crests of the Hogsback, with black trees thinning out to pine and the gleam of snow along the upper ridges far beyond. A door banged sharply in the still air, Leonce Fabrizius entering his new house. Good-bye, Trangsted—good-bye, Pil. Airar shook his head, trudging along, and the tall archer leaned down:

"Cheer up, younker, you have the world to make. What you need is a couple of nights with one of Madame Korin's girls at Naaros. That'll fix you up."

The horse's hoofs went klop-klop on the frozen road and Airar said nothing.

"You get over it. Why, when I was a lad we were taxed out ourselves—that was up in West Lacia in the days of the old Count and how I came into service, scrubbing armor at Briella, when the old man went down there and hired himself out for a cook in the castle, at the time of the Count's war with the heathens."

Not a word said Airar, and the tall archer tapped the neck of his horse with one glove.

"Now take yourself," he went on. "Here you are, a free man, no debts, or service due, and a figure to make some of those court

fillies prance to be ridden or a baron glad to have you at his gate.
The world's not perfect, but a young fellow is a fool not to make
the best out of what he has given him. Set yourself up for an
archer, younker, or a billman, which is easier; you'll be noticed,
never doubt it. I've done all right at Briella and here I am with a
face to scare mice. But you're a Dalecarle, not so? Well, then, try
Salmonessa; Duke Roger keeps lively girls there and I have heard
he keeps an agent in Naaros to wage men. I'll even give you a
word. What do you say?"

"No, bugger Roger of Salmonessa."

"Why, you sguittard, you milk-sucker, if—"

He jerked hard on the rein and Airar looked up angry into a face
unlike most Vulkings, long, lean, and lined from nose to jaw. "Oh,
sir," he cried, all his black mood running off as soon as it had accomplished its object of reaching another, "I cry your pardon.
There must be a doom on me that always I strike at those who
would be my friends. But in fact you speak at a hard time when I
have lost everything and can gain nothing, being clerk but kept by
law from it, nor carry weapons in Dalarna that is my home, nor
have even a roof to my head."

The tall archer dropped rein and hand, now mollified. "No matter, younker. I grant you grace. Aye, it would be an ill life, playing
tomcat to one of Duke Roger's bawds. Duke! Why, he's only a
hedge-duke, or duke of the rabbits, not worth sitting at the feet of a
simple count. Now—"

He left it unfinished and for a while they strode and rode along
with communication silently established past the stead where the
three sons of Viclid used to live. There were a couple of Micton
slaves in the barnyard, trying to persuade a bullock to some mysterious doing, trotting around incompetently with many cries, the
slow beef pulling from their grasp. The young man thought of these
clumsy fools tracking mud across the floors of Trangsted. Presently
the place and the hill on which it stood were left behind, the noise
behind them still, and the tall archer said:

"My name is Pertuit. You are for Naaros, then?"

"Where else?"

"Kinfolk there?"

Airar gave a short, hard laugh, like a bark. "A—a—father's
brother—Tholo hight."

"No friend of mine. But it is said: long is the street where no
sibling sits at the end."

"Aye. Tholo Airarson sits in a street where Leonce Fabrizius' house is and plays his client."

The archer Pertuit whistled. "That's a fine coil. Not that I have anything against Fabrizius, but you were a pig's head sure to be his man, even at the second remove, under the circumstances. Yet what else have you? Hell's broth, it's like being taken by the heathen of Dzik, that offer you a horse—to ride with them to the wars or before them to the scaffold. I was there once, but I found a little black-haired wench who would rather have me play jig on a pallet with her than alone at the end of a rope, therefore escaped."

He shook his head, problem too deep for him, and they came to the crest of another of the long fingers reaching down from the Hogsback. The trees by the roadside dropped away here and a little distance out the knuckle ended, so they could see for miles in the windless clear air out to the west where a clump of wood on the horizon took a nip from the sinking sun. Between were long fields, only a few checkered with winter plowing, the rest brown pasture and animals like toys, moving slowly. Through its center ran the great river, the Naar, dark blue in illumination already becoming uncertain, with flashes of white that caught the last light as ice slid down its floor toward Naaros city.

Pertuit the archer drew rein. "I call this five thousand paces," said he, "and moreover, I'm for supper. Look here, younker, we spend the night at that place of yours, Dingsted or Frogsted or how you call it. But tomorrow I'll be back in the city. Ask for me at the archers' barracks, foot of the citadel, toward evening. We'll toss a pot and think what may be done. You're all right."

He reached down a hand and this time Airar touched it. "Done—at the archers' barracks," Airar said. The archer turned round and with a "Hey Nonnine," to make his horse trot, was gone back down into the shadows of the valley they had just left. Airar Alvarson turned down the opposite slope, alone in the world with his single gold noble, his pack, and his knife, going to the city certainly, but now it struck him for the first time that a city is a big place, not friendly like the steads of the hills, and he would be certain to arrive after dark when the gates were shut with a watch over them. No matter; he had slept abroad before, and in winter, fox-trapping up the Hogsback fells. But it was not comfortable.

So he walked and meditated down into the vale from which the next finger rose to bar the way to Naaros. The sun had gone down,

but up aloft it was still bright. In that dim brightness a big owl flew
out of somewhere and lit on a long branch that overreached the
road. Airar looked up at it. The owl stretched one wing, shifted its
claws on the branch, and said abruptly:

"Airar Alvarson."

Perhaps some other might have doubted his own hearing, but
this young man had long since reached for himself the thought that
the world's not all made of matter. He stopped, gazed, and without
showing whether startled or not, said, "What will you have?"

"Airar Alvarson," repeated the owl.

"Lira-lira-bekki," said Aira, and giving a yank to his pack, which
was growing heavy, put down his head and trudged along. When
he had gone about a hundred yards the owl swept dimly past him
through the gloom and perching on another branch by the roadside,
said once more, "Airar Alvarson."

Ahead, down at the bottom of the valley, someone was coming
out from the city in a cart, the first person Airar had met on that
road. The shape was dim but the horse's hoofbeats could be heard
change sound on the wooden bridge at the bottom, and one of the
wheels needed tallow. A few minutes more and there he was, an old
man with no cap on his white head and a sleepy boy leaning
against him, who gave Airar soft-voiced greeting and nodded his
head to the return. When he was well past and Airar himself was
crossing the bridge, the owl came and sat on the hand-rail at its further end, once more repeating its two-word remark.

—Fabrizius' work, reflected Airar and began looking annoyedly
for a stone to throw, but looking, reflected that one does not get rid
of a sending with a thrown stone, so called up his clerkly knowledge
to mind. The Seven Powers?—would take a spray of witch-hazel
twisted so, and how find it in the dark? Nor the Three Divinities either, which needed a reading from the book, too long to make by
any flicker he might strike from tinder there. So he even had to bear
the sending, plodding along the road through night now complete
with a slice of moon just beginning behind the trees, on the road toward Naaros. It was after all harmless enough to be silly, a big bird
that fluttered a few yards ahead to light and again repeat his name
with idiot persistence, only kept him from bedding down when he
otherwise might.

So they moved, man and owl, over the last of the low ridges
above the plain. There was a stead on the far slope with a light in

the window behind bushes and somebody singing inside; in another mood he might have sought harborage and been happy, but he was feeling all the world lost with the penalties of the afternoon and the owl hooting round his head, so pressed on down the plain, where the lights and towers of the city showed distant beyond the great sweep of the Naar, glittering faintly under its bridges in the starshine.

2

The way led now downhill through a tall alley of trees with more behind them that concealed whatever view there had been from the hilltop. There were hedges of thorn-apple grown rank, their unfriendly spicules outflung against the night sky, when he paused on the uncertain footing to glance at the odd bird which followed him still. Small things moved among hedge and trees; and they reached a place where a path led winding from the road leftward, not wide enough for a cart. Here Airar looked sharp, for something long and grey scuttled across the path, and through the screen of leafless branches a flicker of light seemed to leap and disappear; not warm yellow, but blue foxfire or lightning. The talking owl swung low past his head, to station itself at the very path, and "Airar Alvarson!" cried, a tone higher. It came to the young man's mind that the bird wanted him to enter by that path, but at the same time thinking—What if not?—he set face and foot to the road again.

At once he had the curst bird in his face, wingtip brushing one ear, as it soared away from his clutching hand, shouting "Airar!" again in the new note of urgency. At the same moment from around a corner down the road ahead, there came a faint jingle of accouterment, a laugh and the sound of voices singing discordantly, where some group came from the taverns of Naaros.

Since there was no great loss of honor, a roof for the night possible and avoidance of the roisterers, Airar let himself be schooled to the owl's path; and presently stood before the door of a house set so close round with trees and bush that one could hardly see how from the window, time and time, came the flash of dead-blue light.

The door had no pillars nor carved name. Airar raised a hand to knock, but before touch it sprang open upon a boy or manikin (for the features were of adult proportion to the body) who gave a tittering laugh in his face. "Airar Alvarson," said the owl from right overhead.

"You are expected," said the dwarf, and bowed not too quickly to hide a mocking grin; then turned and led on soft-shod feet through a room larger than it seemed from outside to another with many furnishings. It was hung heavily with old tapestries worked in a design of frightful beasts and human faces twisted with fear, half visible in the light of a single candle. "Wait," said the guide, snickered, ducked under one of the tapestries, and disappeared.

There was a chair of pretense placed beside a table on which an alembic with a broken neck jostled parchments. Airar avoided it, swung down pack, and sat on a stool. Behind the tapestry to his near right occurred a sound that he, woodsman, identified as like a rabbit moving secretly in brush. The tapestry before him parted and a man came in—medium tall, full-bearded and grey, clad in a robe rather ruffled than neat, stained in front and with a rip in it. Thin white hair made a halo in the rising candlelight and threw shadows up deep eye-arches, but his face bore an expression determinedly friendly.

He sat down in the chair. "You are Airar Alvarson," he said, making no offer of hand, "and I am Meliboë."

Airar knew the name and it was not a good one. The other's expression did not alter at the flicker of muscle round the young man's mouth. "I have sent for you because we can do each other service."

"The owl—"

Meliboë waved a deprecatory hand. "A familiar, and harmless. If I had wished to compel your attendance—" he stood up with a motion lithe for such age, talking as he walked, "—I show you this to prove I deal gently and it is alliance not servitude I offer." The tapestry by Airar's side was drawn back and the rustling had been made by a loathsome great worm in a cage, large as a cockadrill, shining in green and yellow, with pairs of clawed feet where its back-armor ran down in joints. It gazed at the young man with multiplex cloudy eyes and made a small mewing sound, blowing bubbles of froth from a hexagonal mouth. Airar wanted to vomit.

"You perceive I have powers," said the enchanter, tranquilly. "You had better endure an adder's bite than even be clasped by his claws. . . . Tsa, bibé!" He dropped the tapestry.

Airar managed to say, "But why me, of all Dalarna?"

"Ha!" Meliboë raised a finger. "You had a visit from Leonce Fabrizius today, I think?" Against expectation he paused to be answered.

"Aye," said the young man.

"Then you are for what place? Naaros, no doubt? To join your father, son of Alvar?"

"My father—"

"Lives with Tholo Airarson as pensioner of that same Fabrizius. I understand, young man. You are of honor, as noble-born. Most fair; I had not sent for you otherwise."

"The more why me? You have powers and I am friendless."

Meliboë swivelled round to look at him full as though here were something caught to surprise. "It is not less than I would have expected, to find you so acute," he said, "and it does my judgment compliment. Well, since I see you will have nothing less than the full tale, here it is: there are not few, and I am among them, who would be less than melancholy to see an alternation in the rule of our good Count Vulk, fourteenth of the name. Yet here am I, court doctor and astrologer; not Dalecarle by birth. Shall I not need an impeccable ambassador before the Iron Ring?"

There was a moment's silence, no sound at all but an intake of breath from Airar as the last words fell. Oh, aye, he knew of iron ring and iron ring—badge worn by Micton slaves and those sentenced for a time to servitude by the Vulking courts; some words half-caught from behind the door of his lock-bed, the night the stranger in the worn blue coat guested at Trangsted, his father saying—"No and no again. What? Leave my stead and my son's future to [here a gap] iron ring?"—the nine days' wonder of old Tyel, who had hanged himself (men said) in the barn of the upper farm at Gräntraen, with an iron ring new forged around his neck. But at the market in Naaros, no one would speak of that. . . .

"I do not know what you mean about the Iron Ring," he said stoutly, but Meliboë laughed. "It is as I would have desired. You are a model of discretion. So let us put it this way; there is a certain group at Naaros with whom I am wishful to strike hands, but may not do so in person. You seek employment; I wage you as plenipotentiary before them and will pay well, from which it will grow that either they send you back to me with another message for a second payment, or find employment enough for you of their own. That it is not altogether without danger I admit. Can you do better unhelped?"

The offer seemed fair enough even though (as Airar noted, secretly amused) the remark about danger was made more for encouragement than fairness. But he was of peasant stock. "How great is the wage?"

"I wonder, did you take the Count's goldpiece? I think you would. No matter; three like it paid down for this one message."

The sum was princely, yet "Is it enough?" asked Airar.

Meliboë looked at him narrowly. "Four then. I am striking too high to haggle." The note was finality.

"And the message?"

"Merely this: that Meliboë, a poor doctor of the philosophies, wishes them well; and as proof that he does so wish them, he is full aware of what the syndics of the guilds of Mariupol propose, but none at the court knows of it else; that a scorpion without a head can sting but not bite, but that by certain philosophic arts one might find a hand to bear a banner."

"To whom given?"

Meliboë twitched lips, but, wise to take substance rather than shadow, answered: "To a certain group who meet at a tavern, called Of The Old Sword, with the arms of the Argimenids before, as though it were imperial property, but differenced as to color. It is in the Street of the Unicorn, hard by the Lady-Chapel, and the hour is one after sunset."

"It smacks of secret. How shall they believe I am to come?"

The philosophic doctor placed his head a little on one side, a long forefinger up the angle of his jaw, the back of his hand ruffling beard under chin. "Your care is admirable," he said; turning, unlocked a drawer Airar had not noticed amid the carving of the table, and drew forth a small ring, intricately wrought in silver. "This be your passport."

To Airar's fingers it felt wholly smooth. He looked up surprised and a smile stretched across the limits of Meliboë's beard. "A small enchantment," said he. "Look you but now." The parchments and desk litter were tossed aside till he found a gugglet of water from which he sprinkled a few drops as Airar held the ring outstretched. It was plain iron with square edges, but when the young man rubbed it dry on the edge of his jerkin there it was again to appearance silver and much carven.

"Put it on." The enchanter waved hands. "You will go then to this tavern; if they make difficulties ask for a few drops of wine or water and show it anew. What do you think?"

"Good. But a ring is not always on the hand of the owner."

"That is thought on. There is also a certain song from one of the old tongues before the heathen. How much clerk are you?"

"Somewhat; but not to practice."

The enchanter laughed shortly. "Not for admission to bailiffs, I know. Well, then, one shall hum to you or sing softly,

Geme, plange, moesto more—

and your reply to the same air is,

Dolorosa Dalarna.

Or you may reverse it, offering the first line in challenge."

Airar caught the air and repeated it readily enough, but Meliboë waved hands and stood up. "So for business; now courtesy. You have supped?"

Said Airar, who was in a state to attack the worm and carve steaks from its ribs, "Not I."

"All my apologies." His host pulled aside another part of the tapestry than the dwarf had used when he entered. "Young sir and partner, come."

There was a passage. At the end of it Meliboë ushered him into an apartment where again one candle burned, this above a bed well furnished. He clapped hands. Airar noticed the door had a lock and was glad; the manikin entered, still smiling at his secret jest, and was told to bring a plate with somewhat to drink. Meliboë remained on his feet and so did Airar for politeness, while time paused, from which the enchanter's eyes rolled suddenly. "You are a lucky man and will do much," he said, "but I do not think your luck will hold against that of the three-fingered lord, though he be himself less than fortunate. A mystery."

Airar stared at him. The dwarf, whom it would be more like to call a small man, since he was in all respects perfectly proportioned, came in with a tray that held meat, drink, and a manchet of bread; but at the moment he entered, there was a frightful dying scream that seemed to run through the whole building and rend one to the very marrow.

The little man set down the tray and tittered. "The leopard is dead," said he.

"Ten thousand furies!" cried Meliboë and dived through the door. Airar drove home the bolt before he addressed himself to the food.

FRITZ LEIBER

THE writers interested in "the Northern thing" are still with us, of course: I will let one last example of this school in before passing to another tradition.

Fritz Leiber (1910–   ), son of the noted Shakespearean actor of the same name, contributed heavily to the fantasy and science fiction magazines from the late 1930s on. His science fiction novels and stories have won him many prizes, including the Hugo Award itself, the science fiction equivalent of the Oscar or the Emmy. But it is with his Fafhrd and the Gray Mouser saga that we are chiefly concerned here. These two inimitable rogues began their swash-buckling career in the pages of John W. Campbell's memorable fantasy magazine, *Unknown,* in 1939. Happily, they are still going strong.

Now Leiber agrees with me on the pre-eminent position of *The Worm Ouroboros* in the genre, and also has a healthy admiration for Fletcher Pratt. In his case, however, a fondness for the Northern sagas is tempered and enriched by an equally powerful fondness for the immensely sophisticated and intricate fantasies written by James Branch Cabell, such as the celebrated *Jurgen*. So . . . from Eddison he drew the highhearted chivalry and noble language, from Pratt, the stinks of the gutter as well as the perfumes of the palace, and from Cabell, the mischievous and playful tinkerings with so-called reality.

The mixture, however, is uniquely Leiber's own brew of word-witchery. As the following delicious tale demonstrates ably.

THE TWO BEST THIEVES IN LANKHMAR

THROUGH the mazy avenues and alleys of the great city of Lankhmar, Night was a-slink, though not yet grown tall enough to whirl her black star-studded cloak across the sky, which still showed pale, towering wraiths of sunset.

The hawkers of drugs and strong drinks forbidden by day had not yet taken up their bell-tinklings and thin, enticing cries. The pleasure girls had not lit their red lanterns and sauntered insolently forth. Bravos, desperadoes, procurers, spies, pimps, conmen, and other malfeasors yawned and rubbed drowsy sleep from eyes yet thick-lidded. In fact, most of the Night People were still at breakfast, while most of the Day People were at supper. Which made for an emptiness and hush in the streets, suitable to Night's slippered tread. And which created a large bare stretch of dark thick, unpierced wall at the intersection of Silver Street with the Street of the Gods, a crossing-point where there habitually foregathered the junior executives and star operatives of the Thieves Guild; also meeting there were the few free-lance thieves bold and resourceful enough to defy the Guild and the few thieves of aristocratic birth, sometimes most brilliant amateurs, whom the Guild tolerated and even toadied to, on account of their noble ancestry, which dignified a very old but most disreputable profession.

Midway along the bare stretch of wall, where none might conceivably overhear, a very tall and a somewhat short thief drifted together. After a while they began to converse in prison-yard whispers.

A distance had grown between Fafhrd and the Gray Mouser during their long and uneventful trek south from the Great Rift Valley. It was due simply to too much of each other and to an ever more bickering disagreement as to how the invisible jewels, gift of Hirriwi and Keyaira, might most advantageously be disposed of—a dispute which had finally grown so acrimonious that they had divided the jewels, each carrying his share. When they finally reached Lankhmar, they had lodged apart and each made his own contact with jeweler, fence or private buyer. This separation had made their relationship quite scratchy, but in no way diminished their absolute trust in each other.

"Greetings, Little Man," Fafhrd prison-growled. "So you've come to sell your share to Ogo the Blind, or at least give him a viewing? —if such expression may be used of a sightless man."

"How did you know that?" the Mouser whispered sharply.

"It was the obvious thing to do," Fafhrd answered somewhat condescendingly. "Sell the jewels to a dealer who could note neither their night-glow nor daytime invisibility. A dealer who must judge by weight, feel, and what they can scratch or be scratched by. Besides, we stand just across from the door to Ogo's den. It's very well guarded, by the by—at fewest, ten Mingol swordsmen."

"At least give me credit for such trifles of common knowledge," the Mouser answered sardonically. "Well, you guessed right; it appears that by long association with me you've gained some knowledge of how my wit works, though I doubt that it's sharpened your own a whit. Yes. I've already had one conference with Ogo, and tonight we conclude the deal."

Fafhrd asked equably, "Is it true that Ogo conducts all his interviews in pitchy dark?"

"Ho! So there are some few things you admit not knowing! Yes, it's quite true, which makes any interview with Ogo risky work. By insisting on absolute darkness, Ogo the Blind cancels at a stroke the interviewer's advantage—indeed, the advantage passes to Ogo, since he is used by a lifetime of it to utter darkness—a long lifetime, since he's an ancient one, to judge by his speech. Nay, Ogo knows not what darkness is, since it's all he's ever known. However, I've a device to trick him there if need be. In my thick, tightly drawstringed pouch I carry fragments of brightest glow-wood, and can spill them out in a trice."

Fafhrd nodded admiringly and then asked, "And what's in that flat case you carry so tightly under your elbow? An elaborate false history of each of the jewels embossed in ancient parchment for Ogo's fingers to read?"

"There your guess fails! No, it's the jewels themselves, guarded in clever wise so that they cannot be filched. Here, take a peek." And after glancing quickly to either side and overhead, the Mouser opened the case a handbreadth on its hinges.

Fafhrd saw the rainbow-twinkling jewels firmly affixed in artistic pattern to a bed of black velvet, but all closely covered by an inner top consisting of a mesh of stout iron wire.

The Mouser clapped the case shut. "On our first meeting, I took two of the smallest of the jewels from their spots in the box and let Ogo feel and otherwise test them. He may dream of filching them all, but my box and the mesh thwart that."

"Unless he steals from you the box itself," Fafhrd agreed. "As for myself, I keep my share of the jewels chained to me." And after such precautionary glances as the Mouser had made, he thrust back his loose left sleeve, showing a stout browned-iron bracelet snapped around his wrist. From the bracelet hung a short chain which both supported and kept tightly shut a small, bulging pouch. The leather of the pouch was everywhere sewed across with fine brown wire. He unclicked the bracelet, which opened on a hinge, then clicked it fast again.

"The browned-iron wire's to foil any cutpurse," Fafhrd explained offhandedly, pulling down his sleeve.

The Mouser's eyebrows rose. Then his gaze followed them as it went from Fafhrd's wrist to his face, while the small man's expression changed from mild approval to bland inquiry. He asked, "And you trust such devices to guard your half of the gems from Nemia of the Dusk?"

"How did you know my dealings were with Nemia?" Fafhrd asked in tones just the slightest surprised.

"Because she's Lankhmar's only woman fence, of course. All know you favor women when possible, in business as well as erotic matters. Which is one of your greatest failings, if I may say so. Also, Nemia's door lies next to Ogo's, though that's a trivial clue. You know, I presume, that seven Kleshite stranglers protect her somewhat overripe person? Well, at least then you know the sort of trap you're rushing into. Deal with a woman!—surest route to disaster. By the by, you mentioned 'dealings.' Does that plural mean this is not your first interview with her?"

Fafhrd nodded. "As you with Ogo. . . . Incidentally, am I to understand that you trust men simply because they're men? That were a greater failing than the one you impute to me. Anyhow, as you with Ogo, I go to Nemia of the Dusk a second time, to complete our deal. The first time I showed her the gems in a twilit chamber, where they appeared to greatest advantage, twinkling just enough to seem utterly real. Did you know, in passing, that she always works in twilight or soft gloom?—which accounts for the second half of her name. At all events, as soon as she glimpsed them, Nemia greatly desired the gems—her breath actually caught in her throat—and she agreed at once to my price, which is not low, as basis for further bargaining. However, it happens that she invariably follows the rule—which I myself consider a sound one—of never completing a transaction of any sort with a member of the opposite sex without first testing them in amorous commerce. Hence this second meeting. If the member be old or otherwise ugly, Nemia deputes the task to one of her maids, but in my case, of course . . ." Fafhrd coughed modestly. "One more point I'd like to make: 'overripe' is the wrong expression. 'Full-bloomed' or 'the acme of maturity' is what you're looking for."

"Believe me, I'm sure Nemia is in fullest bloom—a late August flower. Such women always prefer twilight for the display of their 'perfectly matured' charms," the Mouser answered somewhat stifledly. He had for some time been hard put to restrain laughter, and now it appeared in quiet little bursts as he said, "Oh, you great fool! And you've actually agreed to go to bed with her? And expect not to be parted from your jewels (including family jewels?), let alone not strangled, while at that disadvantage? Oh, this is worse than I thought."

"I'm not always at such a disadvantage in bed as some people may think," Fafhrd answered with quiet modesty. "With me, amorous play sharpens instead of dulls the senses. I trust you have as much luck with a man in ebon darkness as I with a woman in soft gloom. Incidentally, why must you have two conferences with Ogo? Not Nemia's reason, surely?"

The Mouser's grin faded and he lightly bit his lip. With elaborate casualness he said, "Oh, the jewels must be inspected by the Eyes of Ogo—*his* invariable rule. But whatever test is tried, I'm prepared to out-trick it."

Fafhrd pondered, then asked, "And what, or who are, or is, the Eyes of Ogo? Does he keep a pair of them in his pouch?"

"Is," the Mouser said. Then with even more elaborate casualness, "Oh, some chit of a girl, I believe. Supposed to have an intuitive faculty where gems are concerned. Interesting, isn't it, that a man as clever as Ogo should believe such superstitious nonsense? Or depend on the soft sex in any fashion. Truly, a mere formality."

"'Chit of a girl,'" Fafhrd mused, nodding his head again and yet again and yet again. "That describes to a red dot on each of her immature nipples the sort of female you've come to favor in recent years. But of course the amorous is not at all involved in this deal of yours, I'm sure," he added, rather too solemnly.

"In no way whatever," the Mouser replied, rather too sharply. Looking around, he remarked, "We're getting a bit of company, despite the early hour. There's Dickon of the Thieves Guild, that old pen-pusher and drawer of the floor plans of houses to be robbed —I don't believe he's actually worked on a job since the Year of the Snake. And there's fat Grom, their sub-treasurer, another armchair thief. Who comes so dramatically a-slither?—by the Black Bones, it's Snarve, our overlord Glipkerio's nephew! Who's that he speaks to?—oh, only Tork the Cutpurse."

"And there now appears," Fafhrd took up, "Vlek, said to be the Guild's star operative these days. Note his smirk and hear how his shoes creak faintly. And there's that gray-eyed, black-haired amateur, Alyx the Picklock—well, at least her boots don't squeak and I rather admire her courage in adventuring here, where the Guild's animosity toward free-lance females is as ill a byword as that of the Pimps Guild. And, just now turning from the Street of the Gods, who have we but Countess Kronia of the Seventy-seven Secret Pockets, who steals by madness, not method. There's one bone-bag I'd never trust, despite her emaciated charms and the weakness you lay to me."

Nodding, the Mouser pronounced, "And such as these are called the aristocracy of thiefdom! In all honesty I must say that notwithstanding your weaknesses—which I'm glad you admit—one of the two best thieves in Lankhmar now stands beside me. While the other, needless to say, occupies my ratskin boots."

Fafhrd nodded back, though carefully crossing two fingers.

Stifling a yawn, the Mouser said, "By the by, have you yet any thought about what you'll be doing after those gems are stolen from your wrist, or—though unlikely—sold and paid for? I've been approached about—or at any rate been considering a wander toward—in the general direction of the Eastern Lands."

"Where it's hotter even than in this sultry Lankhmar? Such a stroll hardly appeals to me," Fafhrd replied, then casually added, "In any case, I've been thinking of taking ship—er—northward."

"Toward that abominable Cold Waste once more? No, thank you!" the Mouser answered. Then, glancing south along Silver Street, where a pale star shone close to the horizon, he went on still more briskly, "Well, it's time for my interview with Ogo—and his silly girl Eyes. Take your sword to bed with you, I advise, and look to it that neither Graywand nor your more vital blade are filched from you in Nemia's dusk."

"Oh, so first twinkle of the Whale Star is the time set for your appointment too?" Fafhrd remarked, himself stirring from the wall. "Tell me, is the true appearance of Ogo known to anyone? Somehow the name makes me think of a fat, old, and overlarge spider."

"Curb your imagination, if you please," the Mouser answered sharply. "Or keep it for your own business, where I'll remind you that the only dangerous spider is the female. No, Ogo's true appearance is unknown. But perhaps tonight I'll discover it!"

"I'd like you to ponder that your besetting fault is over-curiosity," said Fafhrd, "and that you can't trust even the stupidest girl to be always silly."

The Mouser turned impulsively and said, "However tonight's interviews fall out, let's rendezvous after. The Silver Eel?"

Fafhrd nodded and they gripped hands together. Then each rogue sauntered toward his fateful door.

The Mouser crouched a little, every sense a-quiver, in space utterly dark. On a surface before him—a table, he had felt it out to be —lay his jewel box, closed. His left hand touched the box. His right gripped Cat's Claw and with that weapon nervously threatened the inky darkness all around.

A voice which was at once dry and thick croaked from behind him, "Open the box!"

The Mouser's skin crawled at the horror of that voice. Nevertheless, he complied with the direction. The rainbow light of the meshed jewels spilled upward, dimly showing the room to be low-ceilinged and rather large. It appeared to be empty except for the table and, indistinct in the far left corner behind him, a dark low shape which the Mouser did not like. It might be a hassock or a fat, round, black pillow. Or it might be . . . The Mouser wished Fafhrd hadn't made his last suggestion.

From ahead of him a rippling, silvery voice quite unlike the first called, "Your jewels, like no others I have ever seen, gleam in the absence of all light."

Scanning piercingly across the table and box, the Mouser could see no sign of the second caller. Evening out his own voice, so it was not breathy with apprehension, but bland with confidence, he said, to the emptiness, "My gems are like no others in the world. In fact, they come not from the world, being of the same substance as the stars. Yet you know by your test that one of them is harder than diamond."

"They are truly unearthly and most beautiful jewels," the sourless silvery voice answered. "My mind pierces them through and through, and they are what you say they are. I shall advise Ogo to pay your asking price."

At that instant the Mouser heard behind him a little cough and a dry, rapid scuttling. He whirled around, dirk poised to strike. There was nothing to be seen or sensed, except for the hassock or whatever, which had not moved. The scuttling was no longer to be heard.

He swiftly turned back, and there across the table from him, her front illumined by the twinkling jewels, stood a slim naked girl with pale straight hair, somewhat darker skin, and overlarge eyes staring entrancedly from a child's tiny-chinned, pouty-lipped face.

Satisfying himself by a rapid glance that the jewels were in their proper pattern under their mesh and none missing, he swiftly advanced Cat's Claw so that its needle point touched the taut skin between the small yet jutting breasts.

"Do not seek to startle me so again!" he hissed. "Men—aye, and girls—have died for less."

The girl did not stir by so much as the breadth of a fine hair; neither did her expression nor her dreamy yet concentrated gaze change, except that her short lips smiled, then parted to say honey-voiced, "So you are the Gray Mouser. I had expected a crouchy, sear-faced rogue, and I find . . . a prince." The very jewels seemed to twinkle more wildly because of her sweet voice and sweeter presence, striking opalescent glimmers from her pale irises.

"Neither seek to flatter me!" the Mouser commanded, catching up his box and holding it open against his side. "I am inured, I'll have you know, to the ensorcelments of all the world's minxes and nymphs."

"I speak truth only, as I did of your jewels," she answered guilelessly. Her lips had stayed parted a little and she spoke without moving them.

"Are you the Eyes of Ogo?" the Mouser demanded harshly, yet drawing Cat's Claw back from her bosom. It bothered him a little, yet only a little, that the tiniest stream of blood, like a black thread, led down for a few inches from the prick his dirk had made.

Utterly unmindful of the tiny wound, the girl nodded. "And I can see through you, as through your jewels, and I discover naught in you but what is noble and fine, save for certain small subtle impulses of violence and cruelty, which a girl like myself might find delightful."

"There your all-piercing eyes err wholly, for I am a great villain," the Mouser answered scornfully, though he felt a pulse of fond satisfaction within him.

The girl's eyes widened as she looked over his shoulder somewhat apprehensively, and from behind the Mouser the dry and thick voice croaked once more, "Keep to business! Yes, I will pay you in gold your offering price, a sum it will take me some hours to assemble. Return at the same time tomorrow night and we will close the deal. Now shut the box."

The Mouser had turned around, still clutching his box, when Ogo began to speak. Again he could not distinguish the source of the voice, though he scanned minutely. It seemed to come from the whole wall.

Now he turned back. Somewhat to his disappointment, the naked girl had vanished. He peered under the table, but there was nothing there. Doubtless some trapdoor or hypnotic device . . .

Still suspicious as a snake, he returned the way he had come. On close approach, the black hassock appeared to be only that. Then as the door to the outside slid open noiselessly, he swiftly obeyed Ogo's last injunction, snapping shut the box, and departed.

Fafhrd gazed tenderly at Nemia lying beside him in perfumed twilight, while keeping the edge of his vision on his brawny wrist and the pouch pendant from it, both of which his companion was now idly fondling.

To do Nemia justice, even at the risk of imputing a certain cattiness to the Mouser, her charms were neither overblown, nor even ample, but only . . . sufficient.

From just behind Fafhrd's shoulder came a spitting hiss. He quickly turned his head and found himself looking into the crossed blue eyes of a white cat standing on the small bedside table beside a bowl of bronze chrysanthemums.

"Ixy!" Nemia called remonstratingly yet languorously.

Despite her voice, Fafhrd heard behind him, in rapid succession, the click of a bracelet opening and the slightly louder click of one closing.

He turned back instantly, to discover only that Nemia had meanwhile clasped on his wrist, beside the browned-iron bracelet, a golden one around which sapphires and rubies marched alternately in single file.

Gazing at him from betwixt the strands of her long dark hair, she said huskily, "It is only a small token which I give to those who please me . . . greatly."

Fafhrd drew his wrist closer to his eyes to admire his prize, but mostly to palpate his pouch with the fingers of his other hand, to assure himself that it bulged as tightly as ever.

It did, and in a burst of generous feeling he said, "Let me give you one of my gems in precisely the same spirit," and made to undo his pouch.

Nemia's long-fingered hand glided out to prevent. "No," she breathed. "Let never the gems of business be mixed with the jewels of pleasure. Now if you should choose to bring me some small gift tomorrow night, when at the same hour we exchange your jewels for my gold and my letters of credit on Glipkerio, underwritte by Hisvin the Grain Merchant . . ."

"Right," Fafhrd said briefly, concealing the relief he felt. He'd been an idiot to think of giving Nemia one of the gems—and with it a day's opportunity to discover its abnormalities.

"Until tomorrow," Nemia said, opening her arms to him.

"Until tomorrow, then," Fafhrd agreed, embracing her fervently, yet keeping his pouch clutched in the hand to which it was chained —and already eager to be gone.

The Silver Eel was far less than half filled, its candles few, its cupbearers torpid, as Fafhrd and the Gray Mouser entered simultaneously by different doors and made for one of the many empty booths.

The only eye to watch them at all closely was a gray one above a narrow section of pale cheek bordered by dark hair, peering past the curtain of the backmost booth.

When their thick table-candles had been lit and cups set before them and a jug of fortified wine, and fresh charcoal tumbled into the red-seeded brazier at table's end, the Mouser placed his flat box on the table and, grinning, said, "All's set. The jewels passed the test of the Eyes—a toothsome wenchlet; more of her later. I get the cash tomorrow night—all my offering price! But you, friend, I hardly thought to see you back alive. Drink we up! I take it you escaped from Nemia's divan whole and sound in organs and limbs —as far as you yet know. But the jewels?"

"They came through too," Fafhrd answered, swinging the pouch lightly out of his sleeve and then back in again. "And I get my money tomorrow night . . . the full amount of my asking price, just like you."

As he named those coincidences, his eyes went thoughtful.

They stayed that way while he took two large swallows of wine. The Mouser watched him curiously.

"At one point," Fafhrd finally mused, "I thought she was trying the old trick of substituting for mine an identical but worthlessly filled pouch. Since she'd seen the pouch at our first meeting, she could have had a similar one made up, complete with chain and bracelet."

"But was she—?" the Mouser asked.

"Oh no, it turned out to be something entirely different," Fafhrd said lightly, though some thought kept two slight vertical furrows in his forehead.

"That's odd," the Mouser remarked. "At one point—just one, mind you—the Eyes of Ogo, if she'd been extremely swift, deft, and silent, might have been able to switch boxes on me."

Fafhrd lifted his eyebrows.

The Mouser went on rapidly, "That is, if my box had been closed. But it was open, in darkness, and there'd have been no way to reproduce the varicolored twinkling of the gems. Phosphorus or glow-wood? Too dim. Hot coals? No, I'd have felt the heat. Besides, how get that way a diamond's pure white glow? Quite impossible."

Fafhrd nodded agreement, but continued to gaze over the Mouser's shoulder.

The Mouser started to reach toward his box, but instead with a small self-contemptuous chuckle picked up the jug and began to pour himself another drink in a careful small stream.

Fafhrd shrugged at last, used the back of his fingers to push over his own pewter cup for a refill, and yawned mightily, leaning back a little and at the same time pushing his spread-fingered hands to either side across the table, as if pushing away from him all small doubts and wonderings.

The fingers of his left hand touched the Mouser's box.

His face went blank. He looked down his arm at the box.

Then to the great puzzlement of the Mouser, who had just begun to fill Fafhrd's cup, the Northerner leaned forward and placed his head ear-down on the box.

"Mouser," he said in a small voice, "your box is buzzing."

Fafhrd's cup was full, but the Mouser kept on pouring. Heavily fragrant wine puddled and began to run toward the glowing brazier.

"When I touched the box, I felt vibration," Fafhrd went on bemusedly. "It's buzzing. It's still buzzing."

With a low snarl, the Mouser slammed down the jug and snatched the box from under Fafhrd's ear. The wine reached the brazier's hot bottom and hissed.

He tore the box open, opened also its mesh top, and he and Fafhrd peered in.

The candlelight dimmed, but by no means extinguished the yellow, violet, reddish, and white twinkling glows rising from various points on the black velvet bottom.

But the candlelight was quite bright enough also to show, at each such point, matching the colors listed, a firebeetle, glowwasp, nightbee, or diamondfly, each insect alive but delicately affixed to the floor of the box with fine silver wire. From time to time the wings or wingcases of some buzzed.

Without hesitation, Fafhrd unclasped the browned-iron bracelet from his wrist, unchained the pouch, and dumped it on the table.

Jewels of various sizes, all beautifully cut, made a fair heap.

But they were all dead black.

Fafhrd picked up a big one, tried it with his fingernail, then whipped out his hunting knife and with its edge easily scored the gem.

He carefully dropped it in the brazier's glowing center. After a bit it flamed up yellow and blue.

"Coal," Fafhrd said.

The Mouser clawed his hands over his faintly twinkling box, as if about to pick it up and hurl it through the wall and across the Inner Sea.

Instead he unclawed his hands and hung them decorously at his sides.

"I am going away," he announced quietly, but very clearly, and did so.

Fafhrd did not look up. He was dropping a second black gem in the brazier.

He did take off the bracelet Nemia had given him; he brought it close to his eyes, said, "Brass . . . glass," and spread his fingers to let it drop in the spilled wine. After the Mouser was gone, Fafhrd drained his brimming cup, drained the Mouser's and filled it again, then went on supping from it as he continued to drop the black jewels one by one in the brazier.

Nemia and the Eyes of Ogo sat cosily side by side on a luxurious divan. They had put on negligees. A few candles made a yellowish dusk.

On a low, gleaming table were set delicate flagons of wines and liqueurs, slim-stemmed crystal goblets, golden plates of sweetmeats and savories, and in the center two equal heaps of rainbow-glowing gems.

"What a quaint bore barbarians are," Nemia remarked, delicately stifling a yawn, "though good for one's sensuous self, once in a great while. This one had a little more brains than most. I think he might have caught on, except that I made the two clicks come so exactly together when I snapped back on his wrist the bracelet with the false pouch and at the same time my brass keepsake. It's amazing how barbarians are hypnotized by brass along with any odd bits of glass colored like rubies and sapphires—I think the three primary colors paralyze their primitive brains."

"Clever, *clever* Nemia," the Eyes of Ogo cooed with a tender caress. "My little fellow almost caught on too when I made the switch, but then he got interested in threatening me with his knife. Actually jabbed me between the breasts. I think he has a dirty mind."

"Let me kiss the blood away, darling Eyes," Nemia suggested. "Oh, dreadful . . . dreadful."

While shivering under her treatment—Nemia had a slightly bristly tongue—Eyes said, "For some reason he was quite nervous about Ogo." She made her face blank, her pouty mouth hanging slightly open.

The richly draped wall opposite her made a scuttling sound and then croaked in a dry, thick voice, "Open your box, Gray Mouser. Now close it. Girls, girls! Cease your lascivious play!"

Nemia and Eyes clung to each other laughing. Eyes said in her natural voice, if she had one, "And he went away still thinking there was a real Ogo. I'm quite certain of that. My, they both must be in a froth by now."

Sitting back, Nemia said, "I suppose we'll have to take some special precautions against their raiding us to get their jewels back."

Eyes shrugged. "I have my five Mingol swordsmen."

Nemia said. "And I have my three and a half Kleshite stranglers."

"Half?" Eyes asked.

"I was counting Ixy. No, but seriously."

Eyes frowned for half a heartbeat, then shook her head decisively. "I don't think we need worry about Fafhrd and the Gray Mouser raiding us back. Because we're girls, their pride will be hurt, and they'll sulk a while and then run away to the ends of the earth on one of those adventures of theirs."

"Adventures!" said Nemia, as one who says, "Cesspools and privies!"

"You see, they're really weaklings," Eyes went on, warming to her topic. "They have no drive whatever, no ambition, no true passion for money. For instance, if they did—and if they didn't spend so much time in dismal spots away from Lankhmar—they'd have known that the King of Ilthmar has developed a mania for gems that are invisible by day, but glow by night, and has offered half his kingdom for a sack of star-jewels. And then they'd never have had even to consider such an idiotic thing as coming to us."

"What do you suppose he'll do with them? The King, I mean."

Eyes shrugged. "I don't know. Build a planetarium. Or eat them." She thought a moment. "All things considered, it might be as well if we got away from here for a few weeks. We deserve a vacation."

Nemia nodded, closing her eyes. "It should be absolutely the opposite sort of place to the one in which the Mouser and Fafhrd will have their next—ugh!—adventure."

Eyes nodded too and said dreamily, "Blue skies and rippling water, spotless beach, a tepid wind, flowers and slim slavegirls everywhere . . ."

Nemia said, "I've always wished for a place that has no weather, only perfection. Do you know which half of Ithmar's kingdom has the least weather?"

"Precious Nemia," Eyes murmured, "you're so civilized. And so very, very clever. Next to one other, you're certainly the best thief in Lankhmar."

"Who's the other?" Nemia was eager to know.

"Myself, of course," Eyes answered modestly.

Nemia reached up and tweaked her companion's ear—not too painfully, but enough.

"If there were the least money depending on that," she said quietly but firmly, "I'd teach you differently. But since it's only conversation . . ."

"Dearest Nemia."

"Sweetest Eyes."

The two girls gently embraced and kissed each other fondly.

The Mouser glared thin-lipped across a table in a curtained booth in the Golden Lamprey, a tavern not unlike the Silver Eel.

He rapped the teak before him with his fingertip, and the perfumed stale air with his voice, saying, "Double those twenty gold pieces and I'll make the trip and hear Prince Gwaay's proposal."

The very pale man opposite him, who squinted as if even the candlelight were a glare, answered softly, "Twenty-five—and you serve him for one day after arrival."

"What sort of ass do you take me for?" the Mouser demanded dangerously. "I might be able to settle all his troubles in one day—I usually can—and what then? No, no preagreed service; I hear his proposal only. And . . . thirty-five gold pieces in advance."

"Very well, thirty gold pieces—twenty to be refunded if you refuse to serve my master, which would be a risky step, I warn you."

"Risk is my bed-mate," the Mouser snapped. "Ten only to be refunded."

The other nodded and began slowly to count rilks onto the teak. "Ten *now*," he said. "Ten when you join our caravan tomorrow morning at the Grain Gate. And ten when we reach Quarmall."

"When we first glimpse the spires of Quarmall," the Mouser insisted.

The other nodded.

The Mouser moodily snatched the golden coins and stood up. They felt very few in his fist. For a moment he thought of returning to Fafhrd and with him devising plans against Ogo and Nemia.

No, never! He realized he couldn't in his misery and self-rage bear the thought of even looking at Fafhrd.

Besides, the Northerner would certainly be drunk.

And two, or at most three, rilks would buy him certain tolerable

and even interesting pleasures to fill the hours before dawn brought
him release from this hateful city.

Fafhrd was indeed drunk, being on his third jug. He had burnt
up all the black jewels and was now with the greatest delicacy and
most careful use of the needle point of his knife, releasing unharmed
each of the silver-wired firebeetles, glowwasps, nightbees, and
diamondflies. They buzzed about erratically.

Two cupbearers and the chucker-out had come to protest, and
now Slevyas himself joined them, rubbing the back of his thick
neck. He had been stung and a customer too. Fafhrd had himself
been stung twice, but hadn't seemed to notice. Nor did he now pay
the slightest attention to the four haranguing him.

The last nightbee was released. It careened off noisily past
Slevyas' neck, who dodged his head with a curse. Fafhrd sat back,
suddenly looking very wretched. With varying shrugs the master of
the Silver Eel and his three servitors made off, one cupbearer making swipes at the air.

Fafhrd tossed up his knife. It came down almost point first, but
didn't quite stick in the teak. He laboriously scabbarded it, then
forced himself to take a small sip of wine.

As if someone were about to emerge from the backmost booth,
there was a stirring of its heavy curtains, which like all the others
had stitched to them heavy chain and squares of metal, so that one
guest couldn't stab another through them, except with luck and the
slimmest stilettos.

But at that moment a very pale man, who held up his cloak to
shield his eyes from the candlelight, entered by the side door and
made to Fafhrd's table.

"I've come for my answer, Northerner," he said in a voice soft yet
sinister. He glanced at the toppled jugs and spilled wine. "That is, if
you remember my proposition."

"Sit down," Fafhrd said. "Have a drink. Watch out for the glowwasps—they're vicious." Then, scornfully, "Remember! Prince Hasjarl
of Marquall—Quarmall. Passage by ship. A mountain of gold rilks.
Remember!"

Keeping on his feet, the other amended, "Twenty-five rilks.
Provided you take ship with me at once and promise to render a
day's service to my prince. Thereafter by what further agreement
you and he arrive at."

He placed on the table a small golden tower of precounted coins.

"Munificent!" Fafhrd said, grabbing it up and reeling to his feet. He placed five of the coins on the table and shoved the rest in his pouch, except for three more, which scattered dulcetly across the floor. He corked and pouched the third wine jug. Coming out from behind the table, he said, "Lead the way, comrade," gave the squinty-eyed man a mighty shove toward the side door, and went weaving after him.

In the backmost booth, Alyx the Picklock pursed her lips and shook her head disapprovingly.

III.
Fantasy
as
Parable

EDGAR ALLAN POE

TURNING from the fantasy as saga, let us explore a very different tradition, that of the fantasy as parable or prose poem. The crafting of brief, pointed, episodic tales written in a prose intensely lyrical was essentially an art form invented, or at least perfected, during the 19th century, where it came into being under the hands of writers such as Aloysius Bertrand and Charles Baudelaire. In this country, it attracted the rare genius of Poe; during his brief, unhappy life (1809–49) he enhanced or initiated many innovative forms of the short story—the weird tale, the detective story, and even the science fiction story. To this list we must add the parable.

The two samples of Poe's work in this genre I include here were written in 1835 and 1839, respectively. They were perhaps inordinately admired by prose stylists of subsequent generations, and traces of their influence can be seen, I think, in writers as far removed in taste and sensibility as Edgar Saltus and H. P. Lovecraft, James Branch Cabell and Clark Ashton Smith.

Of the two, "Silence" is by far the better known and more easily accessible: the earlier prose-poem, "Shadow," seems never before to have been anthologized.

SHADOW

A PARABLE

Yea! though I walk through the valley of the *Shadow*—
Psalm of David [XXIII.]

YE who read are still among the living: but I who write shall have long since gone my way into the region of shadows. For indeed strange things shall happen, and secret things be known, and many centuries shall pass away, ere these memorials be seen of men. And, when seen, there will be some to disbelieve, and some to doubt, and yet a few who will find much to ponder upon in the characters here graven with a stylus of iron.

The year had been a year of terror, and of feelings more intense than terror for which there is no name upon the earth. For many prodigies and signs had taken place, and far and wide, over sea and land, the black wings of the Pestilence were spread abroad. To those, nevertheless, cunning in the stars, it was not unknown that the heavens wore an aspect of ill; and to me, the Greek Oinos, among others, it was evident that now had arrived the alternation of that seven hundred and ninety-fourth year when, at the entrance of Aries, the planet Jupiter is conjoined with the red ring of the terrible Saturnus. The peculiar spirit of the skies, if I mistake not greatly, made itself manifest, not only in the physical orb of the earth, but in the souls, imaginations, and meditations of mankind.

Over some flasks of the red Chian wine, within the walls of a

noble hall, in a dim city called Ptolemais, we sat, at night, a company of seven. And to our chamber there was no entrance save by a
lofty door of brass: and the door was fashioned by the artisan
Corinnos, and, being of rare workmanship, was fastened from
within. Black draperies, likewise, in the gloomy room, shut out from
our view the moon, the lurid stars, and the peopleless streets—but
the boding and the memory of Evil, they would not be so excluded.
There were things around us and about of which I can render no
distinct account—things material and spiritual—heaviness in the
atmosphere—a sense of suffocation—anxiety—and, above all, that
terrible state of existence which the nervous experience when the
senses are keenly living and awake, and meanwhile the powers of
thought lie dormant. A dead weight hung upon us. It hung upon
our limbs—upon the household furniture—upon the goblets from
which we drank; and all things were depressed, and borne down
thereby—all things save only the flames of the seven iron lamps
which illumined our revel. Uprearing themselves in tall slender
lines of light, they thus remained burning all pallid and motionless;
and in the mirror which their lustre formed upon the round table
of ebony at which we sat, each of us there assembled beheld the
pallor of his own countenance, and the unquiet glare in the
downcast eyes of his companions. Yet we laughed and were merry
in our proper way—which was hysterical; and sang the songs of
Anacreon—which are madness; and drank deeply—although the
purple wine reminded us of blood. For there was yet another tenant
of our chamber in the person of young Zoilus. Dead, and at full
length he lay, enshrouded;—the genius and the demon of the scene.
Alas! he bore no portion in our mirth, save that his countenance,
distorted with the plague, and his eyes in which Death had but half
extinguished the fire of the pestilence, seemed to take such interest
in our merriment as the dead may haply take in the merriment of
those who are to die. But although I, Oinos, felt that the eyes of the
departed were upon me, still I forced myself not to perceive the bit-
terness of their expression, and, gazing down steadily into the
depths of the ebony mirror, sang with a loud and sonorous voice
the songs of the son of Teios. But gradually my songs they ceased,
and their echoes, rolling afar off among the sable draperies of the
chamber, became weak, and undistinguishable, and so faded away.
And lo! from among those sable draperies where the sounds of the
song departed, there came forth a dark and undefined shadow—a
shadow such as the moon, when low in heaven, might fashion from

the figure of a man: but it was the shadow neither of man, nor of God, nor of any familiar thing. And, quivering awhile among the draperies of the room, it at length rested in full view upon the surface of the door of brass. But the shadow was vague, and formless, and indefinite, and was the shadow neither of man, nor of God— neither God of Greece, nor God of Chaldæa, nor any Egyptian God. And the shadow rested upon the brazen doorway, and under the arch of the entablature of the door, and moved not, nor spoke any word, but there became stationary and remained. And the door whereupon the shadow rested was, if I remember aright, over against the feet of the young Zoilus enshrouded. But we, the seven there assembled, having seen the shadow as it came out from among the draperies, dared not steadily behold it, but cast down our eyes, and gazed continually into the depths of the mirror of ebony. And at length I, Oinos, speaking some low words, demanded of the shadow its dwelling and its appellation. And the shadow answered, "I am SHADOW, and my dwelling is near to the Catacombs of Ptolemais, and hard by those dim plains of Helusion which border upon the foul Charonian canal." And then did we, the seven, start from our seats in horror, and stand trembling, and shuddering, and aghast: for the tones in the voice of the shadow were not the tones of any one being, but of a multitude of beings, and, varying in their cadences from syllable to syllable, fell duskily upon our ears in the well-remembered and familiar accents of many thousand departed friends.

SILENCE

A FABLE

Εὕδουσιν δ᾽ ὀρέων κορυφαί τε καὶ φάραγγες
Πρώονες τε καὶ χαράδραι.

ALCMAN. [60 (10), 646.]

The mountain pinnacles slumber; valleys, crags, and caves *are silent*.

"LISTEN to *me*," said the Demon, as he placed his hand upon my head. "The region of which I speak is a dreary region in Libya, by the borders of the river Zaïre. And there is no quiet there, nor silence.

"The waters of the river have a saffron and sickly hue; and they flow not onwards to the sea, but palpitate forever and forever beneath the red eye of the sun with a tumultuous and convulsive motion. For many miles on either side of the river's oozy bed is a pale desert of gigantic water-lilies. They sigh one unto the other in that solitude, and stretch towards the heaven their long and ghastly necks, and nod to and fro their everlasting heads. And there is an indistinct murmur which cometh out from among them like the rushing of subterrene water. And they sigh one unto the other.

"But there is a boundary to their realm—the boundary of the dark, horrible, lofty forest. There, like the waves about the Hebrides, the low underwood is agitated continually. But there is no wind throughout the heaven. And the tall primeval trees rock eternally hither and thither with a crashing and mighty sound. And from their high summits, one by one, drop everlasting dews. And at the roots strange poisonous flowers lie writhing in perturbed slumber. And overhead, with a rustling and loud noise, the grey clouds rush westwardly forever, until they roll, a cataract, over the fiery wall of the horizon. But there is no wind throughout the heaven. And by the shores of the river Zaïre there is neither quiet nor silence.

"It was night, and the rain fell; and, falling, it was rain, but having fallen, it was blood. And I stood in the morass among the tall lilies, and the rain fell upon my head—and the lilies sighed one unto the other in the solemnity of their desolation.

"And, all at once, the moon arose through the thin ghastly mist, and was crimson in colour. And mine eyes fell upon a huge grey rock which stood by the shore of the river, and was lighted by the light of the moon. And the rock was grey, and ghastly, and tall, —and the rock was grey. Upon its front were characters engraven in the stone; and I walked through the morass of water-lilies, until I came close unto the shore, that I might read the characters upon the stone. But I could not decipher them. And I was going back into the morass, when the moon shone with a fuller red, and I turned and looked again upon the rock, and upon the characters;— and the characters were DESOLATION.

"And I looked upwards, and there stood a man upon the summit of the rock; and I hid myself among the water-lilies that I might discover the actions of the man. And the man was tall and stately in form, and was wrapped up from his shoulders to his feet in the toga of old Rome. And the outlines of his figure were indistinct—but his features were the features of a deity; for the mantle of the night, and of the mist, and of the moon, and of the dew, had left uncovered the features of his face. And his brow was lofty with thought, and his eye wild with care; and in the few furrows upon his cheek I read the fables of sorrow, and weariness, and disgust with mankind, and a longing after solitude.

"And the man sat upon the rock, and leaned his head upon his hand, and looked out upon the desolation. He looked down into the low unquiet shrubbery, and up into the tall primeval trees, and up higher at the rustling heaven, and into the crimson moon. And I lay close within shelter of the lilies, and observed the actions of the man. And the man trembled in the solitude;—but the night waned, and he sat upon the rock.

"And the man turned his attention from the heaven, and looked out upon the dreary river Zaïre, and upon the yellow ghastly waters, and upon the pale legions of the water-lilies. And the man listened to the sighs of the water-lilies, and to the murmur that came up from among them. And I lay close within my covert and observed the actions of the man. And the man trembled in the solitude;—but the night waned and he sat upon the rock.

"Then I went down into the recesses of the morass, and waded

afar in among the wilderness of the lilies, and called unto the hippopotami which dwelt among the fens in the recesses of the morass.
And the hippopotami heard my call, and came, with the behemoth,
unto the foot of the rock, and roared loudly and fearfully beneath
the moon. And I lay close within my covert and observed the actions of the man. And the man trembled in the solitude;—but the
night waned and he sat upon the rock.

"Then I cursed the elements with the curse of tumult; and a
frightful tempest gathered in the heaven where, before, there had
been no wind. And the heaven became livid with the violence of
the tempest—and the rain beat upon the head of the man—and the
floods of the river came down—and the river was tormented into
foam—and the water-lilies shrieked within their beds—and the
forest crumbled before the wind—and the thunder rolled—and the
lightning fell—and the rock rocked to its foundation. And I lay
close within my covert and observed the actions of the man. And
the man trembled in the solitude;—but the night waned and he sat
upon the rock.

"Then I grew angry and cursed, with the curse of *silence,* the
river, and the lilies, and the wind, and the forest, and the heaven,
and the thunder, and the sighs of the water-lilies. And they became
accursed, and *were still.* And the moon ceased to totter up its path-
way to heaven—and the thunder died away—and the lightning did
not flash—and the clouds hung motionless—and the waters sunk to
their level and remained—and the trees ceased to rock—and the
water-lilies sighed no more—and the murmur was heard no longer
from among them, nor any shadow of sound throughout the vast
illimitable desert. And I looked upon the characters of the rock, and
they were changed;—and the characters were SILENCE.

"And mine eyes fell upon the countenance of the man, and his
countenance was wan with terror. And, hurriedly, he raised his
head from his hand, and stood forth upon the rock and listened.
But there was no voice throughout the vast illimitable desert, and
the characters upon the rock were SILENCE. And the man shuddered, and turned his face away, and fled afar off, in haste, so that I
beheld him no more."

Now there are fine tales in the volumes of the Magi—in the iron-
bound, melancholy volumes of the Magi. Therein, I say, are
glorious histories of the Heaven, and of the Earth, and of the
mighty sea—and of the Genii that over-ruled the sea, and the earth,

and the lofty heaven. There was much lore too in the sayings which were said by the Sibyls; and holy, holy things were heard of old by the dim leaves that trembled around Dodona—but, as Allah liveth, that fable which the Demon told me as he sat by my side in the shadow of the tomb, I hold to be the most wonderful of all! And as the Demon made an end of his story, he fell back within the cavity of the tomb and laughed. And I could not laugh with the Demon, and he cursed me because I could not laugh. And the lynx which dwelleth forever in the tomb, came out therefrom, and lay down at the feet of the Demon, and looked at him steadily in the face.

CLARK ASHTON SMITH

IF ever a man was born in the wrong time and place, it was the reclusive California artist Clark Ashton Smith (1893–1961). By any standard of justice, he should have been a European, born a generation earlier. His tales, darkly begemmed with exotic verbal ornament, savoring of Beckford and of the Flaubert of *Salammbô*, should have appeared in *The Yellow Book* with illustrations by Aubrey Beardsley; his poems, echoing Swinburne and Poe and the Oscar Wilde of *The Sphinx*, should have been published by John Lane at The Bodley Head. His bizarre paintings and drawings, his inimitable sculptures, belong in Parisian galleries of the Nineties beside the work of Gustave Moreau and Redon.

Unfortunately for Smith, he was born in a small town in rural California where he lived for most of his life, having little to do with his contemporaries, dreaming his own antique dreams, drawing and painting and carving as he wished. Fortunately for us, his unusual genius was so distinct that even in backwoods seclusion his work emerged to the attention of a small but delighted audience. In the decade and a half since his death, that audience has steadily grown larger, until he seems posthumously on the brink of that wider recognition which avoided him in his life as it did Poe in his.

Smith taught himself French in order to translate Baudelaire, with whom he felt in empathy. And he admitted to being powerfully influenced by Poe, both in prose and verse. Of the parables, or "prose pastels" (as he called them), which I include here, the first, "Sadastor," so obviously derives from Poe's own "Silence" that comment would be a redundancy.

FABLES FROM THE EDGE OF NIGHT

I. SADASTOR

LISTEN, for this is the tale that was told to a fair lamia by the demon Charnadis as they sat together on the top of Mophi, above the sources of the Nile, in those years when the sphinx was young. Now the lamia was vexed, for her beauty was grown an evil legend in both Thebais and Elephantine; so that men were become fearful of her lips and cautious of her embrace, and she had no lover for almost a fortnight. She lashed her serpentine tail on the ground, and moaned softly, and wept those mythical tears which a serpent weeps. And the demon told this tale for her comforting:

Long, long ago, in the red cycles of my youth (said Charnadis), I was like all young demons, and was prone to use the agility of my wings in fantastic flights; to hover and poise like a gier-eagle above Tartarus and the pits of Python; or to lift the broad blackness of my vans on the orbit of stars. I have followed the moon from evening twilight to morning twilight; and I have gazed on the secrets of that Medusean face which she averts eternally from the earth. I have read through filming ice the ithyphallic runes on columns yet extant in her deserts; and I know the hieroglyphs which solve forgotten riddles, or hint eonian histories, on the walls of her cities taken by ineluctable snow. I have flown through the triple ring of Saturn, and have mated with lovely basilisks, on isles towering league-high from stupendous oceans where each wave is like the rise and fall of

Himalayas. I have dared the clouds of Jupiter, and the black and freezing abysses of Neptune, which are crowned with eternal starlight; and I have sailed beyond to incommensurable suns, compared with which the sun that thou knowest is a corpse-candle in a stinted vault. There, in tremendous planets, I have furled my flight on the terraced mountains, large as fallen asteroids, where, with a thousand names and a thousand images, undreamt-of Evil is served and worshipt in unsurmisable ways. Or, perched in the flesh-colored lips of columnar blossoms, whose perfume was an ecstasy of incommunicable dreams, I have mocked the wiving monsters, and have lured their females, that sang and fawned at the base of my hiding-place.

Now, in my indefatigable questing among the remoter galaxies, I came one day to that forgotten and dying planet which in the language of its unrecorded peoples was called Sadastor. Immense and drear and gray beneath a waning sun, far-fissured with enormous chasms, and covered from pole to pole with the never-ebbing tides of the desert sand, it hung in space without moon or satellite, an abomination and a token of doom to fairer and younger worlds. Checking the speed of my interstellar flight, I followed its equator with a poised and level wing, above the peaks of cyclopean volcanoes, and bare, terrific ridges of elder hills, and deserts pale with the ghastliness of salt, that were manifestly the beds of former oceans.

In the very center of one of these ocean-beds, beyond sight of the mountains that formed its primeval shoreline, and leagues below their level, I found a vast and winding valley that plunged even deeplier into the abysses of this dreadful world. It was walled with perpendicular cliffs and buttresses and pinnacles of a rusty-red stone, that were fretted into a million bizarrely sinister forms by the sinking of the olden seas. I flew slowly among these cliffs as they wound ever downward in tortuous spirals for mile on mile of utter and irredeemable desolation, and the light grew dimmer above me as ledge on ledge and battlement on battlement of that strange red stone upreared themselves between my wings and the heavens. Here, when I rounded a sudden turn of the precipice, in the profoundest depth where the rays of the sun fell only for a brief while at noon, and the rocks were purple with everlasting shadow, I found a pool of dark-green water—the last remnant of the former ocean, ebbing still amid steep, insuperable walls. And from this pool there cried a voice, in accents that were subtly sweet as the mortal wine of mandragora, and faint as the murmuring of shells. And the voice said:

"Pause and remain, I pray, and tell me who thou art, who comest thus to the accursed solitude wherein I die."

Then, pausing on the brink of the pool, I peered into its gulf of shadow, and saw the pallid glimmering of a female form that upreared itself from the waters. And the form was that of a siren, with hair the color of ocean-kelp, and berylline eyes, and a dolphin-shapen tail. And I said to her:

"I am the demon Charnadis. But who art thou, who lingerest thus in this ultimate pit of abomination, in the depth of a dying world?"

She answered: "I am a siren, and my name is Lyspial. Of the seas wherein I swam and sported at leisure many centuries ago, and whose gallant mariners I drew to an enchanted death on the shores of my disastrous isle, there remains only this fallen pool. Alas! For the pool dwindles daily, and when it is wholly gone I too must perish."

She began to weep, and her briny tears fell down and were added to the briny waters.

Fain would I have comforted her, and I said:

"Weep not, for I will lift thee upon my wings and bear thee to some newer world, were the sky-blue waters of abounding seas are shattered to intricate webs of wannest foam, on low shores that are green and aureate with pristine spring. There, perchance for eons, thou shalt have thine abode, and galleys with painted oars and great barges purpureal-sailed shall be drawn upon thy rocks in the red light of sunsets domed with storm, and shall mingle the crash of their figured prows with the sweet sorcery of thy mortal singing."

But still she wept, and would not be comforted, crying:

"Thou art kind, but this would avail me not, for I was born of the waters of this world, and with its waters I must die. Alas! my lovely seas, that ran in unbroken sapphire from shores of perennial blossoms to shores of everlasting snow! Alas! the sea-winds, with their mingled perfumes of brine and weed, and scents of ocean flowers and flowers of the land, and far-blown exotic balsams! Alas! the quinquiremes of cycle-ended wars, and the heavy-laden argosies with sails and cordage of byssus, that plied between barbaric isles with their cargoes of topaz or garnet-colored wines and jade and ivory idols, in the antique summers that now are less than legend! Alas! the dead captains, the beautiful dead sailors that were borne by the ebbing tide to my couches of amber seaweed, in my caverns underneath a cedared promontory! Alas! the kisses that I laid on their cold and hueless lips, on their sealed marmorean eyelids!"

And sorrow and pity seized me at her words, for I knew that she spoke the lamentable truth, that her doom was in the lessening of the bitter waters. So, after many proffered condolences, no less vague than vain, I bade her a melancholy farewell and flew heavily away between the spirail cliffs where I had come, and clomb the somber skies till the world Sadastor was only a darkling mote far down in space. But the tragic shadow of the siren's fate, and her sorrow, lay grievously upon me for hours, and only in the kisses of a beautiful fierce vampire, in a far-off and young and exuberant world, was I able to forget it. And I tell thee now the tale thereof, that haply thou mayest be consoled by the contemplation of a plight that was infinitely more dolorous and irremediable than thine own.

II. THE PASSING OF APHRODITE

In all the lands of Illarion, from mountain-valleys rimmed with unmelting snow, to the great cliffs of sard whose reflex darkens a sleepy, tepid sea, were lit as of old the green and amethyst fires of summer. Spices were on the wind that mountaineers had met in the high glaciers; and the eldest wood of cypress, frowning on a sky-clear bay, was illumined by scarlet orchids. . . . But the heart of the poet Phaniol was an urn of black jade overfraught by love with sodden ashes. And because he wished to forget for a time the mockery of myrtles, Phaniol walked alone in the waste bordering upon Illarion; in a place that great fires had blackened long ago, and which knew not the pine or the violet, the cypress or the myrtle. There, as the day grew old, he came to an unsailed ocean, whose waters were dark and still under the falling sun, and bore not the memorial voices of other seas. And Phaniol paused, and lingered upon the ashen shore; and dreamt awhile of that sea whose name is Oblivion.

Then, from beneath the westering sun, whose bleak light was prone on his forehead, a barge appeared and swiftly drew to the land: albeit there was no wind, and the oars hung idly on the foamless wave. And Phaniol saw that the barge was wrought of ebony fretted with curious anaglyphs, and carved with luxurious forms of gods and beasts, of satyrs and goddesses and women; and the figurehead was a black Eros with full unsmiling mouth and implacable sapphire eyes averted, as if intent upon things not lightly to be named or revealed. Upon the deck of the barge were two women, one pale as the northern moon, and the other swart as equatorial midnight. But both were clad imperially, and bore the mien of goddesses or of those who dwell near to the goddesses. Without word or gesture, they regarded Phaniol; and, marvelling, he inquired, "What seek ye?"

Then, with one voice that was like the voice of hesperian airs among palms at evening twilight in the Fortunate Isles, they answered, saying:

"We wait the goddess Aphrodite, who departs in weariness and sorrow from Illarion, and from all the lands of this world of petty loves and pettier mortalities. Thou, because thou art a poet, and hast known the great sovereignty of love, shall behold her departure. But they, the men of the court, the marketplace and the temple, shall receive no message nor sign of her going-forth, and will scarcely dream that she is gone. . . . Now, O Phaniol, the time, the goddess and the going-forth are at hand."

Even as they ceased, One came across the desert; and her coming was a light on the far hills; and where she trod the lengthening shadows shrunk, and the grey waste put on the purple asphodels and the deep darkening legend and a dust of mummia. Even to the shore she came and stood before Phaniol, while the sunset greatened, filling sky and sea with a flush as of new-blown blossoms, or the inmost rose of that coiling shell which was consecrate to her in old time. Without robe or circlet or garland, crowned and clad only with the sunset, fair with the dreams of man but fairer yet than all dreams: thus she waited, smiling tranquilly, who is life or death, despair or rapture, vision or flesh, to gods and poets and galaxies unknowable. But, filled with a wonder that was also love, or much more than love, the poet could find no greeting.

"Farewell, O Phaniol," she said, and her voice was the sighing of remote waters, the murmur of waters moon-withdrawn, forsaking not without sorrow a proud island tall with palms. "Thou has known me and worshipped all thy days till now, but the hour of my departure is come: I go, and when I am gone, thou shalt worship still and shalt not know me. For the destinies are thus, and not forever to any man, to any world or to any god, is it given to possess me wholly. Autumn and spring will return when I am past, the one with yellow leaves, the other with yellow violets; birds will haunt the renewing myrtles; and many little loves will be thine. Not again to thee or to any man will return the perfect vision and the perfect flesh of the goddess."

Ending thus, she stepped from that ashen strand to the dark prow of the barge; and even as it had come, without wafture of wind or movement of oar, the barge put out on a sea covered with the fallen fading petals of sunset. Quickly it vanished from view, while the desert lost those ancient asphodels and the deep verdure it had worn again for a little. Darkness, having conquered Illarion, came slow and furtive on the path of Aphrodite; shadows mustered innumerably to the grey hills; and the heart of the poet Phaniol was an urn of black jade overfraught by love with sodden ashes.

III. FROM THE CRYPTS OF MEMORY

Aeons of aeons ago, in an epoch whose marvelous worlds have crumbled, and whose mighty suns are less than shadow, I dwelt in a star whose course, decadent from the high, irremeable heavens of the past, was even then verging upon the abyss in which, said astronomers, its immemorial cycle should find a dark and disastrous close.

Ah, strange was that gulf-forgotten star—how stranger than any dream of dreamers in the spheres of to-day, or than any vision that hath soared upon visionaries, in their retrospection of the sidereal past! There, through cycles of a history whose piled and bronze-writ records were hopeless of tabulation, the dead had come to outnumber infinitely the living. And built of a stone that was indestructible save in the furnace of suns, their cities rose beside those of the living like the prodigious metropoli of Titans, with walls that overgloom the vicinal villages. And over all was the black funereal vault of the cryptic heavens—a dome of infinite shadows, where the dismal sun, suspended like a sole, enormous lamp, failed to illumine, and drawing back its fires from the face of the irresolvable ether, threw a baffled and despairing beam on the vague remote horizons, and shrouded vistas illimitable of the visionary land.

We were a sombre, secret, many-sorrowed people—we who dwelt beneath that sky of eternal twilight, pierced by the towering tombs and obelisks of the past. In our blood was the chill of the ancient night of time; and our pulses flagged with a creeping prescience of the lentor of Lethe. Over our courts and fields, like invisible sluggish vampires born of mausoleums, rose and hovered the black hours, with wings that distilled a malefic languor made from the shadowy woe and despair of perished cycles. The very skies were fraught with oppression, and we breathed beneath them as in a sepulcher, forever sealed with all its stagnancies of corruption and slow decay, and darkness impenetrable save to the fretting worm.

Vaguely we lived, and loved as in dreams—the dim and mystic dreams that hover upon the verge of fathomless sleep. We felt for our women, with their pale and spectral beauty, the same desire that the dead may feel for the phantom lilies of Hadean meads. Our days were spent in roaming through the ruins of lone and immemorial cities, whose palaces of fretted copper, and streets that ran between lines of carven golden obelisks, lay dim and ghastly with the dead light, or were drowned forever in seas of stagnant shadow; cities whose vast and iron-builded fanes preserved their gloom of primordial mystery and awe, from which the simulacra of century-forgotten gods looked forth with unalterable eyes to the hopeless heavens, and saw the ulterior night, the ultimate oblivion. Languidly we kept our gardens, whose grey lilies concealed a necromantic perfume, that had power to evoke for us the dead and spectral dreams of the past. Or, wandering through ashen fields of perennial autumn, we sought the rare and mystic immortelles, with sombre leaves and pallid petals, that bloomed beneath willows of wan and veil-like foliage: or wept with a sweet and nepenthe-laden dew by the flowing silence of Acherontic waters.

And one by one we died and were lost in the dust of accumulated time. We knew the years as a passing of shadows, and death itself as the yielding of twilight unto night.

ROBERT H. BARLOW

ANOTHER writer who explored the possibilities of the minor art of the parable was this promising young writer, who corresponded with both Lovecraft and Smith and was one of the first fantasy connoisseurs in America to recognize the values of their fiction. Barlow (1918–51) lived only thirty-three years, but crammed considerable life experience into so brief a span. Amateur publisher, Mayan scholar, Guggenheim Fellow and poet of considerable gifts, Barlow was born in Kansas and raised in Florida where he played host to Lovecraft on one of his rare visits. He later became an archaeologist on the staff of the University of Mexico and his pioneering work on Mayan antiquities earned him the unofficial sobriquet of Father of Mexican Archaeology.

During the decade of the thirties, under the influence of Smith, Lovecraft and Dunsany, he composed a sequence of short prose parables issued under the generic title *Annals of the Jinns*. The germ of the notion came from a phrase in *Vathek:* "thither Ganigul often retired in the daytime to read in quiet the marvelous Annals of the Jinns, the chronicles of ancient worlds, and the prophecies relating to the worlds that are yet to be born."

Admittedly minor, Barlow's fables have a quaint charm and an element of grotesquerie which I find pleasing. The one I have selected here appeared in an amateur magazine in 1934 and has never previously been reprinted or anthologized in any form, which is to be regretted for these fables are exquisite dark miniatures, like tiny cameos carved in onyx.

THE TOMB OF THE GOD

FOR days the band of explorers from Phoor had been excavating the ancient and immemorial tomb of Krang on the edge of the desert. The sands had been blowing ceaselessly, even as they had done for ages before the coming of man. The tomb had been built long before any human had walked the world; it had been built by evil powers that had reigned unchecked in that unthinkable age when all the desert had been a verdant garden through which had stalked yellow giants of small intelligence but of prodigious strength; it had been they who had built the tower and the city of the most powerful Lord Krang. And even before that, Krang had been: he had existed for aeons, and had come hither from a remote planet (it was told in runes inscribed in a dead language, the lan-

guage of the Old Gods) in a time when dark magical powers had
battled for possession of the universe. And Krang had won that battle, Krang the Old One, the monstrous dark thing, that planned and
ruled and malefically twisted the futures of world. But the time
came that none had foreseen and Krang the Ancient fell into the
semblance of death, though his flesh rotted not nor did his aspect
change. So the people of that time gathered together in a vast fu-
neral procession and conveyed him to an enormous tomb carven of
living blue stone in the side of the mountain, and they sealed him in
and forever departed from his worship. For a god should not die.
And the years and the decades and the centuries and the unthinkable aeons came and went, and the sands of the desert swirled over
the mouth of the tomb, and the door was obliterated, and at length
none knew where Krang the Elder God lay in stupendous slumber.

Then audacious mortals had unwittingly found traces of the mau-
soleum that even legend had discredited, and they had resolved to
open it and seek the great body of the Old Thing that had lain un-
moving since the world was young and green, slumbering ages by
the while the gardens withered and the deserts grew and all that
land became a barrenness.

It was said that there had been sealed in the tomb of Krang
treasures that made avarice pale and gems the like of which man no
longer knew, for such jewels had come from worlds afar in the
dawn of time, worlds that had died and returned again; and strange
manuscripts with the lost Hsothian chants inscribed upon them,
and other equally desirable and precious things. Therefore, many
had set out to reach the far-off site of the ancient tomb, but few
had lived to attain the goal of their questing. Some had fallen prey
to the hateful green things that lay in wait for unwary travelers beneath the surface of the sands, and that sprang up therefrom to
drag their victims down to a horrible death. Those who had lived to
reach their goal scratched and chipped at the sealed entrance, but
it was as the gnawing of rats upon mighty doors, and before they
could penetrate those portals they had mysteriously vanished from
human ken, nor were they ever seen or heard of thereafter. Yet
even this did not discourage others who remained unharmed; for
the desire for power will lead men to great heights of fortitude, and
power there was within the tomb of Krang.

They were engaged in chipping away the obstruction of the ages,
and were making slight headway therein, when one of their
members chanced upon an orifice in the rock into which he cu-

riously thrust his arm. Deep within he touched some secret mechanism, and, Lo! the huge door grated outwards inexorably, ruthlessly, and ground him beneath its ponderous moving weight, leaving of him naught but a smear of slime and an unpleasant smell. And the door was opened. Paralyzed, the survivors did not act until it had swung firmly back into place again, and was immovable save by a repetition of the same catastrophe. So, though they could spare him but ill, they forced one of the brown slave-men from Leek to perform the suicidal opening of the portal; and he whimpered, and would have refused, but they discouraged this by subtle and hastily improvised tortures, and he eventually complied.

They stepped squeamishly over the brown smear that had been a slave from Leek, and caught the door before it could swing to again and cost them yet another of their few remaining slaves, and placed obstructions in its way, so that it might stay open. And then they entered in, the first living creatures to penetrate the sanctity of the tomb since their race had appeared in the world.

The air was foul as the bed of an ancient sea exposed to the merciless rays of the sun, and the stench thereof was beyond description. All about the giant vault were great fragments of richly colored crystal cut in curious facets, with cryptic inscriptions thereon. The central object was the tomb of Lord Krang, where a vast body reposed upon a slab of figured chalcedony. Terrible to gaze upon was Krang, for even after this immense period of time he still bore semblance of the hideous aspect traditionally assigned by legend.

And the explorers who had entered the tomb gathered about the monstrous slab in awe, but only for a moment, for they were soon distracted from their solemnity by the glittering wealth that lay carelessly scattered about. And a sort of madness came upon them at the sight of the infinite riches; they stroked the jewels and clung to them, babbling and crooning.

But what happened next, none can tell with certainty. For the two of their number left to guard the portal without that tomb, lest it should somehow close again, heard from within a peculiar sound like a *slithering*—then a screaming—and then the great door swung shut again, despite the stone block they had placed so as to obstruct it. And this time it could not be opened.

AND the tomb of Krang once again became buried beneath the drifting sands; and for all the immensity of wealth hidden therein, never thereafter did a man from Phoor dare venture near.

For the Lord Krang had roused him from his age-long sleep and had feasted, and now he slept again, but whether he slept lightly, none could say. And wealth is no value to one being slowly digested in the belly of a god.

IV.
Fantasy
as
Anecdote

T. H. WHITE

LET us turn from the parable to another miniature form, which might be called the fantasy as humorous anecdote. Such stories tend either to be brief ones, since the anecdotal structure has built-in frailties which tend to collapse under the weight of extended length, or, when used in the novel, such novels tend to be very episodic.

Such is the case with one of the most marvelous and delectable fantasy novels published in our time, *The Sword in the Stone* (1939). Ostensibly a children's book, the story was filmed by Walt Disney a few years ago; predictably, he failed to capture its charming whimsy. White, a British writer (1906–64) was born in Bombay and educated at Cambridge, and later made his home first in Ireland then in the Channel Islands. His book about the boyhood of the future King Arthur was so well received that he later published two sequels, and in 1958 rewrote the entire trilogy, adding a new novella, as a huge book called *The Once and Future King;* this later became the basis for a Broadway musical called *Camelot* and a film of the same name.

While *The Once and Future King* is, I think, unquestionably the most perfect fantasy masterpiece of its length, in his revision of earlier work White often was arbitrary and even ruthless, cutting or changing entire scenes which linger in the memory as favorite passages. The one scene I remember most fondly from *The Sword in the Stone,* the magic duel in Chapter 6 between Merlyn and the witch, Madame Mim, is, for instance, completely eliminated in the second version, which superseded the original book seventeen years ago.

Seventeen years is too long a time for a scene as good as this one to lapse into oblivion, unavailable to a readership unable to find a secondhand copy of the original edition. As the most hilarious single scene in what must surely be the most hilarious of all modern fantasy novels, it does not deserve to remain a "lost chapter." Hence I have repeated it here, exactly as it first appeared, picking the scene up at the point where White ended it in his revision.

The boys, Wart and his foster-brother, Kay, have been out playing that afternoon with their bows along the edge of the woods which ring in the Castle. Their tutor, the irascible and fussy old magician, Merlyn, has warned them not to go into the Forest Sauvage, but they do anyway, in search of a lost arrow. What follows is much too funny to be permitted to be forgotten.

MERLYN VS. MADAME MIM

THE Wart watched his arrow go up. The sun was already westing towards evening, and the trees where they were had plunged them into a partial shade. So, as the arrow topped the trees and climbed into sunlight, it began to burn against the evening like the sun itself. Up and up it went, not weaving as it would have done with a snatching loose, but soaring, swimming, aspiring towards heaven, steady, golden and superb. Just as it had spent its force, just as its ambition had been dimmed by destiny and it was preparing to faint, to turn over, to pour back into the bosom of its mother earth, a terrible portent happened. A gore-crow came flapping wearily before the approaching night. It came, it did not waver, it took the arrow. It flew away, heavy and hoisting, with the arrow in its beak.

Kay was frightened by this, but the Wart was furious. He had loved his arrow's movement, its burning ambition in the sunlight, and, besides, it was his best arrow. It was the only one which was perfectly balanced, sharp, tight-feathered, clean-nocked, and neither warped nor scraped.

"It was a witch," said Kay.

"I don't care if it was ten witches," said the Wart. "I am going to get it back."

"But it went towards the Forest."

"I shall go after it."

"You can go alone, then," said Kay. "I'm not going into the Forest Sauvage, just for a putrid arrow."

"I shall go alone."

"Oh, well," said Kay, "I suppose I shall have to come too, if you're so set on it. And I bet we shall get nobbled by Wat."

"Let him nobble," said the Wart. "I want my arrow."

They went in the Forest at the place where they had last seen the bird of carrion.

In less than five minutes they were in a clearing with a well and a cottage just like Merlyn's.

"Goodness," said Kay, "I never knew there were any cottages so close. I say, let's go back."

"I just want to look at this place," said the Wart. "It's probably a wizard's."

The cottage had a brass plate screwed on the garden gate. It said:

MADAME MIM, B.A. (Dom-Daniel)
PIANOFORTE
NEEDLEWORK
NECROMANCY

No Hawkers, circulars
or Income Tax.
Beware of the Dragon.

The cottage had lace curtains. These stirred ever so slightly, for behind them there was a lady peeping. The gore-crow was standing on the chimney.

"Come on," said Kay. "Oh, do come on. I tell you, she'll never give it us back."

At this point the door of the cottage opened suddenly and the witch was revealed standing in the passage. She was a strikingly beautiful woman of about thirty, with coal-black hair so rich that it had the blue-black of the maggot-pies in it, silky bright eyes and a general soft air of butter-wouldn't-melt-in-my-mouth. She was sly.

"How do you do, my dears," said Madame Mim. "And what can I do for you today?"

The boys took off their leather caps, and Wart said, "Please, there is a crow sitting on your chimney and I think it has stolen one of my arrows."

"Precisely," said Madame Mim. "I have the arrow within."

"Could I have it back, please?"

"Inevitably," said Madame Mim. "The young gentleman shall have his arrow on the very instant, in four ticks and ere the bat squeaks thrice."

"Thank you very much," said the Wart.

"Step forward," said Madame Mim. "Honor the threshold. Accept the humble hospitality in the spirit in which it is given."

"I really do not think we can stay," said the Wart politely. "I really think we must go. We shall be expected back at home."

"Sweet expectation," replied Madame Mim in devout tones.

"Yet you would have thought," she added, "that the young gentlemen could have found time to honor a poor cottager, out of politeness. Few can believe how we ignoble tenants of the lower classes value a visit from the landlord's sons."

"We would like to come in," said the Wart, "very much. But you see we shall be late already."

The lady now began to give a sort of simpering whine. "The fare is lowly," she said. "No doubt it is not what you would be accustomed to eating, and so naturally such highly born ones would not care to partake."

Kay's strongly developed feeling for good form gave way at this. He was an aristocratic boy always, and condescended to his inferiors so that they could admire him. Even at the risk of visiting a witch, he was not going to have it said that he had refused to eat a tenant's food because it was too humble.

"Come on, Wart," he said. "We needn't be back before vespers."

Madame Mim swept them a low curtsey as they crossed the

threshold. Then she took them each by the scruff of the neck, lifted them right off the ground with her strong gypsy arms, and shot out of the back door with them almost before they had got in at the front. The Wart caught a hurried glimpse of her parlor and kitchen. The lace curtains, the aspidistra, the lithograph called the Virgin's Choice, the printed text of the Lord's Prayer written backwards and hung upside down, the sea-shell, the needle-case in the shape of a heart with A Present from Camelot written on it, the broom sticks, the cauldrons, and the bottles of dandelion wine. Then they were kicking and struggling in the back yard.

"We thought that the growing sportsmen would care to examine our rabbits," said Madame Mim.

There was, indeed, a row of large rabbit hutches in front of them, but they were empty of rabbits. In one hutch there was a poor ragged old eagle owl, evidently quite miserable and neglected: in another a small boy unknown to them, a wittol who could only roll his eyes and burble when the witch came near. In a third there was a moulting black cock. A fourth had a mangy goat in it, also black, and two more stood empty.

"Grizzle Greediguts," cried the witch.

"Here, Mother," answered the carrion crow.

With a flop and a squawk it was sitting beside them, its hairy black beak on one side. It was the witch's familiar.

"Open the doors," commanded Madame Mim, "and Greediguts shall have eyes for supper, round and blue."

The gore-crow hastened to obey, with every sign of satisfaction, and pulled back the heavy doors in its strong beak, with three times three. Then the two boys were thrust inside, one into each hutch, and Madame Mim regarded them with unmixed pleasure. The doors had magic locks on them and the witch had made them to open by whispering in their keyholes.

"As nice a brace of young gentlemen," said the witch, "as ever stewed or roast. Fattened on real butcher's meat, I daresay, with milk and all. Now we'll have the big one jugged for Sunday, if I can get a bit of wine to go in the pot, and the little one we'll have on the moon's morn, by jing and by jee, for how can I keep my sharp fork out of him a minute longer it fair gives me the croup."

"Let me out," said Kay hoarsely, "you old witch, or Sir Ector will come for you."

At this Madame Mim could no longer contain her joy. "Hark to

the little varmint," she cried, snapping her fingers and doing a
bouncing jig before the cages. "Hark to the sweet, audacious,
tender little veal. He answers back and threatens us with Sir Ector,
on the very brink of the pot. That's how I faint to tooth them, I do
declare, and that's how I will tooth them ere the week be out, by
Scarmiglione, Belial, Peor, Ciriato Sannuto and Dr. D."

With this she began bustling about in the back yard, the herb
garden and the scullery, cleaning pots, gathering plants for the
stuffing, sharpening knives and cleavers, boiling water, skipping for
joy, licking her greedy lips, saying spells, braiding her night-black
hair, and singing as she worked.

First she sang the old witch's song:

> Black spirits and white, red spirits and gray,
> Mingle, mingle, mingle, you that mingle may.
>> Here's the blood of a bat,
>> Put in that, oh, put in that.
>> Here's libbard's bane.
>> Put in again.
> Mingle, mingle, mingle, you that mingle may.

Then she sang her work song:

>> Two spoons of sherry
>> Three oz. of yeast,
>> Half a pound of unicorn,
>> And God bless the feast.
>> Shake them in a collander,
>> Bang them to a chop,
>> Simmer slightly, snip up nicely,
>> Jump, skip, hop.

> Knit one, knot one, purl two together,
>> Pip one and pop one and pluck the secret
>>> feather.
>> Baste in a mod. oven.
>> God bless our coven.
>> Tra-la la!
>> Three toads in a jar.
>> Te-he-he!
>> Put in the frog's knee.

Peep out of the lace curtain.
There goes the Toplady girl, she's up to
no good that's certain.
Oh, what a lovely baby!
How nice it would go with gravy.
Pinch the salt.

Here she pinched it very nastily.

Turn the malt

Here she began twiddling round widdershins, in a vulgar way.

With a hey-nonny-nonny and I don't mean maybe.

At the end of this song, Madame Mim took a sentimental turn
and delivered herself of several hymns, of a blasphemous nature,
and of a tender love lyric which she sang sotto-voce with trills. It
was:

My love is like a red, red nose
His tail is soft and tawny,
And everywhere my lovely goes
I call him Nick or Horny.

She vanished into the parlor, to lay the table.
Poor Kay was weeping in a corner of the end hutch, lying on his
face and paying no attention to anything. Before Madame Mim had
finally thrown him in, she had pinched him all over to see if he was
fat. She had also slapped him, to see, as the butchers put it, if he
was hollow. On top of this, he did not in the least want to be eaten
for Sunday dinner and he was miserably furious with the Wart for
leading him into such a terrible doom on account of a mere arrow.
He had forgotten that it was he who had insisted on entering the
fatal cottage.
The Wart sat on his haunches, because the cage was too small for
standing up, and examined his prison. The bars were of iron and
the gate was iron too. He shook all the bars, one after the other, but
they were as firm as rock. There was an iron bowl for water—with
no water in it—and some old straw in a corner for lying down. It
was verminous.

"Our mistress," said the mangy old goat suddenly from the next pen, "is not very careful of her pets."

He spoke in a low voice, so that nobody could hear, but the carrion crow which had been left on the chimney to spy upon them noticed that they were talking and moved nearer.

"Whisper," said the goat, "if you want to talk."

"Are you one of her familiars?" asked the Wart suspiciously.

The poor creature did not take offense at this, and tried not to look hurt.

"No," he said. "I'm not a familiar. I'm only a mangy old black goat, rather tattered as you see, and kept for sacrifice."

"Will she eat you too?" asked the Wart, rather tremblingly.

"Not she. I shall be too rank for her sweet tooth, you may be sure. No, she will use my blood for making patterns with on Walpurgis Night."

"It's quite a long way off, you know," continued the goat without self-pity. "For myself I don't mind very much, for I am old. But look at that poor old owl there, that she keeps merely for a sense of possession and generally forgets to feed. That makes my blood boil, that does. It wants to fly, to stretch its wings. At night it just runs round and round and round like a big rat, it gets so restless. Look, it has broken all its soft feathers. For me, it doesn't matter, for I am naturally of a sedentary disposition now that youth has flown, but I call that owl a rare shame. Something ought to be done about it."

The Wart knew that he was probably going to be killed that night, the first to be released out of all that band, but yet he could not help feeling touched at the great-heartedness of this goat. Itself under sentence of death, it could afford to feel strongly about the owl. He wished he were as brave as this.

"If only I could get out," said the Wart. "I know a magician who would soon settle her hash, and rescue us all."

The goat thought about this for some time, nodding its gentle old head with the great cairngorm eyes. Then it said, "As a matter of fact I know how to get you out, only I did not like to mention it before. Put your ear nearer the bars. I know how to get you out, but not your poor friend there who is crying. I didn't like to subject you to a temptation like that. You see, when she whispers to the lock I have heard what she says, but only at the locks on either side of mine. When she gets a cage away she is too soft to be heard. I know the words to release both you and me, and the black cock here too, but not your young friend yonder."

"Why ever haven't you let yourself out before?" asked the Wart, his heart beginning to bound.

"I can't speak them in human speech, you see," said the goat sadly, "and this poor mad boy here, the wittol, he can't speak them either."

"Oh, tell them me."

"You will be safe then, and so would I and the cock be too, if you stayed long enough to let us out. But would you be brave enough to stay, or would you run at once? And what about your friend and the wittol and the old owl?"

"I should run for Merlyn at once," said the Wart. "Oh, at once, and he would come back and kill this old witch in two twos, and then we should all be out."

The goat looked at him deeply, his tired old eyes seeming to ask their way kindly into the bottom of his heart.

"I shall tell you only the words for your own lock," said the goat at last. "The cock and I will stay here with your friend, as hostages for your return."

"Oh, goat," whispered the Wart. "You could have made me say the words to get you out first and then gone your way. Or you could have got the three of us out, starting with yourself to make sure, and left Kay to be eaten. But you are staying with Kay. Oh, goat, I will never forget you, and if I do not get back in time I shall not be able to bear my life."

"We shall have to wait till dark. It will only be a few minutes now."

As the goat spoke, they could see Madame Mim lighting the oil lamp in the parlor. It had a pink glass shade with patterns on it. The crow, which could not see in the dark, came quietly closer, so that at least he ought to be able to hear.

"Goat," said the Wart, in whose heart something strange and terrible had been going on in the dangerous twilight, "put your head closer still. Please, goat, I am not trying to be better than you are, but I have a plan. I think it is I who had better stay as hostage and you who had better go. You are black and will not be seen in the night. You have four legs and can run much faster than I. Let you go with a message for Merlyn. I will whisper you out, and I will stay."

He was hardly able to say the last sentence, for he knew that Madame Mim might come for him at any moment now, and if she came before Merlyn it would be his death warrant. But he did say it, pushing the words out as if he were breathing against water, for he knew that if he himself were gone when Madame came for him, she would certainly eat Kay at once.

"Master," said the goat without further words, and it put one leg out and laid its double-knobbed forehead on the ground in the salute which is given to royalty. Then it kissed his hand as a friend.

"Quick," said the Wart, "give me one of your hoofs through the bars and I will scratch a message on it with one of my arrows."

It was difficult to know what message to write on such a small space with such a clumsy implement. In the end he just wrote KAY. He did not use his own name because he thought Kay more important, and that they would come quicker for him.

"Do you know the way?" he asked.

"My grandam used to live at the castle."

"What are the words?"

"Mine," said the goat, "are rather upsetting."

"What are they?"

"Well," said the goat, "you must say: Let Good Digestion Wait on Appetite."

"Oh, goat," said the Wart in a broken voice. "How horrible. But run quickly, goat, and come back safely, goat, and oh, goat, give me one more kiss for company before you go." The goat refused to kiss him. It gave him the Emperor's salute, of both feet, and bounded away into the darkness as soon as he had said the words.

Unfortunately, although they had whispered too carefully for the crow to hear their speech, the release words had had to be said rather loudly to reach the next-door keyhole, and the door had creaked.

"Mother, Mother!" screamed the crow. "The rabbits are escaping."

Instantly Madame Mim was framed in the lighted doorway of the kitchen.

"What is it, my Grizzle?" she cried. "What ails us, my halcyon tit?"

"The rabbits are escaping," shrieked the crow again.

The witch ran out, but too late to catch the goat or even to see him, and began examining the locks at once by the light of her fingers. She held these up in the air and a blue flame burned at the tip of each.

"One little boy safe," counted Madame Mim, "and sobbing for his dinner. Two little boys safe, and neither getting thinner. One mangy goat gone, and who cares a fiddle? For the owl and the cock are left, and the wittol in the middle."

"Still," added Madame Mim, "it's a caution how he got out, a proper caution, that it is."

"He was whispering to the little boy," sneaked the crow, "whispering for the last half-hour together."

"Indeed?" said the witch. "Whispering to the little dinner, hey? And much good may it do him. What about a sage stuffing, boy, hey? And what were you doing, my Greediguts, to let them carry on like that? No dinner for you, my little painted bird of paradise so you may just flap off to any old tree and roost."

"Oh, Mother," whined the crow. "I was only adoing of my duty."

"Flap off," cried Madame Mim. "Flap off, and go broody if you like."

The poor crow hung its head and crept off to the other end of the roof, sneering to itself.

"Now, my juicy toothful," said the witch, turning to the Wart and opening his door with the proper whisper of Enough-Is-As-Good-As-A-Feast, "we think the cauldron simmers and the oven is mod. How will my tender sucking pig enjoy a little popping lard instead of the clandestine whisper?"

The Wart ran about in his cage as much as he could, and gave as much trouble as possible in being caught, in order to save even a little time for the coming of Merlyn.

"Let go of me, you beast," he cried. "Let go of me, you foul hag, or I'll bite your fingers."

"How the creature scratches," said Madame Mim. "Bless us, how he wriggles and kicks, just for being a pagan's dinner."

"Don't you dare kill me," cried the Wart, now hanging by one leg. "Don't you dare to lay a finger on me, or you'll be sorry for it."

"The lamb," said Madame Mim. "The partridge with a plump breast, how he does squeak."

"And then there's the cruel old custom," continued the witch, carrying him into the lamplight of the kitchen where a new sheet was laid on the floor, "of plucking a poor chicken before it is dead. The feathers come out cleaner so. Nobody could be so cruel as to do that nowadays, by Nothing or by Never, but of course a little boy doesn't feel any pain. Their clothes come off nicer if you take them off alive, and who would dream of roasting a little boy in his clothes, to spoil the feast?"

"Murderess," cried the Wart. "You will rue this ere the night is out."

"Cubling," said the witch. "It's a shame to kill him, that it is. Look how his little downy hair stares in the lamplight, and how his poor eyes pop out of his head. Greediguts will be sorry to miss those eyes, so she will. Sometimes one could almost be a vegetarian, when one has to do a deed like this."

The witch laid Wart over her lap, with his head between her knees, and carefully began to take his clothes off with a practiced hand. He kicked and squirmed as much as he could, reckoning that every hindrance would put off the time when he would be actually knocked on the head, and thus increase the time in which the black goat could bring Merlyn to his rescue. During this time the witch sang her plucking song, of:

> Pull the feather with the skin,
> Not against the grain—o.
> Pluck the soft ones out from in,
> The great with might and main—o.
> Even if he wriggles,
> Never heed his squiggles,
> For mercifully little boys are quite immune to pain—o.

She varied this song with the other kitchen song of the happy cook:

> Soft skin for crackling,
> Oh, my lovely duckling,
> The skewers go here,
> And the string goes there
> And such is my scrumptious suckling.

"You will be sorry for this," cried the Wart, "even if you live to be a thousand."

"He has spoken enough," said Madame Mim. "It is time that we knocked him on the napper."

> Hold him by the legs, and
> When up goes his head,
> Clip him with the palm-edge, and
> Then he is dead.

The dreadful witch now lifted the Wart into the air and prepared to have her will of him; but at that very moment there was a fizzle of summer lightning without any crash and in the nick of time Merlyn was standing on the threshold.

"Ha!" said Merlyn. "Now we shall see what a double-first at Dom-Daniel avails against the private education of my master Bleise."

Madame Mim put the Wart down without looking at him, rose from her chair, and drew herself to her full magnificent height. Her glorious hair began to crackle, and sparks shot out of her flashing eyes. She and Merlyn stood facing each other a full sixty seconds, without a word spoken, and then Madame Mim swept a royal curtsey and Merlyn bowed a frigid bow. He stood aside to let her go first out of the doorway and then followed her into the garden.

It ought perhaps to be explained, before we go any further, that in those far-off days, when there was actually a college for Witches and Warlocks under the sea at Dom-Daniel and when all wizards were either black or white, there was a good deal of ill-feeling between the different creeds. Quarrels between white and black were settled ceremonially, by means of duels. A wizard's duel was run like this. The two principals would stand opposite each other in some large space free from obstructions, and await the signal to begin. When the signal was given they were at liberty to turn themselves into things. It was rather like the game that can be played by two people with their fists. They say One, Two, Three, and at Three they either stick out two fingers for scissors, or the flat palm for paper, or the clenched fist for stone. If your hand becomes paper when your opponent's become scissors, then he cuts you and wins: but if yours has turned into stone, his scissors are blunted, and the win is yours. The object of the wizard in the duel was, to turn himself into some kind of animal, vegetable or mineral which would destroy the particular animal, vegetable or mineral which had been selected by his opponent. Sometimes it went on for hours.

Merlyn had Archimedes for his second, Madame Mim had the gore-crow for hers, while Hecate, who always had to be present at these affairs in order to keep them regular, sat on the top of a step-ladder in the middle, to umpire. She was a cold, shining, muscular lady, the color of moonlight. Merlyn and Madame Mim rolled up their sleeves, gave their surcoats to Hecate to hold, and the latter put on a celluloid eye-shade to watch the battle.

At the first gong Madame Mim immediately turned herself into a dragon. It was the accepted opening move and Merlyn ought to have replied by being a thunderstorm or something like that. Instead, he caused a great deal of preliminary confusion by becoming a field mouse, which was quite invisible in the grass, and nibbled Madame Mim's tail, as she stared about in all directions, for about five minutes before she noticed him. But when she did notice the nibbling, she was a furious cat in two flicks.

Wart held his breath to see what the mouse would become next —he thought perhaps a tiger which could kill the cat—but Merlyn merely became another cat. He stood opposite her and made faces. This most irregular procedure put Madame Mim quite out of her stride, and it took her more than a minute to regain her bearings and become a dog. Even as she became it, Merlyn was another dog standing opposite her, of the same sort.

"Oh, well played, sir!" cried the Wart, beginning to see the plan.

Madame Mim was furious. She felt herself out of her depth against these unusual stone-walling tactics and experienced an internal struggle not to lose her temper. She knew that if she did lose it she would lose her judgment, and the battle as well. She did some quick thinking. If whenever she turned herself into a menacing animal, Merlyn was merely going to turn into the same kind, the thing would become either a mere dog-fight or stalemate. She had better alter her own tactics and give Merlyn a surprise.

At this moment the gong went for the end of the first round. The combatants retired into their respective corners and their seconds cooled them by flapping their wings, while Archimedes gave Merlyn a little massage by nibbling with his beak.

"Second round," commanded Hecate. "Seconds out of the ring. . . . Time!"

Clang went the gong, and the two desperate wizards stood face to face.

Madam Mim had gone on plotting during her rest. She had decided to try a new tack by leaving the offensive to Merlyn, beginning by assuming a defensive shape herself. She turned into a spreading oak.

Merlyn stood baffled under the oak for a few seconds. Then he most cheekily—and, as it turned out, rashly—became a powdery little blue-tit, which flew up and sat perkily on Madame Mim's branches. You could see the oak boiling with indignation for a moment; but then its rage became icy cold, and the poor little blue-tit was sitting, not on an oak, but on a snake. The snake's mouth was open, and the bird was actually perching on its jaws. As the jaws clashed together, but only in the nick of time, the bird whizzed off as a gnat into the safe air. Madame Mim had got it on the run, however, and the speed of the contest now became bewildering. The quicker the attacker could assume a form, the less time the fugitive had to think of a form which would elude it, and now the changes were as quick as thought. The gnat was scarcely in the air when the snake had turned into a toad whose curious tongue, rooted at the front instead of the back of the jaw, was already unrolling in the flick which would snap it in. The gnat, flustered by the sore pursuit, was bounced into an offensive role, and the hard-pressed Merlyn now stood before the toad in the shape of a mollern which could attack it. But Madame Mim was in her element. The game was going according to the normal rules now, and in less than an eye's blink the toad had turned into a peregrine falcon which was diving at two hundred and fifty miles an hour upon the heron's back. Poor Merlyn, beginning to lose his nerve, turned wildly into an elephant—this move usually won a little breathing space—but Madame Mim, relentless, changed from the falcon into an aullay on the instant. An aullay was as much bigger than an elephant as an elephant is larger than a sheep. It was a sort of horse with an elephant's trunk. Madame Mim raised this trunk in the air, gave a shriek like a railway engine, and rushed upon her panting foe. In a flick Merlyn had disappeared.

"One," said Hecate. "Two. Three. Four. Five. Six. Seven. Eight. Nine—"

But before the fatal Ten which would have counted him out, Merlyn reappeared in a bed of nettles, mopping his brow. He had been standing among them as a nettle.

The aullay saw no reason to change its shape. It rushed upon the man before it with another piercing scream. Merlyn vanished again just as the thrashing trunk descended, and all stood still a moment, looking about them, wondering where he would step out next.

"One," began Hecate again, but even as she proceeded with her counting, strange things began to happen. The aullay got hiccoughs, turned red, swelled visibly, began whooping, came out in spots, staggered three times, rolled its eyes, fell rumbling to the ground. It groaned, kicked and said Farewell. The Wart cheered, Archimedes hooted till he cried, the gore-crow fell down dead, and Hecate, on the top of her ladder, clapped so much that she nearly tumbled off. It was a master stroke.

The ingenious magician had turned himself successively into the microbes, not yet discovered, of hiccoughs, scarlet fever, mumps, whooping cough, measles and heat spots, and from a complication of all these complaints the infamous Madame Mim had immediately expired.

L. SPRAGUE DE CAMP

ANOTHER modern fantast whose fictions most generally fall into the category of the humorous anecdote is my friend L. Sprague de Camp, who will, I feel certain, appreciate a place in this anthology immediately following T. H. White, whom he admires and enjoys almost as much as I do.

Born in New York City in 1907, de Camp showed no early aptitude for fantasy writing. He took degrees in aeronautical engineering and economics, and his first books bear forbidding titles like *The Evolution of Naval Weapons* and *Patents and their Management.* Happily for all of us who like good storytelling, he soon switched to the concocting of delightful modern fantasies, at first in collaboration with Fletcher Pratt in such books as *The Castle of Iron* and *The Incomplete Enchanter,* and later on his own with novels such as *The Goblin Tower* and *The Clocks of Iraz.*

De Camp's sense of humor is too powerful to permit him to write straightforward heroica, even here, when he is attempting something essentially in the vein of Robert E. Howard's Conan stories. His feel for the ridiculous element in human affairs always seizes command; over the years, he has learned to yield gracefully to this bent.

Laid in the age after Atlantis, these "Pusâdian tales" (as he calls them) have proved so popular that they have all been reprinted in various anthologies. The single exception is "The Owl and the Ape," which follows next. It has never been anthologized until now. I cannot permit such a lapse in taste to continue uncorrected.

THE OWL AND THE APE

JARRA was always promising to complete Gezun Lorska's education for him and never getting around to it. This was one of the times:

". . . so if you'll come into the garden after the supper-hour, Gezun, I'll show you some of the singular things one of Father's sailors taught me . . ."

Gezun said: "Meseems I've heard all that before." He grasped her wrist. "I suspect that what you really yearn for, my lass—"

"My goodness, Gezun!" she said. "Aren't you strong! Are you *sure* you're only fourteen?"

"Quite certain." (Actually, he thought that his fourteenth birthday was yet some days off. In the year since he had been sold to Sancheth Sar he had somewhat lost track of time, and moreover the calendar used here in Gadaira differed from that of his native Lorsk. Still, her question had cogency, for a fourteen-year-old Pusâdian like Gezun might well be as tall as a mature Euskerian.)

"As I was saying," he continued, "I'm a peaceable wight, and don't like to slay folk save those who wantonly offend me. But I take not teasing kindly, and am minded to drag you back into this fabulous garden of yours—"

"Not *now!*" she squeaked. "Mother's hanging out the—"

"*Gezun! Gezun Lorska!*" came the familiar caw of Sancheth Sar. "Boy! Hither, forthwith!"

Gezun dropped Jarra's wrist. "Run along, Jarra; this is men's business."

He stuck his thumbs into the belt of his kilt and ambled around to the front of Sancheth's house, fast enough to avoid serious trouble with his owner but not so fast as to give the old wizard exaggerated ideas of his submissiveness. He was secretly grateful to Sancheth for rescuing him from what might, as a result of his own youthful ignorance, have developed into an embarrassing situation. What if Jarra had said "Yes"?

"You take long enough, you young bull-mammoth," said Sancheth Sar, leaning on his stick and glaring down his hawk's nose. Though in former years the sorcerer had stood a good span taller than Gezun did now, age had bowed him until the difference was no longer great.

"Yessir sorrysir."

"When you apologize, speak distinctly and run not all your words together; else the whole effect be lost." The sorcerer blew his nose upon his mystic robe and continued: "Where was I? Ah, yes, the auction."

"What auction, Master?"

"Why, lout, the auction of Dauskezh Van, what else? But I forget; I've not advised you thereof. Dauskezh, wishing to retire from active practice of the sorcerous and thaumaturgic arts, has—"

"Who's Dauskezh Van?"

"Such ignorance! He's the greatest, the wisest, the profoundest magician ever to practice in the Tartessian Empire. But now, despite all that longevity and rejuvenation spells can do, age claims him for its hoary own. Where was I?"

"You were telling me about the auction."

"So I was. Well, wishing to retire from practice and spend the balance of his life in peace, he's selling off all his magical talismans, tokens, sigils, relics, and other accessories. I was to have departed to wend my way to his cave on Tadhik Mountain in rocky Dzen beginning on the morrow, but now that Nikurteu has sent this cursed tisick upon me I must remain at home to nurse my infirmities." He sneezed.

"You mean you wish *me* to go to Dzen in your stead?" cried Gezun, torn between excitement and apprehension.

"With admirable promptitude you grasp my meaning ere I've formulated it in words. Aye, boy, the task is yours to dare and do."

"What do you wish me to seek to buy? Anything that seems good?"

"By no means! But one particular item, namely: the Hordhun Manuscript."

"What's that?" said Gezun.

"As the name implies, a set of waxen sheets with pictographs inscribed thereon."

"I mean, what's in it?"

"Spells."

"What sort of spells?"

"Curse you for a nosey quidnunc! But then, perhaps indeed you ought to know, that you shall watch well where you place those monstrous feet of yours. As you're no doubt aware, your land of Poseidonis is slowly, in the course of many earthquakes, sinking beneath the waters of the Western Sea."

"So I've heard. It's said that one can take a boat in the harbor of Amferé on a calm day and through the water see the ruins of former edifices, once on dry land but now paving the harbor-bottom."

"Just so. My reckonings show that in three thousand years there'll be nought left of Pusâd save chains of islands, now the tops of mountains."

"What difference does it make what happens thousands of years hence?"

"To you none, stripling, but kings must take a view that's longer than the span of their own petty lifetimes—at least if they'd rise above the level of mere crowned beasts—and it is with kings I'd deal. The Hordhun Manuscript, 'tis rumored, harbors spells of such puissance that they'll either halt or speed this continental settling. With that in my hands, do you see in what an advantageous site I'd be respecting the Pusâdian kinglets?"

"I see. Do these spells really work?"

"That I know not; but even if they don't, they'll furnish a lever wherewith to pry open the bulging coffers of Lorsk and Parsk and the rest."

"Then I saddle up Dostaen tomorrow, ride to Dauskezh's cave, and out-bid our rivals when this work comes up?"

"Yes, but it's not quite so simple. For this auction entails two unique attributes. First, you'll not see the faces of your fellow-bidders, because 'tis one of Dauskezh's crotchets to make all who'd attend his auction wear masks resembling the visages of animals."

"Do I don such a mask here?" Gezun had an unpleasant mental picture of himself wearing the head of a leopard or an ibex and jogging through Gadaira on his mule, to the uproarious mirth of his fellow-striplings.

"Nay; Dauskezh will furnish them on your arrival, assigning to each the semblance of the beast his hoary fancy thinks that bidder most in soul and character resembles. And that fact provides you with your only clue to the second difficulty, to wit: that neither will the items to be sold be openly displayed, but be identified by number merely."

"What japery! How shall I know the Hordhun Manuscript when it's offered?"

"'Tis the conceit of Dauskezh that a true magician can perceive without being told; and in sooth, were I there, I'd no doubt contrive to make head against his quillets. Lacking such skills, you must devise another means. Now, there's no doubt that Nikurteu Balya, may the gods blast his leprous soul, is also bent upon procurement of this manuscript. And if you rate the wizards of Tartessia in order of intelligence, Dauskezh stands first, myself second, and Nikurteu third. It follows that of all who come in masks to this event, Nikurteu'll be the most sagacious. Therefore you should know him by his mask, which I presume will be that of an owl since that bird is universally conceded to be the wisest of the brute kingdom. And when you perceive that he displays unwonted interest in some item, you may infer that that's the manuscipt in question, and bid the limit."

"But," said Gezun Lorska, "what's to hinder this same Nikurteu from casting on me some baneful spell that shall strike me immobile or speechless till the bidding be completed?"

"Oh, a trifle, a trifle that had slipped my old mind. I'll put on you a counter-spell that should endure till your return, so that such unnatural assaults shall rebound and recoil upon the sender."

"Why not lend me the ring of star-metal?"

Gezun indicated the band of metal, like silver but duller, that encircled the finger of Sancheth Sar. What the metal was none knew, save that it was harder than the toughest bronze, and was said to have come from a stone that fell from the sky. The stone itself had passed through many hands—those of King Awoggas of Belem and Prince Vakar of Lorsk among others—and the material was so effective as a repellant for all sorts of spells and spirits, that Gezun's master had to doff it before he could undertake any magical operation himself.

"Heh-heh, and have you defy my commands with impunity, you young coystril? Not likely!" said Sancheth.

"Huh. You don't care what becomes of me, it seems, but only for your art. Some day I'll slay myself in sheer despite."

"Oh, come now . . . I'll tell you. You've been a good boy, though betimes exasperating; in recognition whereof I'll make you a bargain. I have another of these rings, raped from the same sky-stone, and if you procure this manuscript despite all perils, I'll give you this spare ring to keep."

Gezun Lorska grinned under his mop of black Pusâdian curls. "I'll fetch your zany writing, Master, or perish in the trying! You'll faithfully feed my beasts whilst I'm gone?"

"Aye; though I know not why I submit to having my house turned into a menagerie. Go now, fetch our supper, for your tomorrow commences ere dawn."

Gezun rode his mule a week down the coast, and then for three days into the deep defiles and gloomy mountains of the haunted peninsula of Dzen, with plenty of time to think.

He wondered, for instance, at his master's plan to extort treasure from the kinglets of Poseidonis by means of the Hordhun Manuscript and its alleged spells. These kinglets included his own former sovereign, Vuar the Capricious of Lorsk. Now, whither lay his primary duty, towards King Vuar or towards Sancheth Sar? This was his first real chance to ponder such problems since his purchase from the pack of Aremorian pirates a year before. Ever since he had been kidnapped while exploring his family's estate on the supposedly safe western shores of Lorsk he had lived in too constant a ferment of sudden terrors and new experience to have time to think.

He was hazy as to what rights a slave had. If he ran away but was recaptured before leaving the confines of the Tartessian Empire, he knew he'd be forcibly returned to Sancheth's custody, minus an ear as a reminder. On the other hand if he crossed the Sirenian Sea to Poseidonis he would, he thought, be safe; and once in Lorsk his family's influence could interpose an army between him and any pursuers.

Unfortunately there lay that somber sea between himself and home, and passage would not easily be arranged for a fourteen-year-old boy with a slave-brand on his hand.

And how eager was he to escape, really? To him enslavement was one of the normal risks of life, and he would no more have thought of attacking the institution as a whole merely because it had caught him in its toils than he would have thought of proposing a law against dying.

All things considered, he had gotten off rather well. Sancheth had not inflicted on him any mutilation besides the pirates' brand, and had, in his erratic and absent-minded way, treated him kindly enough, so that Gezun had become warily fond of the old man. Or as fond as any adolescent normally becomes of an adult master. His real friends were those of his own age in Gadaira, whom he dominated partly by a certain amiable ingenuity in plotting forays against the common enemy, the adult world; partly by the glamour of his magical apprenticeship; and partly by sheer size.

If he continued to work with reasonable fidelity for this strange master, he thought, he might even look forward to stepping into the wizard's shoes some day. Such a career might well provide more fun and glory than life as a petty lordling on the bison-swarming plains of windy Lorsk. Perhaps he could set up headquarters in lordly Torrutseish, whence Sancheth had originally come. Maybe he could win a daughter of the king of Tartessia to concubine; become vizier, or even king himself . . .

Another thought made him grin: He certainly wouldn't leave Gadaira until he had had a showdown with Jarra on that matter of completing his education.

When the mountains of Dzen had grown so tall that they seemed to lean over and glower down upon him, Gezun came to Mount Tadhik and the cave of Dauskezh Van, which opened out into a natural amphitheater among the crags. A small almost-human being came up and took Gezun's mule and led it to where other beasts of burden were tethered, then returned to Gezun. It laid a finger on its lips and led him into the mouth of the cave, picking up a small copper oil-lamp whose flame cast a meager yellow glow into the dark.

"You were almost too late," it whispered, tugging Gezun along the rocky corridor. "Wait here."

It disappeared into a side-cave or room and came out again with a curious object: a hollow head-mask in the form of a lamb's head. Gezun remembered his master's warning about Dauskezh's custom of making the bidders don masks that symbolized their respective natures, and felt anger stir within him.

"Why you—" he began, but just then the creature popped the object over his head and tied it in place with a draw-string before he could avert the event.

Gezun's anger subsided and he allowed himself a chuckle. Let them think him a lamb; the reputation of being a simpleton might be an asset to a man—provided he were not one in fact.

Then the being led him swiftly further back into the labyrinth of caves where Dauskezh made his home. Here and there the little lamp showed where the wizard and his helpers had improved the natural formations for their own conveniences, enlarging a minor vug to serve as a storage space or shoring up a precarious bit of cave-roof with planks and props. Then they entered a large cavern lit by several lamps, in which were gathered Gezun's fellow-bidders, seated on the swept stone floor in concentric crescents and wrapped in the black mantles of the Euskerian peoples.

As the being pushed Gezun into a vacant place in the last row, most of the heads of the earlier arrivals turned towards him, exhibiting, not human faces, but more animal-masks. Through the eye-holes in his mask he saw a horse, a lion, an aurochs, a fallow-deer, a rhinoceros, a badger—even one grotesque simulacrum in miniature of a mammoth's head, complete with curling tusks and dangling trunk.

By the lamplight he could discern along the walls row after row of dim-lit painting of animals, executed in a lively and life-like though archaic style. There were mammoths and bison and the giant deer now found only in savage Ierarné. This, then, must be one of the caves of which the legends of Poseidonis told, where his forebears had lived scores of centuries earlier, before the gods had taught men the copper-smelting art—before the short sharpbrowed Euskerians had driven the Pusâdians across the Sirenian Sea and made all of Tartessia theirs. His people, though individually larger than the Euskerians by the length of a foot, had been too much absorbed in their art, their songs, their totemistic religion, and their intertribal feuds to resist these taciturn and tenacious newcomers, who swarmed ino the land like hornets, bringing a new and deadly sting: the bow and arrow.

Now the Pusâdians on their sea-girt land painted new pictures and dreamed dreams of returning to their homeland. The animals on the wall reminded Gezun that he was a Pusâdian too, and that his real name was Döpueng Shysh, not this servile cognomen his master had imposed upon him as easier for Euskerian vocal organs to pronounce than the vowels of Poseidonis. Gezun wondered whether he could, by taking Sancheth's place and becoming the greatest wizard in the Tartessian Empire, expedite this homecoming before all of Poseidonis sank beneath the Western Sea.

But right now he had to pick Nikurteu Balya out of the crowd without a face to go by. Sancheth had hinted that Nikurteu, for his sagacity, might be honored with an owl's head. Gezun, however, knew a lot about animals. He had kept as a pet practically everything short of a bison, both home in Poseidonis and here in Tartessia, and had given Sancheth a terrific turn by producing a pair of snakes at supper. Unknown on Poseidonis, these reptiles had fascinated Gezun's artistic eye by their grace, and fortunately they were not of a venomous species.

Gezun knew that the owl, for all its sage appearance, was no more intelligent than any other bird—if anything rather less so.

He peered through the crowd, picking out a leopard, a hyena, a bear, a wolverine, a wild ass, and a monkey. He had also had to do with monkeys, and knew something of their trickiness and resource. It seemed to him that if Dauskezh were as wise as he was alleged to be, and were going to choose an animal to symbolize the character of Nikurteu, he could hardly select a more suitable symbol than the monkey.

Well, he'd be taking a chance either way, so he might as well take it his way as another's. The ape it should be.

Leather curtains rustled and Dauskezh Van came in. He was even older than Sancheth Sar, and in the dim light he seemed to Gezun to be already dead and reanimated by some not altogether successful witchery.

"Bids on One," whispered Dauskezh.

"Fourteen nasses of gold," responded a wizard with the head of a chamois.

"Fifteen," said a beaver.

"Sixteen," said the owl.

Gezun Lorska felt an urge to jump to the conclusion that the owl was Nikurteu after all, and begin bidding against him. He restrained himself, bearing in mind that he had reached his decision dispassionately, uninfluenced by the excitement of the moment, and had better stick to it.

Item Number One went to the chamois and Two came up. It was a very dull business, and Gezun almost fell asleep when a bid on Number Twenty-three from the direction of the monkey brought him sharply out of his doze.

"Twelve nasses," said the monkey.

"Fifteen," said Gezun, heart pounding.

"Twenty."

"Twenty-five," said Gezun, thankful now that Sancheth had forced him to learn simple sums.

They went on up in jumps of five until they neared fifty, Sancheth's limit. It was a formidable price; not only for Sancheth, but also, apparently, for his rival, for the monkey-head began slowing down as they neared it.

"Forty-eight," said the monkey.

"Forty-nine," said Gezun.

"Forty-nine and a half."

"Fifty."

Now Gezun waited, feeling as though his heart would burst through his chest. All the monkey had to do was add another fraction of a nas, no matter how small, and take the item . . .

"Sold!" croaked Dauskezh. "Item Number Twenty-four . . ."

Gezun relaxed, letting his breath out—then caught it again as another fear fingered his windpipe. Suppose he had been mistaken and the ape was not Nikurteu after all? Or suppose Number Twenty-three were not the Hordhun Manuscript?

It would all come out in due time. If he had gone astray he could at best expect a beating from Sancheth—not that he held Sancheth's beatings in much awe, for the old wizard no longer had the strength even to raise a welt on Gezun's tough hide. More serious was the prospect of having Sancheth cast upon him some bothersome curse, like muteness or inability to touch water—but then, he now carried a protective spell from Sancheth himself, and by the time it wore off, the sorcerer would have simmered down and forgotten his costly error.

Item Thirty proved the last of the lot. The near-human thing touched Gezun and beckoned while the others kept their places. Gezun inferred that under Dauskezh's quaint rules the bidders were allowed to depart at intervals only, so as not to see each other's faces. He, being the last to arrive, would go first.

So it proved. The being stopped Gezun at the anteroom, took the lamb's head from him, and handed him a cylindrical package wrapped in lambskin and tied with a string of esparto grass. In return Gezun handed over the entire contents of the bag of golden rings and wedges which Sancheth had sent with him. The being weighed the gold with care before letting Gezun go.

Once free, Gezun wasted no time but rode off on Dostaen at once, chewing a great chunk of barley-bread from his scrip.

The sun was sending a last red ray through a notch in the mountains of Dzen, and Gezun Lorska was lolling on his mule and humming a song of Poseidonis, when two men sprang out from behind the rocks. One, who carried a big bronze sword, seized Dostaen's bridle; the other made at Gezun with a hunting-spear.

As the man with the spear drew it back for a stab, Gezun

tumbled off his mule's back, so that the bronze spearhead darted like a snake's tongue through the empty space where Gezun had just been. He scrambled to his feet on the leeward side of the mule and made off up the nearest slope as fast as he could.

Gezun's ear caught a fragment of speech between the men: something like ". . . you hold the mule whilst I . . ." A glance showed the spearman coming after him, bounding with great leaps from rock to rock, his black cloak flapping like bat's wings. Though more agile than the man, Gezun had a horrid feeling that the fellow would run him down in the long run. And he had nothing but a modest bronze knife to fight with.

He ran on anyway. The slope narrowed to a tongue of land as Gezun neared the summit of a small hill which on the far side dropped away in sheer precipices. A quick look showed no way down on that side. He was cornered.

The panting breaths of the pursuer came louder and louder to Gezun's ears; any second the man would appear. The knife would be of little use. So would his sandals. His only other possessions at the moment were the Hordhun Manuscript (if such it was), his kilt, and the broad leather belt that held the kilt in place. His cloak he had shed at the start of the chase. The bronze buckle on the end of the belt might prove useful . . .

A jumble of rocks lay about the hilltop; one nearly the size of his head and of curious elongated shape, like an enlarged fingerbone. Gezun whipped off his belt, letting his kilt fall; made a loop of his belt, and slipped the loop over the narrow place in the middle of the stone.

When the spearman topped the rise, Gezun rushed at him, screeching in hope of disconcerting him. First he threw the rolled-up kilt at the man's face. The man dodged, but his attention was distracted long enough for Gezun to step in close, whirling the stone around his head on the end of the belt-loop. The spearman was scarcely taller than he was, and the slope gave Gezun some slight advantage.

The stone struck the side of the man's head with a solid sound of crunching bone, and the man fell sidewise across his dropped spear. Gezun made sure the fellow was dead by cutting his throat; then pondered. He could not press his luck too far. The other man, he was sure, would recognize him the minute he appeared, and would be ready to meet him with sword and rolled-up cloak. Craft was indicated.

Gezun Lorska therefore donned the dead man's clothes, pulling the black mantle over his head as these Euskerians did at night. Then, picking up the spear, he swaggered back down the slope. The sun had disappeared.

The swordsman, still holding the mule, looked up as Gezun approached and said: "Did you get it?"

"Uh-huh," grunted Gezun, striving to imitate with his changing voice the deeper accents of his victim. When he was close he said: "Take it."

But as the swordsman tucked his sword under his left arm and put out his right hand, what Gezun laid on the hand was not the Hordhun Manuscript, but the freshly-severed head of the spear-man, which he had been carrying under the cloak.

The swordsman gave a cry of horror and dropped the head with a thud. Gezun whipped up the spear and plunged the point into his foe's thick body. When his young muscles failed to drive it very far in on the first thrust, he shoved on the shaft with all his might, pushing the man back from him.

The man dropped his sword with a clatter and tried to recover it, but another push by Gezun forced him off-balance and he fell. He tried to wrestle the spear-shaft out of his body, but Gezun kept pushing it in. Then he tried to reach Gezun, who was now at the far end of the spear and beyond reach. At last the man threw himself away from Gezun, tearing the spear-shaft out of his grasp.

Gezun danced back as the man rounded on him and pulled the spear out of his side, hobbled back to where he had dropped his sword, picked it up too, and set out after Gezun with a weapon in each hand. Gezun ran—not uphill this time, but down. Behind him the man plowed through the scrub and scrambled over the rocks, cursing by his various gods in a gasping undertone.

The chase went on until Gezun realized that the gasping breath and the muttered curses were no longer keeping up with him. He looked back and saw a dark shape sprawled on the hillside among the boulders.

He scouted cautiously towards it. The man was lying and holding his side, but as Gezun approached he sat up and hurled the spear at him. It was a bad throw, for the spear slewed sidewise in the air and the shaft hit Gezun on the forearm he threw up to ward it off—a bruising knock but not crippling. Gezun picked up the spear and backed as the man tried to rush with his sword. Lacking the strength to make it, the fellow sank down again among the rocks.

Gezun sat down on a boulder and waited warily for the man to weaken further. Darkness deepened; the evening star appeared. The gasping breath became a rattle and then stopped. Gezun rose, bounded around behind the man, and drove the spear into his back to make sure he was dead. He looted the corpse with swift efficiency and found his way back up to the road, where Dostaen placidly munched the scanty herbage.

A few minutes later, wearing his own clothes and carrying the Hordhun Manuscript and the weapons of his late attackers, he set out again on the way to Gadaira.

"Gezun! Gezun Lorska!" cried a voice.

Gezun recognized it. "Jarra!" he shouted. "What on earth are you doing here?" In his excitement his voice slid up into the high boy's range.

She hopped down to the road and caught his leg. "Oh, right joyful am I that you came! My father brought me on a trading-trip down the coast, and a pack of knaves set upon us and scattered the caravan, though I think my father got away safe. Will you take me back to Gadaira?"

"What think you? Here, catch my hand and hop up behind."

"Won't you dismount a minute first? So weary am I of wandering these forsaken hills, and you can't go much further tonight in any case."

"I'll go far enough to put a healthy distance betwixt me and the ghosts of those I sped!"

"You've been manslaying?"

"Merely in self-defense. There were six, but I drove Dostaen at full gallop into the ruck, slew two at the first onset, and put the rest to rout."

"Marvellous! You shall tell me all about it; but meanwhile dismount. Have you aught to eat? I'm so weak of starvation that without a bite I fear I can go no further."

"Oh, very well." Gezun vaulted off. "But for all these things there is a price, as says the philosopher Goishek."

Laughing she put her face up to be kissed. Although the light was too dim to discern her features clearly, her Euskerian eyebrows, like a pair of little black sickles, showed against the lighter tone of her skin. She melted into his arms and he felt her ripening young body against his. He kissed her frantically, his pulse pounding.

"There's a place—nearby—" she gasped, "where—your education might—"

Somewhere an owl hooted. The sound touched off a train of thought in Gezun's mind, even while he was kissing Jarra. The owl is really a stupid creature, he remembered, for all his appearance of wisdom. Was he playing the owl by any chance?

It was odd that when he had seen Jarra eleven days ago she had said nothing of any such trip. It was odder that Jarra's father, the merchant Berota, a patriarch with strong ideas of the place of women in society, should take his daughter with him on such a commercial foray. And the rocky peninsula of Dzen, haunted by demons and their depraved worshipers, was no profitable field for trade. Perhaps it was more than a coincidence that the type of education which Jarra proposed to give him was precisely that guaranteed to dissolve and cancel the spell that Sancheth had cast upon him to ward off Nikurteu's maleficent magic.

As he hesitated, torn between prudence and passion, the owl hooted again. With that he thrust her to arms' length, looking at her through narrowed eyes.

"What's the name of my mother?" he demanded abruptly.

"Why Gezun, as if I should know that . . ."

"Then be damned to demon-land!" he shouted, vaulting back on the mule. "May all your brats be stillborn! May Dyosizh smite your tenderest parts with an itch! May the teeth rot in your head!"

He trotted off into the night, knowing that the real Jarra knew the names of his parents perfectly well. Hadn't he spent hours telling her of his life in Lorsk?

A glance back showed Jarra standing quietly by the road. As he watched, her features changed into something not quite human, and peals of shrill aged laughter came after him. He spat and wiped his mouth with his mantle.

"Thinks he can befool me with his shape-changing sprites, eh!" he mused. "Me, *me?* Döpueng Shysh of Lorsk, the future king of Tartessia?"

He gestured with the spear against the unresisting night air.

The heart of Gezun Lorska beat high as he rode into Gadaira in the early morning. At the edge of town he dismounted to lead Dostaen the rest of the way, for the narrow streets did not encourage cantering, and anyway Gezun's bottom was sore from days of hard riding.

He paused at the little bridge over the Arrang to watch a gang of workmen digging a foundation for a house. It would be a fine house judging from the size and depth of the excavation. They had dug a trench from the house-hole down to the edge of the little river, and now were laying semicylindrical tiles in the trench to carry off the wastes of the house.

Gezun filed the idea away for his own future use. He became lost in contemplation, thinking of the fine palace he would build when he was king, until a voice behind him roused him:

"Day-dreaming, Gezun? You'll never attain the style of magician by that road!"

It was Nikurteu Balya, riding past on his fine black horse. With a laugh Gezun's master's rival rode on and disappeared.

Gezun pulled himself together and trudged the small remaining distance to Sancheth Sar's house. Sancheth himself hurried to the door at the sound of his approach.

"What news?" creaked the old wizard.

"Success, Master!"

"*Haulae!* Glorious! You're a fine lad, as I've always said!" Years fell away from Sancheth as he waved his stick, did a little dance-step, and thumped Gezun affectionately on the back. "Tell me all about it."

"Here's the manuscript," said Gezun, handing it over. "But before I begin, wasn't there a certain other bargain between us?"

"You mean the ring? Here, take mine; I'll use the other."

Sancheth Sar slipped the ring of sky-metal off and handed it to Gezun, who experimented till he found a finger that it fitted comfortably.

"And now to your tale—wup! What's this?"

As Gezun watched with increasing alarm, Sancheth's eyes widened, the corners of his mouth turned down, and his fingers began to shake.

"Listen," he said in a voice like one of Gezun's pet snakes in a rage:

"'To my esteemed colleague, Sancheth Sar, from his admirer Nikurteu Balya. Your servant bore himself nobly on the mission whereon you sent him. Nevertheless it is written in the Book of Geratun that he who assigns to a boy a task properly appertaining to a man shall rue the day he did so. For Gezun shrewdly surmised which item of the auction was the Hordhun Manuscript and over-bid me; he bravely fought and slew two servants I sent to waylay him; he resisted with inhuman self-control the advances of a sprite I sent to entice him from the path of rectitude in the form of his sweetling. Yet when he entered Gadaira did he stop to watch four men digging a hole in the ground—four men whom I, knowing that no boy can resist the spectacle of an excavation, had hired for the purpose. And so bemused became he that it was no tough task to take the Hordhun Manuscript from his scrip and substitute this commiseratory screed. Farewell!'"

"You!" screamed Sancheth, and his eyes were like those of a hungry eagle. "You bawbling oaf! You imperceiverant hilding! You incondite loon! I'll cast upon you an itch that shall leave you no peace for—"

"Forget not this, Master!" cried Gezun, backing toward the door and holding out the clenched hand that bore the ring of star-metal. "You can't enchant me!"

"But that protects you not from more mundane chastisement!" yelled Sancheth, and went for Gezun with his stick.

And thus it came to pass that the citizens of Gadaira were treated to the diverting if not uplifting spectacle of Gezun Lorska running full-tilt down the main street, while behind him came the town's senior sorcerer, Sancheth Sar, making a speed that none would have expected in a wizard of his centuries, and cleaving the air with his mystic walking-stick.

LIN CARTER

I was born in St. Petersburg, Florida, in 1930, and came to New York to study writing at Columbia University in 1953, following a tour of duty with the infantry in Korea. Here I have stayed ever since.

My very first book, *The Wizard of Lemuria* (1965), was heroic fantasy in the tradition of Robert E. Howard and Edgar Rice Burroughs; it was straighforward Sword and Sorcery, grim and essentially humorless. But there have been forty novels since then, and maybe I have matured, or mellowed, or something. Because recently I find myself injecting humor into my fantasies, which have become lighter and lighter and ever more playful.

The story which follows is a perfect example of this new trend. The first in a new cycle of tales set in the fabulous islands of Antillia, presumed by certain occultists to have flourished between the ages of Lemuria and of Atlantis, it is a humorous anecdote set in magical scenery, written with an impudent style and a surface sparkle that pleases me immensely. Never before published, it appears here in print for the first time. I hope it amuses you as much as it amused me in the writing of it.

THE TWELVE WIZARDS OF ONG

1.

"THE air elemental, Fremmoun, has recently returned to the earth after a journey to the third planet of the star Srendix, where he discovered the long-lost Compendium of the sorcerer Paroul," the demon reported sullenly.

Intrigued at this intelligence, the young karcist, Chan, questioned the captive diabolus further on this point without, however, learning more. Satisfied at length that the infernal spirit possessed no further details on this matter, Chan uttered the Greater Dismissal, broke the circle of luminous powder which had confined the demon, suffumigated the invocatorial chamber with camphor, and strode from his house for a turn or two through his gardens.

Deep in thought, the youthful karcist strolled the gem-strewn path which meandered through his pleasaunce, absently driving an archeopteryx from his mandragora beds by hurling a well-placed opal. With a guttural squawk, the ungainly feathered reptile flapped away through the tall stand of nodding cycads that bordered the garden.

The implications of the demon's message were almost alarming. On a sudden impulse the young karcist returned to his house, belted on his Live Blade, took up his Waystaff and a purse stuffed with potent amulets, and strode off to visit his nearest neighbor.

Chan's house of red stone stood on the southern slopes of Mount Ong; the mountain was a nexus of occult forces and many fellow practitioners of the Secret Sciences made this mountain their home. The domed dwelling of his nearest neighbor, Hormatz, a theomancer, rose on the same slope a bit higher than Chan's house; toward it the impulsive youth headed without further cogitation.

The dome, a handsome edifice of bronze and smoky crystal, stood amidst a grove of feathery tree-fern. Chan found the decrepit theomancer, his senior by a dozen centuries, busied making oblations to a squat yellow jade idol of Muvian craftsmanship. The elder nodded perfunctory greeting at his approach. Without ado the karcist informed his senior colleague of his information regarding the sylph Fremmoun. The old theomancer was not impressed.

"I fail to see the reason for your concern," he said absently. "However I will consult my Eidola if you require further data on the matter."

"I would indeed appreciate it," the youth admitted. "But can you not see the horrendous implications? Paroul was the preëminent sorcerer of the last epoch. It is a matter of common knowledge that Fremmoun is subject to Nelibar Zux. Zux, once he has mastered the Compendium's contents, will thus become the most advanced sorcerer of our day."

"I still fail to perceive the cause of your perturbations," the theomancer reiterated.

"Has not Sarthath Oob, the leader of a rival enclave, sought for some time to enlist the sorcerer in his coven? What a coup it would be for him—and what a loss to us!"

The aged theomancer paled as the full import dawned upon him at last. The wizards who dwelt about Mount Ong had long since formed a local enclave. They were twelve in number, lacking only a final member to total thirteen, at which number they could become a full coven. A rival enclave, that headed by the nefarious Sarthath Oob, was in an identical predicament. Both enclaves had made overtures to the sorcerer Nelibar Zux but without success. Were the nefarious Oob to succeed in persuading Zux to join his group, it would be a coup of considerable value; at once he would achieve full covenhood for his group, thus outranking the enclave of Mount Ong, to say nothing of the prestige he would gain for his group, since Zux, his occult authority newly enhanced by mastery of the long-lost Compendium, would be the supreme sorcerer of the age, his presence lending enormous luster to the coven of Sarthath Oob. The prospect was horrible to contemplate, and Hormatz hurried to consult his collection of gods upon the instant.

These divinities ranged in size from an amulet of blue paste the length of your middle finger to a rough-hewn monolith of porous lava the height of a full-grown stegosaurus. Some were squat and fat, with features jovial, complacent, or sleepy. Others glared beneath crowns of woven vipers, leered with fangs of sparkling black obsidian, or howled in graven wrath, brandishing skulls and scorpions in the grasp of multiplex limbs.

In oracular response to the theomancer's queries, a brass godlet from the Southern Polar Continent informed them that Fremmoun had indeed borne with him from the star Srendix a ponderous volume bound in diplodocus hide, whose contents were, however, unknown to him.

A triple-headed Eidolon from elder and age-lost Hyperborea, fashioned from a pillar of flint, reported that the sorcerer Nelibar Zux had recently canceled a scheduled tour of the astral plane and remained in the seclusion of his subterranean palace, presumably deep in study of the famous Compendium of advanced sorcery.

The remainder of Hormatz' collection of carven gods professed ignorance in the matter.

"Perhaps the brothers, Themnon and Thoy, can inform you as to the current activities of our rival, Sarthath Oob," suggested the decrepit theomancer. The young karcist offered hasty thanks and departed at once for their abode.

The necromancer Themnon and his twin, the warlock Thoy, dwelt together in a manse of gray stone on the east face of Mount Ong. Chan selected the shortest path, but it was late afternoon before he reached their manse, a somber and ominous structure, builded on a glassy scarp of glittering quartz which overhung a deep chasm. The manse bore up a crest of turrets; scarlet lights flickered in its tall, pointed windows; potent runes, cut in pillars of harsh corundum, protected the dwellers therein from unwanted visitors. Before the portal of scaly and verdigris-eaten bronze, a heavy slug-horn hung. Chan set it to his lips and sounded an echoing call. In a few moments the magical fence flickered and went dead; he strode between the pillars and up to the door, which creaked open on rusty hinges. To the worm-eaten lich who served the necromancer and the warlock as butler Chan crisply stated his business and was ushered into a gloomy hall hung with moldy tapestries and thick with neglected cobwebs, while the magically animated cadaver stalked into the further recesses of the manse to fetch his masters.

2.

THEMNON was a tall, gaunt necromancer with dull eyes like unpolished smaragds set in a dour, wrinkled visage. His brother, the warlock Thoy, was short, bald and sleepy. They served the young karcist a black, heady wine of mediocre Atlantean vintage in cups of luminous orichalc and listened without comment to his urgent tale. Chan well knew that naught could stir the gaunt necromancer to a semblance of excitement unless it were a newly excavated mummy or an interesting corpse; but the squat warlock was less phlegmatic and more given to social conviviality.

Upon the conclusion of his account, the twins conducted him into the depths of their gloomy manse. By crumbling stone stairs, made slippery with slimy lichens, they descended to a deep crypt whose stone walls held flaring torches which shed a guttering orange light over a clutter of sarcophagi. Cadavers lay strewn on the stone floor in various stages of advanced decay. Several closed wooden coffins were drawn up beneath the flickering torches; their lids obviously served the brethren in lieu of desks, for portfolios and tomes lay helter-skelter upon them and scrolls of parchment fashioned from the membrane of pterodactyl wings were tumbled about in a litter of periapts and tomb figurines. The stench of the place was frightful.

With the casual ease born of long practice, gaunt Themnon animated a favorite lich, whose degree of decomposition was extraordinary, and queried it as to the current affairs of Sarthath Oob. Chan listened intently but could make nothing from the slurred, liquescent syllables wherewith the animated corpse mumbled its reply. Themnon was accustomed to a certain lack of articulation on the part of his pet corpses, and easily interpreted the slobbering speech: the leader of the rival enclave had departed that noon from his residence amidst the Desolation of Skarm, which lay on the other side of the island, for an unknown destination. Chan could guess all too well that his destination was none other than the famous subterranean palace of the sorcerer Nelibar Zux. He thanked the brothers and hastily departed from that ominous crypt of mouldering corpses and antique mummy cases.

Achieving again the open air, he spied the hut of the fair young witch, Azra, far below him at the base of the mountain, and upon a sudden whim descended the glassy scarp by means of a narrow ledge which zigzagged down the cliffy face to the brink of the chasm.

On his way he passed the hovel of the shaggy and unkempt old alchemist, Phlomel: a miserable lean-to, a mere shack, filled with stenchful reeks and bubbling messes, belching forth at that moment a nauseous yellow smoke. He could picture the wild-eyed old *souffleur* within, acid-stained smock flapping about his skinny shanks, his flying beard smelling of sulphur, as he hopped busily about from alembic to athanor, from crucible to cucurbite, amidst roaring fires, seething smokes, and amazing fluids. Although the alchemist was a fellow member of the enclave, Chan could discern no means by which Phlomel could render assistance in his current plight, and thus he passed his hovel by without a visit.

The pleasant hut of the witch Azra, who was the only feminine member of the Mount Ong wizards, was situated at the base of the eastern slope at the head of a grassy glade hemmed in by tall bamboo. Like Chan, the witch girl was yet in first youth. Indeed the green-haired girl, with her ripe lips and eyes of sparkling quicksilver, had often prompted erotic fancies in the heart of the bold, impulsive young karcist. Her supple, tawny, high-breasted body and long lissom legs were entrancing, as was the languor of her smile and the honeyed warmth of her slow, soft, husky voice. Her tempting charms had inspired him to venture on certain overtures which, however, she laughingly rebuffed in a casual and humorous way, which deprived her refusals of the sting they might otherwise have inflicted on his masculine vanity.

By now the sun had declined the sky and the west was one splendid vault of tangerine flame. A cheerful light shone from the windows of Azra's hut and it guided him across the darkening meadow to her door where the witch girl greeted him with a friendly smile and an invitation to enter. His pulses thrummed at the beauty of her lithe form, which her carefree costume—consisting of a silken scarf tied loosely about her hips and a small idol of green porcelain suspended between her bare, pointed breasts by a thong—did little to conceal.

Azra's hut was cosy and comfortable. A magical fire of sizzling blue flames danced on the stone hearth without need of arboreaceous fuel. A cage of woven rattan housed a tame archeopteryx which squawked, fluttered ungainly wings, and snapped its fanged beak at his entry. A decoction of herb tea simmered in a kettle hung above the flames and fresh mangoes and pawpaws were arrayed temptingly in a wooden bowl on the table. The fragrance of the tea and the glossy rondure of the ripe fruit recalled to Chan the fact that he had not partaken of nutriment since long before his invocation of the diabolus, mid-morn at least; thus without hesitancy he accepted Azra's invitation to dine.

While at table with the nearly nude witch girl, Chan conveyed a brief narrative of the day's adventures and the disappointing failure of their colleagues, Hormatz, Themnon, and Thoy, to suggest a remedy. The green-haired girl responded with sympathy to his woeful tale.

"Tomorrow evening a full meeting of the enclave is scheduled," Azra reminded him helpfully. "Surely our brethren in full council should be informed of these dire events and may perchance arrive at a mode of redressing them."

He agreed that the best course to follow was to lay the matter in the collective laps of the enclave and to postpone any further efforts of his own towards the resolution of the problem until the following eve. Then, warmed by the tea and excited by her casual state of undress, he again made amorous overtures. And again she smilingly denied him her body and gracefully eluded his embrace in such a manner as to cause no affront. His protests that night was upon them and his own house far above, while her bed was capacious enough to shelter both of them, went unheard. And so he was forced to wearily trudge up the mountain again to his own house of red stone and to his empty, lonely bed.

3.

ELDEST and most powerful of the twelve wizards of Ong was the Archimage, Doctor Pellsipher, who resided in a villa of rose-marble and mellow ivory atop the utmost peak and pinnacle of the magic mountain. The Archimage served the local wizards as magister, or presiding officer, of their enclave, and Chan had no doubt but that Doctor Pellsipher would turn a most sympathetic ear to his urgent news. For nothing was more dear to Pellsipher's heart than his ambition to preside over a full, authentic coven, and

the fact that their enclave lacked a thirteenth member, which was
the chief prerequisite for covenhood, was a matter of considerable
complaint by the membership in general and Doctor Pellsipher in
particular. They had often discussed means of enticing or persuading or coercing one more practitioner of the Secret Sciences to join
them on the slopes of Mount Ong, and it was the Archimage himself who most frequently voiced the opinion that their thirteenth
member should be a sorcerer. As the enclave already consisted of
an Archimage, a karcist, a theomancer, a witch, an haruspex, an
alchemist, a warlock, a necromancer, a conjuror, a magician, an astromancer, and a theurgist, there were few occult disciplines not
represented amongst them already. Thus they could pick and
choose between adding to their enclave a diabolist, a sorcerer, a
thaumaturge, or an enchanter. And it was the emphatic opinion of
Doctor Pellsipher that a full-fledged sorcerer was what they most
needed.

Pellsipher's villa was complex and baroque, all balconies and
cupolas and ornamental balustrades, minarets, pavilions, and bel-
vederes. While it clung to the very pinnacle of the mountain's crest,
the remainder of the peak had, by afreets subject to the Doctor's
art, been leveled into artificial terraces, which now bloomed with
lush gardens and exotic pleasurances. Archaic sculpture rose amidst
the nodding cycads; gazebos stood in lotus pools; arched bridges
spanned wandering artificial streamlets; paper lanterns swayed
from the palmy boughs of club-mosses and tree-ferns, glowing like
luminous and cycloptic eyes through the purpureal dusk. The villa
was a faerie structure of carven ornamentation; jeweled mosaics
twinkled through rows of fluted pilasters, fountains splashed in
miniature courts, screens of fretted ivory shielded nooks and niches
where lamps of pierced silver shed a warm luminance through the
gathering twilight.

Despite his concern and the importance of the occasion, for one
reason or another, Chan was the last of the wizards to arrive for the
meeting of the enclave. He was admitted by a voiceless figure of
sparkling brass, one of the marvelous automata from which the
Archimage had been justly famed for several millennia; it looked like
a man in jointed, fantastical armor, the visor of his helm closed. But
Chan knew it was an ingenious clockwork mechanism and neither
alive nor mortal.

He was ushered into the great domed hall, which was roofed by
a vast cupola of milky glass supported atop twenty slender pillars

of spiral-fluted rose-quartz. His eleven colleagues were already in attendance: Spay, Phlomel, Velb the Irithribian, Themnon, Thoy, Master Quinibus, Azra, Hormatz, Kedj the Conjuror, Zoramus of Pankoy, and Doctor Pellsipher. He bowed slightly to their host and magister, and made his apologies for his unseemingly lateness.

"Tut, my boy, not another word! These monthly assemblages are, as ever, mere informal social gatherings, and strict attendance is neither desired nor enforced," the Archimage rejoined in a hearty manner. This Pellsipher was a large, jovial, not-unhandsome man, whose good humor and elephantine courtliness made him generally popular with all, despite his considerable tendency towards a pompous and pontifical tone. He customarily dressed in the height of Antillian fashion, and this evening he was, as usual, resplendent in a nine-tiered hat of scarlet crepe, a many-pleated cloak of striped pink and vermilion taffeta, high-laced buskins of orange plush, and a beautifully draped undertoga of peach silk with a tasselated violet fringe. He wore a jeweled talismanic ring on each finger, and in his left hand he bore an ivory baton carven to the likeness of a winged caduceus. This last was a mere ornament: his Blasting Rod, the badge of his science, was too uncouth an instrument to be borne into polite society.

Patting the young karcist on the shoulder in an affable manner, Pellsipher guided him to a long table where a cold buffet supper had been laid out by mechanical servants. Chan had not eaten before arrival so he did not scruple, but heaped a porcelain plate with stuffed figs, smoked oysters, cheese paté, miniature sandwiches, a dab or two of mint jelly, and small cubes of spiced meat speared through with silver toothpicks. A brass servitor was at his elbow with a crystal goblet of chilled, sparkling yellow wine.

"Ah, my dear friends, how delightful to see you all here, in splendid health, I trust, and making excellent progress in your Art? Azra, my dear, ravishing as always! My good Phlomel, I declare we have civilized you at last: a clean smock, on my aura!" Pellsipher boomed expansively.

Munching away, Chan covertly eyed the witch girl. She was somewhat more formally dressed for this occasion than on their last meeting, although her raiment would still not exactly have pleased a person of puritanical repressions, as it left her deliciously rounded and coral-peaked right breast bare. The rest of her was gowned in platinum lamé: a gorget of iridium was clasped about her throat, set, he observed, with uncut but polished emeralds and moony pearls from the isle of Zatoum, which set off, respectively, her sea-green hair and lovely quicksilver eyes.

Still chatting with Phlomel the wild-eyed old alchemist, who did indeed look somewhat less disreputable this evening than on previous occasions, the hearty and jovial Pellsipher was interrupted by Spay, the tall and bony haruspex, who dourly observed that, clean smock or no, Phlomel's dingy and unclean beard still was redolent of sulphur and chemical messes. Pellsipher nodded, beamed, and overrode this comment by inquiring after the alchemist's progress. In his croaking voice, rusty from disuse, Phlomel reported happily that he had achieved the Green Lion transformation and was well on the way to synthesizing the Azoth, as the ultimate goal of all the sages of his profession was called. Spay grumpily commented that by the time the disheveled old pouffleur achieved his Azoth young Atlantis should have joined elder Mu beneath the waves, but no one was listening as Pellsipher was by then loudly interrogating his colleague, the eminent magician Zoramas on the progress of his breeding vats—Zoramas being currently involved in a century-long experiment in the creation of artificial homunculi.

The suave, courtly magician, a tall and distinguished gentleman in a narrow robe of lavender satin embellished with minute golden amulets sprinkled through the folds, silver slippers and a heavy pectoral of massy gold which was, Chan knew, a genuine magical relic of antique Hyperborean work, quietly rejoined that his latest mutations were only partially satisfactory. He was then attempting to breed a flower-headed human, but the hybrid proved cretinous and had to be dissolved in the acid tanks.

"Regrettable, most regrettable," tut-tutted Pellsipher. "Your vat creatures will yet earn you the well-deserved applause of your fellow magicians; persevere, my dear chap, persevere!"

"Such is my intention, Magister," Zoramus assured him, smoothing his neat silver beard with a carefully manicured left hand. "The error doubtless lies in the blending of nutrients, for I embued the creature with an excellent brain and his idiocy must be traceable to the causation of a faulty blend of protein froth. I know the brain was of the finest for I procured it myself from a strapping young male slave from the island of Thang, and before attempting the surgical transference I myself tended to the slave's tutoring."

"Splendid, my dear fellow! Persevere; success will yet crown your endeavors, I am certain of it!" beamed the Archimage.

As the magician stepped to the buffet to select refreshment, their genial host turned to query the languid and dreamy-eyed astrologer who stood at his elbow.

"Master Quinibus, I will have your opinion on a most interesting artifact I recently procured on the isle of Ompharos; it was uncovered in the Valley of Silver Tombs by a ghoul of my acquaintance; a fellow of disgusting habits, of course, but no mean antiquarian, I assure you!" Drawing the languid astrologer aside, he indicated a ceramic cylinder of brick-red, incised with time-worn cuneiform, which stood on a jasper pedestal.

His plate empty, Chan left it on the table and followed Themnon and Velb and Zoramus who were drifting into an antechamber where low curule chairs of mastodon ivory were drawn in a half-circle about a modest podium. Once these mandatory social amenities were concluded, the business session would commence and he could present his information to general discussion.

4.

AS Chan expected, his presentation of the matter to the assembled wizards threw the throng into a fury of consternation and repeated remonstrances by their magister failed to restore the enclave to quietude.

When at last order was established, Pellsipher asked for suggestions from the floor.

"As you all know," he said in a taut state of quivering agitation, "this matter lies close to my heart, and I cannot but hold it a problem of the gravest import. We all owe a debt of gratitude to our young karcist for pursuing the event and thus bringing it to our attention. I will now hear queries or notions from the floor. Ah, my dear Velb, your hand is raised: may we have silence for our esteemed theurgical colleague.

Velb the Irithribian, a dwarvish little theurgist noted for his waspish temper, spoke up first.

"Sorcery is a discipline alien to my own studies," he observed. "What is this Compendium and who is this Paroul?" In his pontifical, expansive manner, the Archimage explained that the sorcerer Paroul had been an ornament to the reign of Gledrion, Grand Prince of Ib, an island to the east, in a remote epoch. "The practice of sorcery," he went on, "employs spoken spells, mantra, and cantrips. A master sorcerer, such as the distinguished Paroul, bends his efforts to composing new, more complex and powerful cantrips. Of such is the famous Compendium composed; possession of the volume gives one access to the most advanced mantra ever created."

Velb the Irithribian tugged at his perfumed indigo beard. "Very well! But what is all this about the star Srendix, a luminary, I believe, found in the constellation of the Gargoyle? How did this book find its way thither?"

"Since a sorcerer's power lies in written spells, anyone who captures such a volume from its rightful owner gains possession of his full art," Pellsipher explained. "Unlike, for example, a witch—such as our charming Mistress Azra, here—whose supernatural powers derive from a learned knowledge of herbal lore and natural philosophy; or for that matter, a theurgist such as you yourself, who commands the diabolic and celestial intelligences through usage of the Names of Power, which reside in your memory and not on the parchment page."

"Yes, yes," Velb snapped pettishly. "But what of Srendix?"

"To insure his privacy and safety from envious and malign fellow practitioners of the Art Sorcerous, the distinguished Paroul caused a winged elemental to transport himself and the contents of his librarium to this distant orb whereon certain efreets bound to his service constructed a palatial abode to his own design. Millennia passed, and eventually Paroul succumbed to his innate mortality—which can be postponed but for an era or two, as every wizard knows, but which cannot be put off forever."

"Whereafter this Nelibar Zux dispatched his sylph to this ultratelluric abode and thus gained possession of the precious Compendium, I see, I see." Having the matter thus detailed to his satisfaction, the theurgist Velb lapsed into thoughtful silence.

Some further discussion eventuated; at length the obvious course was agreed upon: the Ong enclave would send a delegation to the subterranean palace of the augmented Zux and reiterate their offer of membership. As night was wearing on and argumentation over the precise composition of the delegation might well consume the remainder of the nighted hours, Pellsipher took the matter into his own hands with a commendable display of managerial decision.

"Naturally, I, as magister of the enclave shall head the delegation and tender our invitation in person as a mark of respect. As to the further members of the party, I select our young karcist, Chan, who, as the individual most responsible for bringing these events to our attention, has a vested personal interest in their successful conclusion. Yet a third representative is needed; I suggest our esteemed colleague Zoramus."

"Alas, my latest crop of vat creatures are approaching their maturity and I cannot, at present, spare the time," responded that individual.

"Very well; Master Quinibus, then."

The astromancer declined as well, pleading a rare conjugation of the planets demanded his full attentions. Pellsipher became disconcerted. The remainder of the enclave were disappointing choices: Phlomel made a poor appearance; Spay the haruspex was distinguished enough in his person, but his Art, like that of Kedj, was hardly high enough in the hierarchy of the Secret Sciences to form a good impression on the mind of Nelibar Zux. He was debating between the remainder when the witch girl stood, her lithe figure sheathed in sparkling lamé, her sea-green hair pouring down her slender tawny shoulders.

"If the magister will permit, my work does not demand my presence for some days and I will be happy to join the expedition," she said in her warm, throaty voice.

And thus it was decided. They would depart at dawn.

5.

CHAN rose before dawn, nibbled absently at a hearty meal laid out for him by captive spirits, while selecting his wardrobe and magical appurtenances for the voyage to Zatoum, where dwelt the sorcerer. He chose high scarlet boots, a brief kilt of rust and umber wool, patterned after his tribal tartan, and a loose white silk blouse to be worn under a tough jerkin of canary leather. Around his shoulders he slung his famous Live Blade in its dragonhide scabbard and baldric; to his shoulder tabs he affixed a cunningly designed Weather Cloak with cairngorm brooches; and he took up his Waystaff, although it did not seem likely he would need it. Still: you never know.

Thus accoutered, he summoned his attendant spirits, demons, afreets, and intelligences, sternly bade them keep to the premises, tend to his various long-term magical experiments, ward against intruders, rogues, thieves, and interlopers. He then sealed the windows and portals with potent Wards which could be released only by the proximity of his own aura, and strode up the mountain to Pellsipher's villa.

In a columned arcade of the eastern wing he found the jubilant Archimage and the witch girl preparing Pellsipher's rare aerial gondola for the sky voyage. The Archimage affected an elaborate undertoga of mauve gauze, pleated and gathered in many folds, over which he wore an expensive Armor Cloak that was a product of Troglodytic enchanters. A quiver strapped to the magister's back contained slim homotropic javelins of frail glass suffused with the venom of the horned Cerastes serpent, a loathly ophidian found in the Gorgon Isles. The old magister bore with him his mighty Blasting Rod which hummed and thrummed with power. His far-seeing helm of magical crystalloid he wore upon his brows: it gave him an unwontedly martial and even heroic appearance.

The witch girl was clad in an abbreviated tunic of tough woven silver fibers, magically rendered supple; high-laced sandals and sparkling greaves of perdurable orichalc guarded her lovely shins; her breasts were protected in cups of silver filigree; and a small oval buckler composed of seven thicknesses of brontosaurus hide, tanned in the bile of basilisks and riveted together with diamond screws, was strapped to her forearm. She wore a coronet of silver set with fire opals and her seaweed-green hair flowed unbound over her shoulders. Chan found her ravishing, her usual nymphine beauty enhanced by the Amazonian war-dress. She bore no visible weapons, but pouches and flasks of potent liqueurs and powders hung from her metallic girdle.

As he approached through the slim alabaster columns of the arcade, Chan observed the famous gondola which lay on the tesselated pave of alternate squares of iridescent black jade and lapis lazuli. The slim-hulled boat was constructed of light, polished wood: perhaps twenty feet from stem to stern, it was equipped with three comfortable chairs bound firmly to the inner structure with leathern thongs. A silken canopy, raised on twisting, gilded poles, shielded the occupants from the sun and the elements. Gondola-like, poop and prow rose in graceful spiraling foliations. Chan had heard much of the famous vessel but had never chanced to see it before, and much less to venture upon the unstable winds therein.

"Ah, my boy, a perfectly timed arrival," the genial Archimage beamed at his approach. "My aerial contrivance is prepared and ready; naught restrains us from an immediate departure. After you, my dear!"

Helping the witch girl clamber aboard, Doctor Pellsipher guided her to the rearmost of the three chairs, indicated that Chan should make himself comfortable in the midmost, while clambering with agility surprising for one of his not-inconsiderable millennia into the foremost.

Ingenious belts strapped them securely in place, so that a chance wind might not dislodge them from their seats. When his colleagues were securely harnessed, the magister activated the magical adjuncts of the vessel. These consisted of a bulbous flask of thick crystal wherein a mixture of pulverized cinnabar, powdered emeralds, crushed orichalcum nuggets, and desiccated moontree seeds seethed in a slime of hissing acids. Pellsipher had timed the transformation to a nicety: as the last belt was buckled, a sudden flash of nine-colored radiance illuminated the glassy globe. Chan perceived a rolling vapor exuded by the potent mixture. The hue of mingled azure and chartreuse was the tincture of the uncanny mist, which thickened visibly, filling the sphere until it became opaque.

Upon the same instant, the aerial gondola became buoyant. It trembled, shivered, wobbled—and floated up from the tesselated pave. Pellsipher uttered a Word; the prow veered to portside and the contrivance glided between two pillars and drifted out over the gardens. Now a strong up-draft caught and cupped the knife-slim hull. The vessel inclined steeply and shot skywards with alacrity. Achieving a height of five thousand feet, Pellsipher halted the upward motion with a second Word; next he directed the floating skyboat due west with a third powerful vocable. And the voyage was begun!

Mount Ong is situated towards the thickly-jungled interior of Thosk, which is the larger of the two westernmost of the isles of Antillia. Thosk, indeed, is the second largest of the isles and its extent is considerable. Zatoum, their goal, is far smaller, and is itself the very westernmost of the archipelago.

Soon the mountain of the twelve wizards dwindled behind them. They passed over the Ymbrian Hills. They traversed the Green Plains of Nool, observing with delighted amusement a grazing herd of burly aurochs reduced to the stature of Minnikins from the perspective of their height. They flew across the Rivers of Ska and Osk. They approached the outer suburbs of Palmyrium, the capital of the isle and the residence of the current Emperor, Mnumivor, twenty-third regnant monarch of that name.

Azra's quicksilver eyes sparkled with interest as she gazed down on this splendid metropolis. She had yet to visit it; this was, in fact, the first time she had even seen it: and to observe it from this unique aerial vantage-point lent an extra fillip of excitement to the experience.

In truth, it was a most fair city, splendid with domes of green copper, superb with thronged minarets of alabaster, pink coral, and yellow sandstone. Broad boulevards and awning-shaded arcades stretched beneath them. Quaint houses roofed with indigo tile cupped secluded gardens where palmy cycads were mirrored in still ponds. Bazaars seethed with market-day throngs, crowded booths, strolling jugglers.

The imperial city passed slowly beneath them. Now the blue harbour lay below. High-prowed galleys from young Atlantis swayed at anchor along stone quays. As well, stately triremes with sails of purple and orange lay at anchor, come from the last few surviving isles of floundering Mu. Fat-bellied merchant ships from remote Antichthon, as the mysterious South Continent was named, lay berthed beside rakish corsair galleys with slim black hulls and ominous scarlet sails.

Now they flew beyond the harbour and out over the Deep Green Sea. Thosk receded behind them; Zatoum, the last isle of Antillia, lay dead ahead.

6.

SUDDENLY a hoarse, raucous cry broke the whispering silence of their windy height. Chan jerked about from his dreamy contemplation of dwindling Thosk to observe a horrendous peril flapping swiftly towards them.

It was a monstrous flying reptile with clawed, batlike wings, fanged jaws agape, red eyes burning like coals. Even an aerial voyage, the karcist discovered, is not without its hazards.

The predator of the upper air, a gigantical pteranodon, swept down upon them with such velocity that it had struck their craft before any of them could utter a protective Name or direct a single blast of deathly force. In an instant its terrible bird-claws squeaked and crunched and clung to the edge of the hull. They stared into blind, mad eyes of depthless rapacity. Its stinking breath blew over them like the reek of an open grave. Even Pellsipher sat frozen, immobile, voiceless.

But Chan's Live Blade was indoctrinated for such a moment and it flashed from its scabbard and slapped its hilt into his lax palm. Almost before his fingers could curl about the pommel the curved blade of the ensorcelled scimitar had hissed in a sparkling stroke, slashing deep in the lean, scaly throat of the pteranodon. Vile, oily reptilian gore leaked from the great wound, gliding down the length of the extended neck in nauseous rivulets.

The Live Blade swung back for another stroke, dragging Chan's arm with it unresistingly. The round sentient yellow crystal set in the pommel of the scimitar glittered alertly like a living eye.

But the aerial reptile had suffered a terrible wound and had momently lost its appetite. Voicing an ear-splitting screech it abandoned its prey and swerved fluttering away, the skyboat wobbling at an unstable pitch as it loosed its clutches on the gunwals.

So swiftly had the attack occurred and so swiftly had Chan's sword beaten off the attacker that the occupants of the gondola still sat frozen in shock. But Chan fancied he caught a certain unwonted warmth in the gaze Azra turned upon him: a certain admiration shone in her sparkling quicksilver eyes.

Had there been sufficient leisure to indulge in so luxurious an emotion as self-congratulation, Chan doubtless would have basked in a feeling of heroic manliness. But, alas, new perils were upon the travelers in the next instant.

The Archimage paled, gave voice to an inarticulate cry of alarm, and called their attention to the globe which contained the levitational vapor. In its precipitous retreat from the skyboat, the pteranodon must have struck either its gaunt claws or the hard bony fore-edge of a wing against the sphere, for it had cracked badly and the magical vapor of buoyancy was escaping with rapidity.

Consternation seized the voyagers. As yet they had not achieved even the beaches of Zatoum. Still the briny waves of the Deep Green Sea dashed below the keel of their aerial craft. True, the small jungle isle was visible on the expanse of ocean ahead . . . but already the ensorcelled gondola was losing altitude, sinking with alarming velocity towards the foam-crested waves.

Pellsipher pressed the talismanic alexandrite he wore on his left thumb to the broken sphere and activated a potent Sealing Spell, thus halting the escape of any further vapors. The black zigzag cracks melted from view as the glassy substance healed its fractures. A portion of the buoyant vapor still remained within the crystal orb, but not, however, enough to markedly alleviate their misfortunate decline towards the watery abyss.

But wizards are seldom at a complete loss to arrest an unhappy turn of events.

Doctor Pellsipher activated his Flying Ring, a fiery carnelian set in a hoop of black silver on his left index finger.

Azra plucked from her knap a packet of iridescent powder and sprinkled it about the gondola: this, we may assume, engendered weightlessness and was used by sorceresses of her rank to fly to the sabbat.

As for Chan the karcist, he uttered a summoning Word which commanded a minor sylph, and bade the airy spirit to sustain the sinking gondola with all its strength.

Between the three varieties of magic and what little remained of the buoyant vapor in the flask, the gondola managed to reach the shores of Zatoum safely, permitting the exhausted voyagers to disembark on dry land. But having done so, the craft, its sustaining powers vitiated, lay lifeless on the coral sand and would fly no more.

Drained by the tension, anxiety, and precipitous employment of their wizardly powers, the three adventurers sprawled gasping on the shores of the jungle island. A league of dense vegetation, crawling with venomous reptiles and a-prowl with hungry predators, lay between them and the subterranean palace of Nelibar Zux. Formerly they had intended to loll idly at their ease in the flying gondola while it traversed these steaming fens and thick jungles; now they must perform the arduous task afoot.

These were the thoughts which raced through their minds as they sprawled on the powdery sands. Nor were they pleasant thoughts to consider.

At length Pellsipher, recovering from the repeated shocks of the horrendous experience, rose and examined his precious craft anxiously.

"I do hope, Magister," said Chan, "that the injuries to your boat are not permanent, else we shall be marooned here without hope of returning to Thosk."

Pellsipher reluctantly shook his head. Sighing, he said: "The craft itself is not injured in the slightest, but without recourse to the lifting powers of the vapor it is as useless to us as if 'twere shivered to splinters."

"Are the vapors dispersed beyond hope?" the witch girl queried. The magister shrugged gloomily. "The admixture of ingredients whose interaction produces the buoyant vapor yet remain within the sphere. In time, I trust the chemical action will generate sufficient of the gas to render my gondola skyworthy again. However, I estimate that it will be no less than twenty hours before we can expect to be airborne."

"Twenty hours!" Chan cried. "And Sarthath Oob departed in his flying chariot yesterday morn! Surely he has arrived long since and is even now seeking to enlist the sorcerer in his abominable coven. All is lost, then."

Pellsipher had, by now, regained much of his former ebullience. "Not so," he countered. "If we cannot fly, we can at least walk. This isle is minuscule compared to Thosk, and surely 'twill take but a few hours to gain the portals of the underground abode of Zux."

Chan glanced dubiously at the jungle which hemmed in the small beach like a solid wall of greenery, but said nothing.

"Come," puffed Pellsipher with determined cheerfulness. "There is no time like the present; well begun is half-done; and the journey of a thousand leagues is conquered in the first step. These and other homely apothegms suggest we had best be up and walking!"

They advanced to the borders of the jungle. Chan drew his scimitar and began to cut a passage through the tangled growth.

7.

AFTER an hour or two, the young karcist was content to pass the sword into Pellsipher's hands and lag behind.

"My Live Blade is tireless," he admitted, "but *I* am not!"

Pellsipher chopped vigorously at the vines and branches which intertwined to obstruct their path. "Tut, my dear boy! No apologies are necessary. This scimitar of yours is marvelously keen, I must say," he paused, admiring the glittering edge. "After being put to this yeoman-labor, 'tis still as sharp as a fine razor." Chan explained that it had been forged, in Tartarean fires, from the burnt-out core of a fallen star, and tempered seven times by plunging the smoking steel into a crucible of seething venom. 'Twas the work, he noted, of cunning Troglodytes.

The dense undergrowth gradually diminished as they penetrated deeper into the jungled interior of the isle. Now the lofty boles of tall Jurassic conifers soared to either side like the columns of some awesome cathedral. In time, Chan resumed the lead; as he hacked a clear path through a bush of bristling spiny leaves, some intuition bade him hesitate.

He uttered an exclamation of surprise and halted, seizing the magister, who was blundering along at his heels, and restraining his progress forcibly.

"What in the name of thirty devils is it, my boy?" the Archimage demanded testily as Chan jostled him aside.

"Look!" Chan cried, pointing downward at the base of the spiny-leaved bush. His companions halted, and Azra sank to her knees with a gasp of marvel and amazement.

A village of Minikins lay at their feet. A cluster of tiny huts, cleverly woven of dried grasses and roofed with thick rubbery leaves. The village warriors had noted the approach of the full-sized humans and had given the alarm. As the travelers bent in fascination over the scene, diminutive mothers, scarce a finger-length in height, scurried for shelters dug under the roots of the bush, bearing to safety babes no bigger than small fat grubs, while the males, armed with slender sharp black thorns, formed a protective ring about the outskirts of the tiny town. They boldly brandished their minuscule weapons, shrilling faint war-cries.

"A rarity! A genuine curiosity!" Pellsipher exclaimed. "Seldom are Minikins observed in their natural habitat these days; pray note, my friends, the cunning of the tiny creatures, whom the chance step of a careless beast could crush to a damp smear: to protect themselves from this ever-present peril they construct their miniature metropolis under this spiny and unpleasant bush whose jag-edged leafage would doubtless be avoided by most tender-skinned animals. Note further the admirable use the small beings have made of the castaway artifacts of nature!" He drew their attention to the war-helms of the Minikin civic guard, which were hard hollow acorns; to their shields, the horny carapace of dead beetles; to their swords, tubular thorns, charged with a poisonous or stinging nettle-venom which oozed in oily droplets from the keen points thereof; and to their armor, consisting of chest-coverings, gauntlets, greaves and loin-guards cut from the dead, discarded skins of serpents.

Chan marveled that a folk so small could be so brave; he reflected that boldness is an attitude of mind, not relative to matters of mere size.

In a low, clear whisper—softened so as not to burst minute eardrums—he said: "Do not fear us, little men; we will not harm you. Observe that I halted my companion lest he unwittingly trample you underfoot."

The leader of the Minikin war band, a handsomely formed young princeling, brandished his thorn and bowed. "Our thanks for your kindness, sir traveler!" he shrilled in a piping voice. "Seldom do we receive aught but brutal and careless treatment from Big Folk, hence forgive our natural alarm and threatening motions, if you please!"

Chan repressed a smile at the thought of being "threatened" by warriors no taller than his forefinger was long, but replied in courteous words to this polite speech. Their alarm ended, the lady Minikins were timidly emerging from their protective burrows under the roots; they clustered in whispering groups, shyly holding up their babes to Azra's admiration, and piping faint comments to each other on her mode of dress, as women will whatever their size. They also eyed the broad shoulders and muscular thighs of the handsome young karcist who stood by her protectively, and giggled to one another.

As for the Minikin juveniles, who were no larger than plump aphids, they rapidly lost their shyness of the Big Folk and scampered and played between the sequoia-vast legs of the visitors. Chan dared not shift his feet lest he inadvertently harm one of the tiny creatures.

The Minikin princeling, whose name was Zixt, engaged Dr. Pellsipher in converse. In a shrill piping voice, whose tones were made more audible as he employed a hollow snail-shell for his speaking-trumpet, he inquired as to their origins, explaining that few Big Folk dwelt on the isle and the presence of a stranger was a rare event. Listening to the exchange, Chan reflected with amusement that to such as the Minikins, the isle of Zatoum was doubtless on the scale of a fair-sized continent. Prince Zixt was also intrigued at their mode of transport hither, when he learned they were visitors from the next isle, come to tender their respects to Zatoum's resident sorcerer. To such as the Minikins, of course, the modest interval of sea between the two islands was a gulf of impassable and oceanic breadth.

These and other queries Pellsipher answered good-humoredly. The conversation terminated in a gracious exchange of compliments and well-wishes, and Pellsipher expressed their desire to continue their journey before nightfall and requested that the Minikin juveniles be withdrawn from their proximity to his boots for their own safety, which plea was granted with all alacrity. The travelers then resumed their expedition without further ado; but the encounter was a rare marvel and one they would long remember.

8.

DURING the several hours consequent to this adventure, the three
envoys traversed the jungles of Zatoum without further incident.
They emerged therefrom, towards sunset, in the vicinity of the residence of the sorcerer, and regarded with some dismay the havoc
their journey had wreaked upon their person: exquisite raiment was
bedraggled, torn by thorny vines, soiled with leaf-mulch, stained
with perspiration exuded from their fatiguing exertions. They
would present a sorry sight in the discriminating eyes of Nelibar
Zux. But at least they had achieved their goal unscathed by the innumerous predators whose hunting cries made the jungle gloom
hideous.

The entrance to the subterranean palace of the celebrated Zux
was the mouth of a cavern which gaped in the flank of a sheer cliff
of glittering quartz. And "mouth" proved a term singularly apt, for
the black gaping portal was hung with dangling stalactites which
almost met the upthrust of squat, tusklike stalagmites, and the
over-all resemblance to the fanged maw of a yawning monster was
shudderingly obvious.

This portal fronted upon a grassy glade, and the plenipotentiaries
from Mount Ong were relieved to observe no visible signs of their
adversary, the nefarious Oob, thereabouts. Was it possible that his
flying chariot had not yet arrived? Had he perchance encountered
ill-luck in his voyage, comparable to their own? Or had he come
and gone, and was his purpose already achieved? Had Nelibar Zux
been enlisted in the rival enclave with all due solemnities, hours
since, while they were busily cutting their path through the
umbrageous foliage?

Unable to resolve these doubts, the travelers straightened and
made as neat as possible their disarranged garments and
approached the black mouth of the cavern, whereupon they lingered for a time, uncertain of the appropriate means whereby to
call their presence to the attention of the resident sorcerer. At
length they entered the gloomy portal, finding themselves at one
end of an unilluminated tunnel hewn—whether by the patient
workings of nature or the deliberate act of art, they could not say—
from the solid mineral of the cliff.

The resourceful Pellsipher evoked the powers latent in one of his several talismanic rings, molding a sphere of pallid and insubstantial radiance out of thin air. This luminous orb floated before them as they cautiously traversed the length of the cavern; it shed a vague but sufficient light whereby they could proceed without fear of treading upon an unseen viper in the dark.

At the nether end of the cavern they observed a portal of red marble, unwholesomely veined with blue and wetly lustrous: with a fastidious *moue* of repugnance, the girl Azra noted the resemblance of this curious mineral to raw human flesh.

Passing therethrough, the envoys discovered a sequence of untenanted apartments decorated with voluptuous luxury, but lapsed most oddly into a neglect which bordered on decay. Floor, walls, and groined and vaulted rooves were faced with marbles similar to those of the portal without, marbles repellently suggestive of raw meat and flayed flesh. The nude stonework, however, was relieved with tapestries of superb antique workmanship whose design and weave were subtly disturbing. Each arras bore curious curvilinear motifs, and it was difficult to perceive the meaning thereof, whether it was meant to suggest entangled human intestines, a nest of squirming serpents, or a congeries of loathsome worms.

The floors of the sumptuous suites wherethrough they ventured were cluttered with a litter of priceless treasure and grisly human remnants. Platinum bowls overflowed with baroque pearls and lucent amethysts; sacks burst with coins of silver, gold, and precious orichalc; chests of sandalwood gaped brokenly, leaking moony opals and winy sapphires. Figurines of jade and malachite lay tossed about helter-skelter amidst tangled carpets of woven and lustrous silks. It would seem they had stumbled upon the treasury of an emperor, or the trove of corsairs who had amassed the plunder of a dozen cities.

But strewn amidst this glittering wealth were white bones and the withered segments of mummies: a dried and severed hand lay half-submerged in uncut zircons looted from the isles that border Atlantis; human knuckle-bones were intermingled in a heap of silver coins cut with cartouches of extinct Lemurian dynasties; a gaunt skull grinned toothily atop a pile of alabaster statuettes of rare Hyperborean craft.

These and other gruesome mementos of mortality, dispersed as they were amidst artifacts of noble metals and precious jewelry, seemed present for no other purpose than to point a moral. Perhaps,

Chan reflected, they were strewn about in such proximity to the
treasures to register a solemn note: to remind the beholder that
wealth is but rubbish, and Death the inexorable terminus of life. If
so, these mementos succeeded, for they cast a ghoulish pall over the
splendid plunder that choked the marble paves.

The apartments wherethrough they wandered in bewilderment
were alit with ten thousand waxen candles, and as no further
increment of luminance was required to augment their vision, Pellsipher dispersed his Witchlight. The forest of tapers rose to every
hand in profusion, weeping thick tears of glutinous wax on gemmed
icons, eidola exquisitely carven from mammoth-ivory, and superb
textiles. But the sheer prodigality of such illumination puzzled the
young karcist: why lighten the gloom of empty and untenanted
chambers with such a largesse of fine tapers? 'Twas but another of
the myriad mysteries of this subterranean realm.

They strolled on through vestibules choked with the dowry of
empresses, through antechambers heaped with wealth sufficient to
ransom a score of satraps, but nowhere in all this echoing and
gruesomely littered redundancy of wealth did they espy a living
thing. But ever and anon, from the corner of their eyes, a flicker of
movement froze them with alarm: but, when they turned, ever and
again it was to observe nothing corporeal. It was a subtle business,
the furtive twitching-aside of the corner of an arras, a stealthy
slither of motion half-glimpsed in a far, dim corner, a fleeting flicker
of something caught in a momentary reflection. But it unnerved
them all; Pellsipher, pale and sweating, wiped his heavy moon-face
on a soiled and thorn-rent sleeve, eyes showing their whites as he
cast a fearful glance at a distant ghost of movement; Azra, clutching at Chan's arm and stifling a half-voiced cry of alarm, at a
mocking swarthy face glimpsed in a flashing silver mirror. But if
they were observed, it was by furtive, slinking things that dared not
challenge them.

Down a vast, uncoiling stairway of porphry they went, whose
ivory balustrade was the single curving horn of some unthinkable
abnormality whose true size they shuddered from guessing; and the
lower levels they found identical to those above: everywhere a
careless profusion of incredible wealth, bestrewn with bony or
mummified reliques of mortality as if in grimly philosophical em-
phasis on the evanescence of human affairs; ever the stealthy and
secretive flicker of movement on the very border of vision, yet never

a firm confrontation with whatever being or essence made of this dreadful treasurehouse its home.

Suddenly, amidst the vastness of a hall of shadowy immensity whose walls were hung with peculiar tapestries of interwoven sword blades and whose portals were hideously veiled by glistening wet human eyeballs threaded like ghastly beads on cords of scarlet silk, they espied a ponderous volume bound in dinosaur-skin. The tome stood atop a pedestal of lead, sealed beneath a dome of perdurable crystal. It was curious that, of all the innumerous compendia of magical and occult science doubtless included in the librarium of Nelibar Zux, one book alone should deserve such protection. They advanced across the glossy floor of mirrorlike blocks of black emerald to peruse this rarity.

As the three travelers approached, there impinged upon their aurae the vibrations of immense magical force. It was Doctor Pellsipher who first guessed the nature of the reverently-enshrined book. He paled and his eyes gleamed with half-fearful triumph.

"Ah, my dear colleagues," he whispered hoarsely, "now I will hazard that this volume is none other than the prestigious and long-sought Compendium of the august Paroul!"

As they came up before the pedestal, Chan perceived this to have been a fortuitous guess. For even his unskillful eyes could read the superscription of glyphs painted upon diplodocus leather, whereof was fashioned the covers of the book, although he was but poorly schooled in the antique charactry current in the remote epoch of Gledrion of Ib.

"You are right!" he exclaimed; "it is the Compendium of Paroul!" His cry rang out in a thousand booming echoes which were followed upon the instant by a terrific detonation of sound, like the knell of Doom itself. For in that fateful instant, as they stood awe-struck before the powerful and supra-significant compendium, the unseen Watcher, who had dogged their steps all this while, struck to immobilize them. With a terrific clangour, as of hollowly metallic moons colliding, impenetrable blocks of adamant fell to seal every egress, save for a slitted window too narrow for human passage, and barred, in any event, with a razory grille. The three wizards hurled against these barriers every thaumaturgy in their repertoire, but, alas, in vain. The potent sorceries of Nelibar Zux were proof against the most persuasive cantrip, spell, potion or invocation they possessed.

They were trapped and helpless, captives in the subterranean lair of Nelibar Zux!

9.

"MY dear young friend," quavered the disheartened Pellsipher, "have you not some powerful diabolus, vowed to your service, who can shift the weight of these adamantine blocks?"

"I fear not, sir," sighed Chan. "Various of the several afreets and elementals sworn to obey my will have strength sufficient to dismember mountains at my word: but adamant, you know, is proof to the lesser sciences. Azra, perchance you came prepared with some terrific acid or all-dissolving alkahest whereby we might yet free ourselves?"

The witch-girl shook her head sadly, tousling her sea-green tresses. "I came prepared for no such exigency as imprisonment," she confessed.

"And my Blasting Rod is charged with energies sufficient to discarnate half an army," groaned Pellsipher, "but the destructive forces would merely rebound from sheer adamant, and, in this confined space, sunder us all to our primal constituents! I fear we are helpless to help ourselves, and must, therefore, wait upon the innate kindness and hospitality of our as-yet-unseen gaoler, who shall doubtless shower us with apologies and gifts, once he discovers us to be accredited envoys of the Mount Ong enclave, and not mere thieves, assassins, or trespassers. . . ."

Through the window-slit that alone gave forth on the outer air they perceived darkness had long-since fallen and a wan and gibbous moon, such as fitfully illuminates the last hours of the doomed and glares down on lonely gibbets where hanged men dance in the toil of mocking winds, gleamed like a cold and ironic eye through the slit upon them.

The dinner-hour had fallen, and to the gloom of their hopeless prisonry was added the discomfort of intense hunger; none of them had partaken of nutriment since breakfast many hours ago, and Pellsipher for one, a gourmet of the first order, felt the lack of sustenance most acutely. Thus none was more delighted than he when there melted suddenly from empty air three tables hung with snowy damask and set with platters of smoking fowl in aspic, dewy goblets of excellent vintage in bowls of snow, mounds of ripely lustrous fruit, and heaps of crusted pastry sprinkled with the rarest of spices. Their senses were assaulted with the succulent odors and their vision caressed by the glitter of silver and crystal; Pellsipher was in rapture.

"Ah! Superb! Our invisible but gracious host, it seems, hath no intent to add starvation to the other injuries he inflicts upon us. Currant-jelly, upon my soul! Pickled baobab-root! Consomme of oyster in cream-sauce: exquisite!"

They fell upon the repast and rapidly consumed the banquet to its final drop of sauce. Replete, they drowsily sought each his place of rest, and though the floor of this hall was devoid of the splendid trash that littered the other chambers, so fatiguing had been this long day of peril, toil and adventure, that the hard floor was to them as the softest of couches.

When they awoke a sanguinary beam struck through the narrow aperture, from which they deduced dawn; that day passed in the utter boredom of their seclusion, broken only by their meals, which appeared like supernatural apparitions: tables draped in snowy napery, aglitter with gold and crystal, laden with fragrant and aromatic foods, flickered into existence, only to melt back into emptiness the moment their appetites were appeased.

Towards evening of the second day of their internment, a singular event broke the monotony of incarceration. A brass mirror, whose surface had gone clouded all this while, cleared suddenly to reveal the similitude of a lean man, cleanly shaven, sallow of skin, with cold, hooded, indifferent eyes, his high-shouldered form draped in somber robes of funereal purple whereupon were sewn many small fierce garnets which twinkled and glittered among the folds of his gown like the eyes of venomous serpents. This mirror apparition looked them over with opaque, supercilious, and insolent gaze.

"Ah!" boomed Pellsipher heartily, "our esteemed host and worthy colleague, the illustrious Master Zux, I assume?"

"The same," a sepulchral voice murmured. "And no doubt you purport to be a deputation from Mount Ong."

It was not a question; nevertheless, Dr. Pellsipher chose to treat it as such.

"To be sure, we are the plenipotentiaries of that excellent fraternity," he beamed. "I am myself the not-unreknowned Iollubus Pellsipherius Senes, Archimagos Maximus et . . ."

"A dear colleague, but recently departed, assured me a party of thieves was en route to my habitation, drawn hither by a despicable greed to seize possession of the Paroul Compendium," the coldly suave tones of Nelibar Zux serenely droned on over the hearty voice of Pellsipher; "and, wary of such, my familiars have been scrutinizing your actions since your temerity in entering my abode uninvited and unwelcome."

"My dear sir! Upon my word as an Archimagos Maximus et . . . !"

"Hence your significant excitement upon discovery of the Paroullian codex can lead me but to one conclusion: you are no gentleman-envoys of the Ong enclave, but scofflaws, booknappers, vile, and despicable burglars! It is even as my colleague predicted . . ."

Dr. Pellsipher purpled at this suave affront and spluttered apoplectically in search of appropriate words whereby to deal with this astonishing accusation. But Chan interposed a swift query—

"Tell me, Master Zux, this colleague whereof you speak—might his name be Sarthath Oob?"

Puzzlement gleamed briefly in the chilly gaze of the mirrored sorcerer.

"Indeed, such is his cognomen, young knave. But how you could have guessed it escapes my comprehension. . . ."

"It is of no importance, sir," Chan smiled grimly. "May I ask towards what eventual punishment we are confined herein?"

Things were moving a bit too fast even for the wits of Nelibar Zux; it seemed that thieves, caught in the very act, who keenly inquired as to their doom were a new breed in his experience. Somewhat flustered, he said he was not yet decided as to whether they should undergo metamorphosis to the form of spiders and beetles, or exposure to the rays of a petrifying lamp which would transform them to marble images: then again there was much to be said for transporting them to the eleventh planet which engirds Aldebaran and which is best described as a wintry hell swept by congealing ammoniac hurricanes . . . but Chan curtly bade him have the simple courtesy to leave them to their several religious devotions until such time as an apt terminus to their earthly careers had occurred to the sorcerer's sense of justice.

His aplomb considerably shaken by the unorthodox behavior of the young karcist, whom he considered a venturesome burglar, the simulacrum of Nelibar Zux obligingly faded from the brass mirror, leaving the adventurers to their solitary meditations.

10.

TOWARDS early morn Chan awoke from a miserable slumber whose serenity was roiled by troublous dreams of torment. Something was buzzing about his face and he batted irritably at the annoying insect which was, he perceived, a dragonfly of considerable size. Driving away the winged pest, he settled again for such repose as one doomed either to be petrified into marble, metamorphosed into a beetle, or transported to a remote orb of superarctic rigor, might expect.

But a small piping voice sounded shrilly in his ear and brought him upright with astonishment. He stared about wildly until a minute figure stepped into view and stood in a moonbeam that filtered through the narrow razor-barred orifice.

"Prince Zixt!" he exclaimed surprisedly, "whatever has brought you all the way into this dismal charnel-house?"

"A debt of gratitude owed to one whose kindness forebore to carelessly tread upon even the smallest of earth's creatures," shrilly proclaimed the princeling of the Minikins. Lowering his voice so as not to awaken his yet-slumbering comrades, the karcist expressed his pleasure at again meeting the tiny potentate, and Prince Zixt explained that it was the common rumor of the night-flying bats that Nelibar Zux had imprisoned the Big Folk under a misapprehension and intended a grim and deplorable doom for them upon the morrow. The word had passed from creature to creature throughout the breadth of the jungle isle, and upon hearing that his courteous friend was thus endangered, Prince Zixt had roused the warriors of the Minikin colony to his aid: mounted on swift dragonflies, whose aid a treasured store of honey-drops had purchased, the minuscule soldiery had traversed the jungle, gaining entry to their prison by the narrow window which was but a slit in the wall to the Big Folk, but as wide as an open gate to the Minikins.

Chan's heart was warmed at the friendliness and courage of the tiny prince, but he could see no method by which the Minikins could assist in alleviating their dangers or in extricating them from the present peril. After all, if he and his comrades were impotent to raise the immense cubes of adamant which blocked their egress from the hall, the tiny strength of the Minikins was likewise of no avail.

"Not so, friend Chan," the princeling piped. "Small feet can sometimes go where Big Folk cannot tread: *behold!*"

And with a flourish, the princeling removed from beneath his spidersilk cloak a topaz scarab-ring, which to his scale had all the girth of a small hogshead.

"And what is this, pray tell?"

"None other than the talisman which controls the adamantine doors which seal you in this prison," announced Prince Zixt pridefully. "I know it to be such for the sorcerer Nelibar Zux had it tucked beneath his pillow as he retired!"

Chan was incredulous: "Is it possible that you dared observe the sorcerer in his own bed-chamber?"

The princeling crowed with laughter like tiny tinkling bells. "Hidden in a tassel on his bed-curtains! Small size hath certain advantages, you see!"

"And small hearts can possess the bravery of many lions!" Chan swore. Awakening his colleagues, he apprised them of the situation; displaying the talismanic ring, he inquired of Pellsipher if his science was sufficient to employ it towards their release.

"Nothing simpler, lad!" the fat old archimage boomed heartily, his spirits much restored by finding an ally even in the very stronghold of the foe. "But even with the adamantine blocks removed and our mode of exeunt clear, how can we hope to elude the vigilance of the many small furtive familiars of the treacherous Zux? Surely, observing our escape, they will arouse their master from his slumbers, and we shall be in trouble all over again."

Again the tiny princeling shrilled with laughter. "The bellowing of thirty Titans in concert," said he, "could not rouse Nelibar Zux this hour—nay, nor for many an hour hence!" He then related that he observed it to be the nightly habit of the subterraneous sorcerer to prepare himself a decoction before slumber, and that this potion had as its base a hot spiced wine whereto the sorcerer added two drops of the juice of crushed black poppies as an aid to slumber. (This intelligence he had learned from a gossipy bachelor spider who made his residence behind a loose wall-tile, and with whom Prince Zixt had struck up a brief but amiable acquaintance while awaiting completion of the nightly ablutions of Nelibar Zux.)

"I took the simple precaution of quadrupling the dosage while Master Zux was still engaged with his toilette," the princeling chuckled. Doctor Pellsipher exclaimed with a glad cry, and performed a brief gavotte.

"Ten drops of poppy-juice will thrust the wily old rogue into the profoundest of slumbers, wherefrom he will emerge sometime next week with a most prodigious headache," he chortled, "which provides us with sufficient time to *swim* back to the isle of Thosk, if such should prove necessary! My dear Prince Zixt, you are one in a million, and should ever you choose to remove your colony to the flanks of Mount Ong, you may rest assured of our benevolent protection and eternal friendship! And now, dear colleagues, gather up your gear and let us be gone from these loathsome and accursed dungeons upon the moment!"

Addressing himself to the topaz ring, Dr. Pellsipher in his most orotund basso solemnly pronounced the prodigious Name of Oommuorondus Smednivlioth—that genie under whose sovereignty the adamantine metal has been ruled since the Creation—and with an earth-shaking and ponderous rumble of subterranean thunder, such as might be rendered audible by the tread of perambulating sierras, the colossal cubes of indestructible metal evaporated into thin air, leaving their free passage unobstructed.

They wasted little time in gaining the open air, with Chan bringing up the rear; and a shrill chorus of cheers arose from the waiting host of Minnikin warrior bedight in beetle-shell breastplates and acorn-helmets, who brandished the stings of wasps for javelins. To this victorious huzzah, Pellsipher bowed magnificently.

Mounted anew on a fleet of fireflies, the Minnikins guided them through the jungles, and, as dawn brightened overhead, they achieved the place whereat they had earlier moored Dr. Pellsipher's aerial gondola; their good fortune continued unimpaired, for the ensuing interval had been sufficient for the sky vessel to renew its store of buoyant gases; thus, as dawn gilded the waves of the Deep Green Sea, they flew safely home to Thosk none the worse for all their perils.

AT the next meeting of the enclave it was, of course, the sad duty of Dr. Pellsipher to announce the utter and complete failure of his mission. His despondency was considerably mitigated, however, at the surprising news volunteered by Velb the Irithribian. It seemed the astral plane was agog: a recent meeting of the Skarm Desert coven had erupted in violent recriminations; Nelibar Zux had resigned amid a storm of allegations, and Sarthath Oob himself, the coven's erstwhile chief executive, had been driven from his high office when he failed lamentably to carry a vote of confidence.

Crushed, the crestfallen Oob had departed on an extended sabbatical to the last isles of foundering Mu. And the Mount Ong enclave, full coven or no, was now supreme in all the isle of Thosk!

"Whatever could have happened?" Pellsipher marveled at this astonishing report.

"I can independently verify brother Velb's intelligence," solemnly intoned Zoramus of Pankoy. "My own sources on the astral plane suggest that in some amazing lapse or negligence, far from his wonted and scrupulous security, the unfortunate Nelibar Zux somehow—*lost*—the Paroullian codex whose acquisition was his paramount claim to supremacy! This misfortune he blamed, for some reason, on none other than the triply unfortunate Sarthath Oob, whose fall from office followed thereafter most precipitously."

Pellsipher seemed dazed: "But how could old Zux have lost his prime and premier treasure . . . yes, my boy? You have something to add to this discussion?"

Chan had arrayed his person with more than his usual meticulous taste; thus, as he rose slowly to address the enclave he cut a striking figure amongst his fellows (and from the corner of his eye he observed the glimmer of an appreciative flash in the quicksilver eyes of the bewitching Azra).

"Yes, indeed," he said modestly. "I believe I can offer some account of what transpired. My colleagues will recall the clever stratagem of our minuscule but lion-hearted savior, Prince Zixt of the Minnikins. I refer, of course, to his theft of the topaz scarab; in imminent peril of discovery, the Minnikin princeling yet retained sufficient coolness of head and fixity of purpose to purloin the talisman that would afford our release from durance vile. I have learned much from the example of Prince Zixt, whose friendship I yet hope to renew on more favorable and leisurely occasions; but in this particular, I have followed his precept to the letter, and, even in our precipitous haste to be gone from the dungeons of Nelibar Zux, I yet lingered for a moment or two, to smash a certain crystal case with a bit of floor-tile. . . ."

And with a flourish the bold young karcist removed from beneath his cloak a certain cumbersome volume, bound in tanned diplodocus hide.

"*The Compendium of Paroul!*" Doctor Pellsipher gasped, clutching the top of the podium as he staggered back with amazement.

Amid the uproarious acclaim of his wizardly brethren, Chan had eyes only for the warm and open admiration in the languorous eyes of the girl Azra. One did not have to be much of a wizard to read the melting adoration in those eyes, or the invitation in those moist and parted, breathless lips. When next he had occasion to visit that cozy hut in the bamboo grove, he knew to what extent he would be welcome.

And if the expedition to Zatoum had failed to enlist a thirteenth member of the enclave, what did it matter? It had at least won him the heart of the fair Azra, of the lissom form, the green hair, and the eyes of sparkling quicksilver.

V.
Fantasy
as
Epic

C. S. LEWIS

YET another variety of fantasy might be called the prose epic: the story of vast length and global or even cosmic events, narrated on a world stage crowded with an immense range of characters. The epic fantasy in our time has been chiefly the province of British writers, the first of whom was the Belfast-born novelist, poet, theologian, literary critic-historian and Oxford don, C. S. (for Clive Staples) Lewis. Lewis (1898–1963) was fascinated by "the Northern thing" early in life, and counted his discovery of the Norse myths and the music of Wagner's *Ring* cycle as powerful influences on his creative life.

In fictions like his famous *Perelandra* trilogy, which was sort of science fiction illuminated with Christian theology, he first demonstrated his remarkable storytelling powers as well as his rare facility for inserting a more substantial philosophical "weight" to his yarns than is commonly found in that genre. In other fictions like *The Screwtape Letters* and *The Great Divorce*, theological matter became central, almost extinguishing the element of story. But when he turned to his marvelous and very popular Narnia books, story again asserted its rightful dominance, and the element of the theological, by now thoroughly digested, was evident throughout but not obtrusive.

The scene which follows, and which has never before been singled out for excerpting, demonstrates the epic power and grandeur of this particular kind of fantasy, its solemnity and strength. What makes the scene all the more astonishing, is that it appears in the midst of something written for the kiddies.

DEEP MAGIC FROM THE DAWN OF TIME

WHEN Edmund had been made to walk far further than he had ever known that anybody *could* walk, the Witch at last halted in a dark valley all overshadowed with fir trees and yew trees. Edmund simply sank down and lay on his face, doing nothing at all and not even caring what was going to happen next provided they would let him lie still. He was too tired even to notice how hungry and thirsty he was. The Witch and the Dwarf were talking close beside him in low tones.

"No," said the Dwarf, "it is no use now, O Queen. They must have reached the Stone Table by now."

"Perhaps the Wolf will smell us out and bring us news," said the Witch.

"It cannot be good news if he does," said the Dwarf.

"Four thrones in Cair Paravel," said the Witch. "How if only three were filled? That would not fulfill the prophecy."

"What difference would that make now that *he* is here?" said the Dwarf. He did not dare, even now, to mention the name of Aslan to his mistress.

"He may not stay long. And then—we would fall upon the three at Cair."

"Yet it might be better," said the Dwarf, "to keep this one" (here he kicked Edmund) "for bargaining with."

"Yes! And have him rescued," said the Witch scornfully.

"Then," said the Dwarf, "we had better do what we have to do at once."

"I would like to have done it on the Stone Table itself," said the Witch. "That is the proper place. That is where it has always been done before."

"It will be a long time now before the Stone Table can again be put to its proper use," said the Dwarf.

"True," said the Witch, and then, "Well, I will begin."

At that moment with a rush and a snarl a Wolf rushed up to them.

"I have seen them. They are all at the Stone Table, with *him*. They have killed my captain, Fenris Ulf. I was hidden in the thickets and saw it all. One of the Sons of Adam killed him. Fly! Fly!"

"No," said the Witch. "There need be no flying. Go quickly. Summon all our people to meet me here as speedily as they can. Call out the giants and the werewolves and the spirits of those trees who are on our side. Call the Ghouls, and the Boggles, the Ogres, and the Minotaurs. Call the Cruels, the Hags, the Spectres, and the people of the Toadstools. We will fight. What? Have I not still my wand? Will not their ranks turn into stone even as they come on? Be off quickly, I have a little thing to finish here while you are away."

The great brute bowed its head, turned, and galloped away.

"Now!" said she, "we have no table—let me see. We had better put it against the trunk of a tree."

Edmund found himself being roughly forced to his feet. Then the Dwarf set him with his back against a tree and bound him fast. He saw the Witch take off her outer mantle. Her arms were bare underneath it and terribly white. Because they were so very white he could not see much else, it was so dark in this valley under the dark trees.

"Prepare the victim," said the Witch. And the Dwarf undid Edmund's collar and folded back his shirt at the neck. Then he took Edmund's hair and pulled his head back so that he had to raise his chin. After that Edmund heard a strange noise—whizz—whizz—whizz. For a moment he couldn't think what it was. Then he realised. It was the sound of a knife being sharpened!

At that very moment he heard loud shouts from every direction—a drumming of hoofs and a beating of wings—a scream from the

Witch—confusion all round him. And then he found he was being untied. Strong arms were round him and he heard big, kind voices saying things like "Let him lie down—give him some wine—drink this—steady now—you'll be all right in a minute."

Then he heard the voices of people who were talking not to him but to one another. And they were saying things like "Who's got the Witch?—I thought you had her—I didn't see her after I knocked the knife out of her hand—I was after the Dwarf— Do you mean to say she's escaped? —A chap can't mind everything at once— What's that? Oh sorry it's only an old stump!" But just at this point Edmund went off in a dead faint.

Presently the centaurs and unicorns and deer and birds (they were of course the rescue party which Aslan had sent in the last chapter) all set off to go back to the Stone Table, carrying Edmund with them. But if they could have seen what happened in that valley after they had gone, I think they might have been surprised.

It was perfectly still and presently the moon grew bright, if you had been there you would have seen the moonlight shining on an old tree-stump and on a fair sized boulder. But if you had gone on looking you would gradually have begun to think there was something odd about both the stump and the boulder. And next you would have thought that the stump did look really remarkably like a little fat man crouching on the ground. And if you had watched long enough you would have seen the stump walk across to the boulder and the boulder sit up and begin talking to the stump; for in reality the stump and the boulder were simply the Witch and the Dwarf. For it was part of her magic that she could make things look like what they weren't, and she had the presence of mind to do so at the very moment when the knife was knocked out of her hand. She had kept hold of her wand also, so it had been kept safe, too.

When the other children woke up next morning (they had been sleeping on piles of cushions in the pavilion) the first thing they heard—from Mrs. Beaver—was that their brother had been rescued and brought into camp late last night; and was at that moment with Aslan. As soon as they had breakfasted they all went out, and there they saw Aslan and Edmund walking together in the dewy grass, apart from the rest of the court. There is no need to tell you (and no one ever heard) what Aslan was saying, but it was a conversation which Edmund never forgot. As the others drew nearer Aslan turned to meet them, bringing Edmund with him.

"Here is your brother," he said, "and—there is no need to talk to him about what is past."

Edmund shook hands with each of the others and said to each of them in turn, "I'm sorry," and everyone said, "That's all right." And then everyone wanted very hard to say something which would make it quite clear that they were all friends with him again—something ordinary and natural—and of course no one could think of anything in the world to say. But before they had time to feel really awkward one of the leopards approached Aslan and said:

"Sire, there is a messenger from the enemy who craves audience."

"Let him approach," said Aslan.

The leopard went away and soon returned leading the Witch's Dwarf.

"What is your message, Son of Earth?" asked Aslan.

"The Queen of Namia and Empress of the Lone Islands desires a safe conduct to come and speak with you," said the Dwarf, "on a matter which is as much to your advantage as to hers."

"Queen of Namia, indeed!" said Mr. Beaver. "Of all the cheek—"

"Peace, Beaver," said Aslan. "All names will soon be restored to their proper owners. In the meantime we will not dispute about noises. Tell your mistress, Son of Earth, that I grant her safe conduct on condition that she leaves her wand behind her at that great oak."

This was agreed to and two leopards went back with the Dwarf to see that the conditions were properly carried out. "But supposing she turns the two leopards into stone?" whispered Lucy to Peter. I think the same idea had occurred to the leopards themselves; at any rate, as they walked off their fur was all standing up on their backs and their tails were bristling—like a cat's when it sees a strange dog.

"It'll be all right," whispered Peter in reply. "He wouldn't send them if it weren't."

A few minutes later the Witch herself walked out on to the top of the hill and came straight across and stood before Aslan. The three children, who had not seen her before, felt shudders running down their backs at the sight of her face; and there were low growls among all the animals present. Though it was bright sunshine everyone felt suddenly cold. The only two people present who seemed to be quite at their ease were Aslan and the Witch herself. It was the oddest thing to see those two faces—the golden face and the dead-white face—so close together. Not that the Witch looked Aslan exactly in his eyes; Mrs. Beaver particularly noticed this.

"You have a traitor there, Aslan," said the Witch. Of course everyone present knew that she meant Edmund. But Edmund had got past thinking about himself after all he'd been through and after the talk he'd had that morning. He just went on looking at Aslan. It didn't seem to matter what the Witch said.

"Well," said Aslan. "His offence was not against you."

"Have you forgotten the Deep Magic?" asked the Witch.

"Let us say I have forgotten it," answered Aslan gravely. "Tell us of this Deep Magic."

"Tell you?" said the Witch, her voice growing suddenly shriller. "Tell you what is written on that very Table of Stone which stands beside us? Tell you what is written in letters deep as a spear is long on the trunk of the World Ash tree? Tell you what is engraved on the sceptre of the Emperor-Beyond-the-Sea? You at least know the magic which the Emperor put into Narnia at the very beginning. You know that every traitor belongs to me as my lawful prey and that for every treachery I have a right to a kill."

"Oh," said Mr. Beaver. "So *that's* how you came to imagine yourself a Queen—because you were the Emperor's hangman. I see."

"Peace, Beaver," said Aslan, with a very low growl.

"And so," continued the Witch, "that human creature is mine. His life is forfeit to me. His blood is my property."

"Come and take it then," said the Bull with the man's head in a great bellowing voice.

"Fool," said the Witch with a savage smile that was almost a snarl, "do you really think your master can rob me of my rights by mere force? He knows the Deep Magic better than that. He knows that unless I have blood as the Law says all Narnia will be overturned and perish in fire and water."

"It is very true," said Aslan; "I do not deny it."

"Oh, Aslan!" whispered Susan in the Lion's ear, "can't we—I mean, you won't, will you? Can't we do something about the Deep Magic? Isn't there something you can work against it?"

"Work against the Emperor's magic?" said Aslan turning to her with something like a frown on his face. And nobody ever made that suggestion to him again.

Edmund was on the other side of Aslan, looking all the time at Aslan's face. He felt a choking feeling and wondered if he ought to say something; but a moment later he felt that he was not expected to do anything except to wait, and do what he was told.

"Fall back, all of you," said Aslan, "and I will talk to the Witch alone."

They all obeyed. It was a terrible time this—waiting and wondering while the Lion and the Witch talked earnestly together in low voices. Lucy said, "Oh, Edmund!" and began to cry. Peter stood with his back to the others looking out at the distant sea. The Beavers stood holding each other's paws with their heads bowed. The centaurs stamped uneasily with their hoofs. But everyone became perfectly still in the end, so that you noticed even small sounds like a bumble bee flying past, or the birds in the forest down below them, or the wind rustling the leaves. And still the talk between Aslan and the White Witch went on.

At last they heard Aslan's voice. "You can all come back," he said. "I have settled the matter. She has renounced the claim on your brother's blood." And all over the hill there was a noise as if everyone had been holding his breath and had now begun breathing again, and then a murmur of talk. They began to come back to Aslan's throne.

The Witch was just turning away with a look of fierce joy on her face when she stopped and said,

"But how do I know this promise will be kept?"

"Wow!" roared Aslan half rising from his throne; and his great mouth opened wider and wider and the roar grew louder and louder, and the Witch, after staring for a moment with her lips wide apart, picked up her skirts and fairly ran for her life.

As soon as the Witch had gone Aslan said, "We must move from this place at once, it will be wanted for other purposes. We shall encamp tonight at the Fords of Beruna."

Of course everyone was dying to ask him how he had arranged matters with the Witch; but his face was stern and everyone's ears were still ringing with the sound of his roar and so nobody dared.

After a meal, which was taken in the open air on the hill-top (for the sun had got strong by now and dried the grass) they were busy for a while taking the pavilion down and packing things up. Before two o'clock they were on the march and set off in a North-Westerly direction, walking at an easy pace for they had not far to go.

During the first part of the journey Aslan explained to Peter his plan of campaign. "As soon as she has finished her business in these parts," he said, "the Witch and her crew will almost certainly fall back to her house and prepare for a siege. You may or may not be able to cut her off and prevent her from reaching it." He then went on to outline two plans of battle—one for fighting the Witch and her people in the wood and another for assaulting her castle. And all the time he was advising Peter how to conduct the operations, saying things like, "You must put your centaurs in such and such a place" or "You must post scouts to see that she doesn't do so-and-so," till at last Peter said,

"But you will be there yourself, Aslan."

"I can give you no promise of that," answered the Lion. And he continued giving Peter his instructions.

For the last part of the journey it was Susan and Lucy who saw most of him. He did not talk very much and seemed to them to be sad.

It was still afternoon when they came down to a place where the river valley had widened out and the river was broad and shallow. This was the Fords of Beruna and Aslan gave orders to halt on this side of the water. But Peter said,

"Wouldn't it be better to camp on the far side—for fear she should try a night attack or anything?"

Aslan who seemed to have been thinking about something else roused himself with a shake of his magnificent mane and said, "Eh? What's that?" Peter said it all over again.

"No," said Aslan in a dull voice, as if it didn't matter. "No. She will not make an attack to-night." And then he sighed deeply. But presently he added, "All the same it was well thought of. That is how a soldier ought to think. But it doesn't really matter." So they proceeded to pitch their camp.

Aslan's mood affected everyone that evening. Peter was feeling uncomfortable too at the idea of fighting the battle on his own; the news that Aslan might not be there had come as a great shock to him. Supper that evening was a quiet meal. Everyone felt how different it had been last night or even that morning. It was as if the good times, having just begun, were already drawing to their end.

This feeling affected Susan so much that she couldn't get to sleep when she went to bed. And after she had lain counting sheep and turning over and over she heard Lucy give a long sigh and turn over just beside her in the darkness.

"Can't you get to sleep either?" said Susan.

"No," said Lucy. "I thought you were asleep. I say, Susan?"

"What?"

"I've a most horrible feeling—as if something were hanging over us."

"Have you? Because, as a matter of fact, so have I."

"Something about Aslan," said Lucy. "Either some dreadful thing that is going to happen to him, or something dreadful that he's going to do."

"There's been something wrong with him all afternoon," said Susan. "Lucy! What was that he said about not being with us at the battle? You don't think he could be stealing away and leaving us to-night, do you?"

"Where is he now?" said Lucy. "Is he here in the pavilion?"

"I don't think so."

"Susan! Lets go outside and have a look round. We might see him."

"All right. Let's," said Susan, "we might just as well be doing that as lying awake here."

Very quietly the two girls groped their way among the other sleepers and crept out of the tent. The moonlight was bright and everything was quite still except for the noise of the river chattering over the stones. Then Susan suddenly caught Lucy's arm and said, "Look!" On the far side of the camping ground, just where the trees began, they saw the Lion slowly walking away from them into the wood. Without a word they both followed him.

He led them up the steep slope out of the river valley and then slightly to the left—apparently by the very same route which they had used that afternoon in coming from the Hill of the Stone Table. On and on he led them, into dark shadows and out into pale moonlight, getting their feet wet with the heavy dew. He looked somehow different from the Aslan they knew. His tail and his head hung low and he walked slowly as if he were very, very tired. Then, when they were crossing a wide open place where there were no shadows for them to hide in, he stopped and looked round. It was no good trying to run away so they came towards him. When they were closer he said,

"Oh, children, children, why are you following me?"

"We couldn't sleep," said Lucy—and then felt sure that she need say no more and that Aslan knew all they had been thinking.

"Please, may we come with you—wherever you're going?" said Susan.

"Well—" said Aslan and seemed to be thinking. Then he said, "I should be glad of company to-night. Yes, you may come, if you will promise to stop when I tell you, and after that leave me to go on alone."

"Oh, thank you, thank you. And we will," said the two girls.

Forward they went again and one of the girls walked on each side of the Lion. But how slowly he walked! And his great, royal head drooped so that his nose nearly touched the grass. Presently he stumbled and gave a low moan.

"Aslan! Dear Alsan!" said Lucy, "what is wrong? Can't you tell us?"

"Are you ill, dear Aslan?" asked Susan.

"No," said Aslan. "I am sad and lonely. Lay your hands on my mane so that I can feel you are there and let us walk like that."

And so the girls did what they would never have dared to do without his permission but what they had longed to do ever since they first saw him—buried their cold hands in the beautiful sea of fur and stroked it and, so doing, walked with him. And presently they saw that they were going with him up the slope of the hill on which the Stone Table stood. They went up at the side where the trees came furthest up, and when they got to the last tree (it was one that had some bushes about it) Aslan stopped and said,

"Oh, children, children. Here you must stop. And whatever happens, do not let yourselves be seen. Farewell."

And both the girls cried bitterly (though they hardly knew why) and clung to the Lion and kissed his mane and his nose and his paws and his great, sad eyes. Then he turned from them and walked out onto the top of the hill. And Lucy and Susan, crouching in the bushes, looked after him and this is what they saw.

A great crowd of people were standing all round the Stone Table and though the moon was shining many of them carried torches which burned with evil-looking red flames and black smoke. But such people! Ogres with monstrous teeth, and wolves, and bull-headed men; spirits of evil trees and poisonous plants; and other creatures whom I won't describe because if I did the grown-ups would probably not let you read this book—Cruels and Hags and Incubuses, Wraiths, Horrors, Efreets, Sprites, Orknies, Wooses, and Ettins. In fact here were all those who were on the Witch's side and whom the Wolf had summoned at her command. And right in the middle, standing by the Table, was the Witch herself.

A howl and a gibber of dismay went up from the creatures when they first saw the great Lion pacing towards them, and for a moment the Witch herself seemed to be struck with fear. Then she recovered herself and gave a wild, fierce laugh.

"The fool!" she cried. "The fool has come. Bind him fast."

Lucy and Susan held their breaths waiting for Aslan's roar and his spring upon his enemies. But it never came. Four hags, grinning and leering, yet also (at first) hanging back and half afraid of what they had to do, had approached him. "Bind him, I say!" repeated the White Witch. The hags made a dart at him and shrieked with triumph when they found that he made no resistance at all. Then others—evil dwarfs and apes—rushed in to help them and between them they rolled the huge Lion round on his back and tied all his four paws together, shouting and cheering as if they had done something brave, though, had the Lion chosen, one of those paws could have been the death of them all. But he made no noise, even when the enemies, straining and tugging, pulled the cords so tight that they cut into his flesh. They they began to drag him towards the Stone Table.

"Stop!" said the Witch. "Let him first be shaved."

Another roar of mean laughter went up from her followers as an ogre with a pair of shears came forward and squatted down by Aslan's head. Snip-snip-snip went the shears and masses of curling gold began to fall to the ground. Then the ogre stood back and the children, watching from their hiding-place, could see the face of Aslan looking all small and different without its mane. The enemies also saw the difference.

"Why, he's only a great cat after all!" cried one.

"Is *that* what we were afraid of?" said another.

And they surged round Aslan jeering at him, saying things like "Puss, Puss! Poor Pussy," and "How many mice have you caught to-day, Cat?" and "Would you like a saucer of milk, Pussums?"

"Oh how *can* they?" said Lucy, tears streaming down her cheeks. "The brutes, the brutes!" for now that the first shock was over the shorn face of Aslan looked to her braver, and more beautiful, and more patient than ever.

"Muzzle him!" said the Witch. And even now, as they worked about his face putting on the muzzle, one bite from his jaws would have cost two or three of them their hands. But he never moved. And this seemed to enrage all that rabble. Everyone was at him now. Those who had been afraid to come near him even after he was bound began to find their courage, and for a few minutes the two girls could not even see him—so thickly was he surrounded by the whole crowd of creatures kicking him, hitting him, spitting on him, jeering at him.

At last the rabble had had enough of this. They began to drag the bound and muzzled Lion to the Stone Table, some pulling and some pushing. He was so huge that even when they got him there it took all their efforts to hoist him onto the surface of it. Then there was more tying and tightening of cords.

"The cowards! The cowards!" sobbed Susan. "Are they *still* afraid of him, even now?"

When once Aslan had been tied (and tied so that he was really a mass of cords) on the flat stone, a hush fell on the crowd. Four Hags, holding four torches, stood at the corners of the Table. The Witch bared her arms as she had bared them the previous night when it had been Edmund instead of Aslan. Then she began to whet her knife. It looked to the children, when the gleam of the torchlight fell on it, as if the knife were made of stone not of steel and it was of a strange and evil shape.

At last she drew near. She stood by Aslan's head. Her face was working and twitching with passion, but his looked up at the sky, still quiet, neither angry nor afraid, but a little sad. Then, just before she gave the blow, she stooped down and said in a quivering voice,

"And now, who has won? Fool, did you think that by all this you would save the human traitor? Now I will kill you instead of him as our pact was and so the Deep Magic will be appeased. But when you are dead what will prevent me from killing him as well? And who will take him out of my hand *then*? Understand that you have given me Narnia forever, you have lost your own life and you have not saved his. In that knowledge, despair and die."

The children did not see the actual moment of the killing. They couldn't bear to look and had covered their eyes.

J. R. R. TOLKIEN

LEWIS and his colleagues used to gather weekly in Lewis' rooms at Magdalen College to drink beer and smoke and talk and to read to each other from their latest works. One of these—the "Inklings," they called themselves—was J. R. R. (for John Ronald Reuel) Tolkien, who taught Anglo-Saxon at Pembroke. Like Lewis, Tolkien was deeply stirred by the Nordic or Germanic lore and literature; and also like him he was a devout Christian, although less interested in purely theological matters.

Out of his scholarly erudition in the field of linguistics, he amused himself by inventing a new language, Elvish; then by imagining the sort of world in which such a tongue might be spoken; from this, it was an easy step to inventing stories about this new world, which he called Middle-earth. The first of these was a children's fantasy novel, *The Hobbit;* but what followed next was no children's book, but an epic fantasy of enormous length, deep seriousness, and powerful dramatic substance. I refer, of course, to *The Lord of the Rings,* the greatest and most popular fantasy of our time.

There is a scene in the first book of this enormous trilogy which moved and thrilled me when I first read it, and still excites me now with undiminished force. Its solemnity and tragic weight makes a perfect match for the episode from Lewis which you have just read. Here, then, is epic fantasy at its most powerful and emotionally moving, chosen from the more than one hundred thousand pages of a modern epic fit to stand on the same shelf with the *Niebelung-enlied* or *Volsunga Saga.*

THE BRIDGE OF KHAZAD-DÛM

THE Company of the Ring stood silent beside the tomb of Balin. Frodo thought of Bilbo and his long friendship with the dwarf, and of Balin's visit to the Shire long ago. In that dusty chamber in the mountains it seemed a thousand years ago and on the other side of the world.

At length they stirred and looked up, and began to search for anything that would give them tidings of Balin's fate, or show what had become of his folk. There was another smaller door on the other side of the chamber, under the shaft. By both the doors they could now see that many bones were lying, and among them were broken swords and axe-heads, and cloven shields and helms. Some of the swords were crooked: orc-scimitars with blackened blades.

There were many recesses cut in the rock of the walls, and in them were large iron-bound chests of wood. All had been broken and plundered; but beside the shattered lid of one there lay the remains of a book. It had been slashed and stabbed and partly burned, and it was so stained with black and other dark marks like old blood that little of it could be read. Gandalf lifted it carefully, but the leaves crackled and broke as he laid it on the slab. He pored over it for some time without speaking. Frodo and Gimli standing at his side could see, as he gingerly turned the leaves, that they were written by many different hands, in runes, both of Moria and of Dale, and here and there in Elvish script.

At last Gandalf looked up. 'It seems to be a record of the fortunes of Balin's folk,' he said. 'I guess that it began with their coming to Dimrill Dale nigh on thirty years ago: the pages seem to have numbers referring to the years after their arrival. The top page is marked *one–three,* so at least two are missing from the beginning. Listen to this!

'*We drove out orcs from the great gate and guard*—I suppose, but it is written *gard,* followed probably by *room—we slew many in the bright*—I think—*sun in the dale. Flói was killed by an arrow. He slew the great.* Then there is a blur followed by *Flói under grass near Mirror mere.* The next line or two I cannot read. Then comes *We have taken the twentyfirst hall of North end to dwell in. There is* I cannot read what. A *shaft* is mentioned. Then *Balin has set up his seat in the Chamber of Mazarbul.'*

'The Chamber of Records,' said Gimli. 'I guess that is where we now stand.'

'Well, I can read no more for a long way,' said Gandalf, 'except the word *gold,* and *Durin's Axe* and something *helm.* Then *Balin is now lord of Moria.* That seems to end a chapter. After some stars another hand begins, and I can see *we found truesilver,* and later the word *wellforged,* and then something, I have it! *mithril;* and the last two lines *Óin to seek for the upper armouries of Third Deep,* something *go westwards,* a blur, *to Hollin gate.'*

Gandalf paused and set a few leaves aside. 'There are several pages of the same sort, rather hastily written and much damaged,' he said; 'but I can make little of them in this light. Now there must be a number of leaves missing, because they begin to be numbered *five,* the fifth year of the colony, I suppose. Let me see! No, they are too cut and stained; I cannot read them. We might do better in the sunlight. Wait! Here is something: a large bold hand using an Elvish script.'

'That would be Ori's hand,' said Gimli, looking over the wizard's arm. 'He could write well and speedily, and often used the Elvish characters.'

'I fear he had ill tidings to record in a fair hand,' said Gandalf. 'The first clear word is *sorrow,* but the rest of the line is lost, unless it ends in *estre.* Yes, it must be *yestre* followed by *day being the tenth of novembre Balin lord of Moria fell in Dimrill Dale. He went alone to look in Mirror mere. an orc shot him from behind a stone. we slew the orc, but many more . . . up from east up the Silverlode.* The remainder of the page is so blurred that I can hardly make anything out, but I think I can read *we have barred the gates,* and then *can hold them long if,* and then perhaps *horrible* and *suffer.* Poor Balin! He seems to have kept the title that he took for less than five years. I wonder what happened afterwards; but there is no time to puzzle out the last few pages. Here is the last page of all.' He paused and sighed.

'It is grim reading,' he said. 'I fear their end was cruel. Listen!
*We cannot get out. We cannot get out. They have taken the Bridge
and second hall. Frár and Lóni and Náli fell there.* Then there are
four lines smeared so that I can only read *went 5 days ago.* The
last lines run *the pool is up to the wall at Westgate. The Watcher
in the Water took Óin. We cannot get out. The end comes,* and
then *drums, drums in the deep.* I wonder what that means. The last
thing written is in a trailing scrawl of elf-letters: *they are coming.*
There is nothing more.' Gandalf paused and stood in silent thought.

A sudden dread and a horror of the chamber fell on the Company. '*We cannot get out,*' muttered Gimli. 'It was well for us that
the pool had sunk a little, and that the Watcher was sleeping down
at the southern end.'

Gandalf raised his head and looked round. 'They seem to have
made a last stand by both doors,' he said; 'but there were not many
left by that time. So ended the attempt to retake Moria! It was valiant but foolish. The time is not come yet. Now, I fear, we must say
farewell to Balin son of Fundin. Here he must lie in the halls of his
fathers. We will take this book, the Book of Mazarbul, and look at
it more closely later. You had better keep it, Gimli, and take it back
to Dáin, if you get a chance. It will interest him, though it will
grieve him deeply. Come, let us go! The morning is passing.'

'Which way shall we go?' asked Boromir.

'Back to the hall,' answered Gandalf. 'But our visit to this room
has not been in vain. I now know where we are. This must be, as
Gimli says, the Chamber of Mazarbul; and the hall must be the
twenty-first of the North-end. Therefore we should leave by the
eastern arch of the hall, and bear right and south, and go downwards. The Twenty-first Hall should be on the Seventh Level, that
is six above the level of the Gates. Come now! Back to the hall!'

Gandalf had hardly spoken these words, when there came a great
noise: a rolling *Boom* that seemed to come from depths far below,
and to tremble in the stone at their feet. They sprang towards the
door in alarm. *Doom, doom* it rolled again, as if huge hands were
turning the very caverns of Moria into a vast drum. Then there
came an echoing blast: a great horn was blown in the hall, and answering horns and harsh cries were heard further off. There was
a hurrying sound of many feet.

'They are coming!' cried Legolas.

'We cannot get out,' said Gimli.

'Trapped!' cried Gandalf. 'Why did I delay? Here we are, caught, just as they were before. But I was not here then. We will see what——'

Doom, doom came the drum-beat and the walls shook.

'Slam the doors and wedge them!' shouted Aragorn. 'And keep your packs on as long as you can: we may get a chance to cut our way out yet.'

'No!' said Gandalf. 'We must not get shut in. Keep the east door ajar! We will go that way, if we get a chance.'

Another harsh horn-call and shrill cries rang out. Feet were coming down the corridor. There was a ring and clatter as the Company drew their swords. Glamdring shone with a pale light, and Sting glinted at the edges. Boromir set his shoulder against the western door.

'Wait a moment! Do not close it yet!' said Gandalf. He sprang forward to Boromir's side and drew himself up to his full height.

'Who comes hither to disturb the rest of Balin Lord of Moria?' he cried in a loud voice.

There was a rush of hoarse laughter, like the fall of sliding stones into a pit; amid the clamour a deep voice was raised in command. *Doom, boom, doom* went the drums in the deep.

With a quick movement Gandalf stepped before the narrow opening of the door and thrust forward his staff. There was a dazzling flash that lit the chamber and the passage outside. For an instant the wizard looked out. Arrows whined and whistled down the corridor as he sprang back.

'There are Orcs, very many of them,' he said. 'And some are large and evil: black Uruks of Mordor. For the moment they are hanging back, but there is something else there. A great cave-troll, I think, or more than one. There is no hope of escape that way.'

'And no hope at all, if they come at the other door as well,' said Boromir.

'There is no sound outside here yet,' said Aragorn, who was standing by the eastern door listening. 'The passage on this side plunges straight down a stair: it plainly does not lead back towards the hall. But it is no good flying blindly this way with the pursuit just behind. We cannot block the door. Its key is gone and the lock is broken, and it opens inwards. We must do something to delay the enemy first. We will make them fear the Chamber of Mazarbul!' he said grimly, feeling the edge of his sword, Andúril.

Heavy feet were heard in the corridor. Boromir flung himself against the door and heaved it to; then he wedged it with broken sword-blades and splinters of wood. The Company retreated to the other side of the chamber. But they had no chance to fly yet. There was a blow on the door that made it quiver; and then it began to grind slowly open, driving back the wedges. A huge arm and shoulder, with a dark skin of greenish scales, was thrust through the widening gap. Then a great, flat, toeless foot was forced through below. There was a dead silence outside.

Boromir leaped forward and hewed at the arm with all his might; but his sword rang, glanced aside, and fell from his shaken hand. The blade was notched.

Suddenly, and to his own surprise, Frodo felt a hot wrath blaze up in his heart. 'The Shire!' he cried, and springing beside Boromir, he stooped, and stabbed with Sting at the hideous foot. There was a bellow, and the foot jerked back, nearly wrenching Sting from Frodo's arm. Black drops dripped from the blade and smoked on the floor. Boromir hurled himself against the door and slammed it again.

'One for the Shire!' cried Aragorn. 'The hobbit's bite is deep! You have a good blade, Frodo son of Drogo!'

There was a crash on the door, followed by crash after crash. Rams and hammers were beating against it. It cracked and staggered back, and the opening grew suddenly wide. Arrows came whistling in, but struck the northern wall, and fell harmlessly to the floor. There was a horn-blast and a rush of feet, and orcs one after another leaped into the chamber.

How many there were the Company could not count. The affray was sharp, but the orcs were dismayed by the fierceness of the defence. Legolas shot two through the throat. Gimli hewed the legs from under another that had sprung up on Balin's tomb. Boromir and Aragorn slew many. When thirteen had fallen the rest fled shrieking, leaving the defenders unharmed, except for Sam who had a scratch along the scalp. A quick duck had saved him; and he had felled his orc: a sturdy thrust with his Barrow-blade. A fire was smouldering in his brown eyes that would have made Ted Sandyman step backwards, if he had seen it.

'Now is the time!' cried Gandalf. 'Let us go, before the troll returns!'

But even as they retreated, and before Pippin and Merry had reached the stair outside, a huge orc-chieftain, almost man-high,

clad in black mail from head to foot, leaped into the chamber;
behind him his followers clustered in the doorway. His broad flat
face was swart, his eyes were like coals, and his tongue was red; he
wielded a great spear. With a thrust of his huge hide shield he
turned Boromir's sword and bore him backwards, throwing him to
the ground. Diving under Aragorn's blow with the speed of a striking snake he charged into the Company and thrust with his spear
straight at Frodo. The blow caught him on the right side, and
Frodo was hurled against the wall and pinned. Sam, with a cry,
hacked at the spear-shaft, and it broke. But even as the orc flung
down the truncheon and swept out his scimitar, Andúril came down
upon his helm. There was a flash like flame and the helm burst
asunder. The orc fell with cloven head. His followers fled howling,
as Boromir and Aragorn sprang at them.

Doom, doom went the drums in the deep. The great voice rolled
out again.

'Now!' shouted Gandalf. 'Now is the last chance. Run for it!'

Aragorn picked up Frodo where he lay by the wall and made for
the stair, pushing Merry and Pippin in front of him. The others
followed; but Gimli had to be dragged away by Legolas: in spite of
the peril he lingered by Balin's tomb with his head bowed. Boromir
hauled the eastern door to, grinding upon its hinges: it had great
iron rings on either side, but could not be fastened.

'I am all right,' gasped Frodo. 'I can walk. Put me down!'

Aragorn nearly dropped him in his amazement. 'I thought you
were dead!' he cried.

'Not yet!' said Gandalf. 'But there is not time for wonder. Off you
go, all of you, down the stairs! Wait a few minutes for me at the
bottom, but if I do not come soon, go on! Go quickly and choose
paths leading right and downwards.'

'We cannot leave you to hold the door alone!' said Aragorn.

'Do as I say!' said Gandalf fiercely. 'Swords are no more use
here. Go!'

The passage was lit by no shaft and was utterly dark. They
groped their way down a long flight of steps, and then looked back;
but they could see nothing, except high above them the faint
glimmer of the wizard's staff. He seemed to be still standing on
guard by the closed door. Frodo breathed heavily and leaned
against Sam, who put his arms about him. They stood peering up
the stairs into the darkness. Frodo thought he could hear the voice

of Gandalf above, muttering words that ran down the sloping roof with a sighing echo. He could not catch what was said. The walls seemed to be trembling. Every now and again the drum-beats throbbed and rolled: *doom, doom.*

Suddenly at the top of the stair there was a stab of white light. Then there was a dull rumble and a heavy thud. The drum-beats broke out wildly: *doom-boom, doom-boom,* and then stopped. Gandalf came flying down the steps and fell to the ground in the midst of the Company.

'Well, well! That's over!' said the wizard struggling to his feet. 'I have done all that I could. But I have met my match, and have nearly been destroyed. But don't stand here! Go on! You will have to do without light for a while: I am rather shaken. Go on! Go on! Where are you, Gimli? Come ahead with me! Keep close behind, all of you!'

They stumbled after him wondering what had happened. *Doom, doom* went the drum-beats again: they now sounded muffled and far away, but they were following. There was no other sound of pursuit, neither tramp of feet, nor any voice. Gandalf took no turns right or left, for the passage seemed to be going in the direction that he desired. Every now and again it descended a flight of steps, fifty or more, to a lower level. At the moment that was their chief danger; for in the dark they could not see a descent, until they came on it and put their feet out into emptiness. Gandalf felt the ground with his staff like a blind man.

At the end of an hour they had gone a mile, or maybe a little more, and had descended many flights of stairs. There was still no sound of pursuit. Almost they began to hope that they would escape. At the bottom of the seventh flight Gandalf halted.

'It is getting hot!' he gasped. 'We ought to be down at least to the level of the Gates now. Soon I think we should look for a left-hand turn to take us east. I hope it is not far. I am very weary. I must rest here a moment, even if all the orcs ever spawned are after us.'

Gimli took his arm and helped him down to a seat on the step. 'What happened away up there at the door?' he asked. 'Did you meet the beater of the drums?'

'I do not know,' answered Gandalf. 'But I found myself suddenly faced by something that I have not met before. I could think of nothing to do but to try and put a shutting-spell on the door. I know many; but to do things of that kind rightly requires time, and even then the door can be broken by strength.

'As I stood there I could hear orc-voices on the other side: at any moment I thought they would burst it open. I could not hear what was said; they seemed to be talking in their own hideous language. All I caught was *ghâsh:* that is 'fire'. Then something came into the chamber—I felt it through the door, and the orcs themselves were afraid and fell silent. It laid hold of the iron ring, and then it perceived me and my spell.

'What it was I cannot guess, but I have never felt such a challenge. The counter-spell was terrible. It nearly broke me. For an instant the door left my control and began to open! I had to speak a word of Command. That proved too great a strain. The door burst in pieces. Something dark as a cloud was blocking out all the light inside, and I was thrown backwards down the stairs. All the wall gave way, and the roof the chamber as well, I think.

'I am afraid Balin is buried deep, and maybe something else is buried there too. I cannot say. But at least the passage behind us was completely blocked. Ah! I have never felt so spent, but it is passing. And now what about you, Frodo? There was not time to say so, but I have never been more delighted in my life than when you spoke. I feared that it was a brave but dead hobbit that Aragorn was carrying.'

'What about me?' said Frodo. 'I am alive, and whole I think. I am bruised and in pain, but it is not too bad.'

'Well,' said Aragorn, 'I can only say that hobbits are made of a stuff so tough that I have never met the like of it. Had I known, I would have spoken softer in the Inn at Bree! That spear-thrust would have skewered a wild boar!'

'Well, it did not skewer me, I am glad to say,' said Frodo; 'though I feel as if I had been caught between a hammer and an anvil.' He said no more. He found breathing painful.

'You take after Bilbo,' said Gandalf. 'There is more about you than meets the eye, as I said of him long ago.' Frodo wondered if the remark meant more than it said.

They now went on again. Before long Gimli spoke. He had keen eyes in the dark. 'I think,' he said, 'that there is a light ahead. But it is not daylight. It is red. What can it be?'

'*Ghâsh!*' muttered Gandalf. 'I wonder if that is what they meant: that the lower levels are on fire? Still, we can only go on.'

Soon the light became unmistakable, and could be seen by all. It was flickering and glowing on the walls away down the passage before them. They could now see their way: in front the road sloped down swiftly, and some way ahead there stood a low archway; through it the growing light came. The air became very hot.

When they came to the arch Gandalf went through, signing to them to wait. As he stood just beyond the opening they saw his face lit by a red glow. Quickly he stepped back.

'There is some new devilry here,' he said, 'devised for our welcome, no doubt. But I know where we are: we have reached the First Deep, the level immediately below the Gates. This is the Second Hall of Old Moria; and the Gates are near: away beyond the eastern end, on the left, not more than a quarter of a mile. Across the bridge, up a broad stair, along a wide road, through the First Hall, and out! But come and look!'

They peered out. Before them was another cavernous hall. It was loftier and far longer than the one in which they had slept. They were near its eastern end; westward it ran away into darkness. Down the centre stalked a double line of towering pillars. They were carved like boles of mighty trees whose boughs upheld the roof with a branching tracery of stone. Their stems were smooth and black, but a red glow was darkly mirrored in their sides. Right across the floor, close to the feet of two huge pillars a great fissure had opened. Out of it a fierce red light came, and now and again flames licked at the brink and curled about the bases of the columns. Wisps of dark smoke wavered in the hot air.

'If we had come by the main road down from the upper halls, we should have been trapped here,' said Gandalf. 'Let us hope that the fire now lies between us and pursuit. Come! There is no time to lose.'

Even as he spoke they heard again the pursuing drum-beat: *Doom, doom, doom.* Away beyond the shadows at the western end of the hall there came cries and horn-calls. *Doom, doom:* the pillars seemed to tremble and the flames to quiver.

'Now for the last race!' said Gandalf. 'If the sun is shining outside, we may still escape. After me!'

He turned left and sped across the smooth floor of the hall. The distance was greater than it had looked. As they ran they heard the beat and echo of many hurrying feet behind. A shrill yell went up, they had been seen. There was a ring and clash of steel. An arrow whistled over Frodo's head.

Boromir laughed. 'They did not expect this,' he said. 'The fire has cut them off. We are on the wrong side!'

'Look ahead!' called Gandalf. 'The Bridge is near. It is dangerous and narrow.'

Suddenly Frodo saw before him a black chasm. At the end of the hall the floor vanished and fell to an unknown depth. The outer door could only be reached by a slender bridge of stone, without kerb or rail, that spanned the chasm with one curving spring of fifty feet. It was an ancient defence of the Dwarves against any enemy that might capture the First Hall and the outer passages. They could only pass across it in single file. At the brink Gandalf halted and the others came up in a pack behind.

'Lead the way, Gimli!' he said. 'Pippin and Merry next. Straight on, and up the stair beyond the door!'

Arrows fell among them. One struck Frodo and sprang back. Another pierced Gandalf's hat and stuck there like a black feather. Frodo looked behind. Beyond the fire he saw swarming black figures: there seemed to be hundreds of orcs. They brandished spears and scimitars which shone red as blood in the firelight. *Doom, doom* rolled the drum-beats, growing louder and louder, *doom, doom.*

Legolas turned and set an arrow to the string, though it was a long shot for his small bow. He drew, but his hand fell, and the arrow slipped to the ground. He gave a cry of dismay and fear. Two great trolls appeared; they bore great slabs of stone, and flung them down to serve as gangways over the fire. But it was not the trolls that had filled the Elf with terror. The ranks of the orcs had opened, and they crowded away, as if they themselves were afraid. Something was coming up behind them. What it was could not be seen: it was like a great shadow, in the middle of which was a dark form, of man-shape maybe, yet greater; and a power and terror seemed to be in it and to go before it.

It came to the edge of the fire and the light faded as if a cloud had bent over it. Then with a rush it leaped across the fissure. The flames roared up to greet it, and wreathed about it; and a black smoke swirled in the air. Its streaming mane kindled, and blazed behind it. In its right hand was a blade like a stabbing tongue of fire; in its left it held a whip of many thongs.

'Ai! ai!' wailed Legolas. 'A Balrog! A Balrog is come!'

Gimli stared with wide eyes. 'Durin's Bane!' he cried, and letting his axe fall he covered his face.

'A Balrog,' muttered Gandalf. 'Now I understand.' He faltered and leaned heavily on his staff. 'What an evil fortune! And I am already weary.'

The dark figure streaming with fire raced towards them. The orcs yelled and poured over the stone gangways. Then Boromir raised his horn and blew. Loud the challenge rang and bellowed, like the shout of many throats under the cavernous roof. For a moment the orcs quailed and the fiery shadow halted. Then the echoes died as suddenly as a flame blown out by a dark wind, and the enemy advanced again.

'Over the bridge!' cried Gandalf, recalling his strength. 'Fly! This is a foe beyond any of you. I must hold the narrow way. Fly!' Aragorn and Boromir did not heed the command, but still held their ground, side by side, behind Gandalf at the far end of the bridge. The others halted just within the doorway at the hall's end, and turned, unable to leave their leader to face the enemy alone.

The Balrog reached the bridge. Gandalf stood in the middle of the span, leaning on the staff in his left hand, but in his other hand Glamdring gleamed, cold and white. His enemy halted again, facing him, and the shadow about it reached out like two vast wings. It raised the whip, and the thongs whined and cracked. Fire came from its nostrils. But Gandalf stood firm.

'You cannot pass,' he said. The orcs stood still, and a dead silence fell. 'I am a servant of the Secret Fire, wielder of the flame of Anor. You cannot pass. The dark fire will not avail you, flame of Udûn. Go back to the Shadow! You cannot pass.'

The Balrog made no answer. The fire in it seemed to die, but the darkness grew. It stepped forward slowly on to the bridge, and suddenly it drew itself up to a great height, and its wings were spread from wall to wall; but still Gandalf could be seen, glimmering in the gloom; he seemed small, and altogether alone: grey and bent, like a wizened tree before the onset of a storm.

From out of the shadow a red sword leaped flaming.

Glamdring glittered white in answer.

There was a ringing clash and a stab of white fire. The Balrog fell back and its sword flew up in molten fragments. The wizard swayed on the bridge, stepped back a pace, and then again stood still.

'You cannot pass!' he said.

With a bound the Balrog leaped full upon the bridge. Its whip whirled and hissed.

'He cannot stand alone!' cried Aragorn suddenly and ran back along the bridge. 'Elendil!' he shouted. 'I am with you, Gandalf!'

'Gondor!' cried Boromir and leaped after him.

At that moment Gandalf lifted his staff, and crying aloud he smote the bridge before him. The staff broke asunder and fell from his hand. A blinding sheet of white flame sprang up. The bridge cracked. Right at the Balrog's feet it broke, and the stone upon which it stood crashed into the gulf, while the rest remained, poised, quivering like a tongue of rock thrust out into emptiness.

With a terrible cry the Balrog fell forward, and its shadow plunged down and vanished. But even as it fell it swung its whip, and the thongs lashed and curled about the wizard's knees, dragging him to the brink. He staggered and fell, grasped vainly at the stone, and slid into the abyss. 'Fly, you fools!' he cried, and was gone.

RICHARD ADAMS

SINCE the three volumes of *The Lord of the Rings* were published in the early years of the 1950s, many a newcomer has appeared whose vision has been shaped or influenced by Tolkien. Without exception, their publishers have hailed the appearance of each of these new fantasy writers as "another Tolkien."

But it remained for a British writer named Richard Adams to write the most popular and successful epic fantasy since *The Lord of the Rings*. His book, *Watership Down*, was published in London in 1972 and promptly became the surprise hit of the publishing season, carrying off the Carnegie Medal and the Guardian Award. Published in America the following year, it became a runaway bestseller and hovered for weeks and weeks and weeks near the top of the *Times*' list. It shows every sign of staying in print forever.

A fate, moreover, which it richly deserves: for it is a gripping, powerful, ingenious, and enthralling story of heroism and courage and survival. The story is so thoroughly fascinating that, even at 430 pages, it is difficult to put down and virtually demands to be read at a single setting. This I know for a fact, because that's the way *I* first read it.

Which is all the more surprising, since the book is about *rabbits*. And not your cutesy-poo humanized rabbits, got up in *pince-nez* and waistcoats like fugitives from Beatrix Potter or Kenneth Grahame, either; but real rabbits—animals, living the life of the hunted, seeking safety and a snug refuge in the modern-day, distinctly *un*magical English countryside.

In many ways, the world of *Watership Down* has nothing in common with the other kingdoms of sorcery we have explored together in this book. There is no magic here, no wizardry, no gods or demons; what "magic" there is in *Watership Down* is the old, familiar, yet rare and always wonderful magic—the magic of storytelling, of a really strong story told really well.

But among the folklore of Mr. Adams' Lapine characters are a number of rabbitish fables and legends which his characters tell to each other throughout the course of the story. I have selected one of the best of them to reprint here, for its first time in an anthology. But not its last, I imagine.

THE STORY OF THE BLESSING OF EL-AHRAIRAH

Why should he think me cruel
Or that he is betrayed?
I'd have him love the thing that was
Before the world was made.

W. B. Yeats,
A Woman Young and Old

"LONG ago, Frith made the world. He made all the stars, too, and the world is one of the stars. He made them by scattering his droppings over the sky and this is why the grass and the trees grow so thick on the world. Frith makes the rivers flow. They follow him as he goes through the sky, and when he leaves the sky they look for him all night. Frith made all the animals and birds, but when he first made them they were all the same. The sparrow and the kestrel were friends and they both ate seeds and flies. And the fox and the rabbit were friends and they both ate grass. And there was plenty of grass and plenty of flies, because the world was new and Frith shone down bright and warm all day.

"Now, El-ahrairah was among the animals in those days and he had many wives. He had so many wives that there was no counting them, and the wives had so many young that even Frith could not count them, and they ate the grass and the dandelions and the lettuces and the clover, and El-ahrairah was the father of them all." (Bigwig growled appreciatively.) "And after a time," went on Dandelion, "after a time the grass began to grow thin and the rabbits wandered everywhere, multiplying and eating as they went.

"Then Frith said to El-ahrairah, 'Prince Rabbit, if you cannot control your people, I shall find ways to control them. So mark what I say.' But El-ahrairah would not listen and he said to Frith, 'My people are the strongest in the world, for they breed faster and eat more than any of the other people. And this shows how much they love Lord Frith, for of all the animals they are the most responsive to his warmth and brightness. You must realize, my lord, how important they are and not hinder them in their beautiful lives.'

"Frith could have killed El-ahrairah at once, but he had a mind to keep him in the world, because he needed him to sport and jest and play tricks. So he determined to get the better of him, not by means of his own great power but by means of a trick. He gave out that he would hold a great meeting and that at that meeting he would give a present to every animal and bird, to make each one different from the rest. And all the creatures set out to go to the meeting place. But they all arrived at different times, because Frith made sure that it would happen so. And when the blackbird came, he gave him his beautiful song, and when the cow came, he gave her sharp horns and the strength to be afraid of no other creature. And so in their turn came the fox and the stoat and the weasel. And to each of them Frith gave the cunning and the fierceness and the desire to hunt and slay and eat the children of El-ahrairah. And so they went away from Frith full of nothing but hunger to kill the rabbits.

"Now, all this time El-ahrairah was dancing and mating and

boasting that he was going to Frith's meeting to receive a great gift. And at last he set out for the meeting place. But as he was going there, he stopped to rest on a soft, sandy hillside. And while he was resting, over the hill came flying the dark swift, screaming as he went, 'News! News! News!' For you know, this is what he has said ever since that day. So El-ahrairah called up to him and said, 'What news?' 'Why,' said the swift, 'I would not be you, El-ahrairah. For Frith has given the fox and the weasel cunning hearts and sharp teeth, and to the cat he has given silent feet and eyes that can see in the dark, and they are gone away from Frith's place to kill and devour all that belongs to El-ahrairah.' And he dashed on over the hills. And at that moment El-ahrairah heard the voice of Frith calling, 'Where is El-ahrairah? For all the others have taken their gifts and gone and I have come to look for him.'

"Then El-ahrairah knew that Frith was too clever for him and he was frightened. He thought that the fox and the weasel were coming with Frith and he turned to the face of the hill and began to dig. He dug a hole, but he had dug only a little of it when Frith came over the hill alone. And he saw El-ahrairah's bottom sticking out of the hole and the sand flying out in showers as the digging went on. When he saw that, he called out, 'My friend, have you seen El-ahrairah, for I am looking for him to give him my gift?' 'No,' answered El-ahrairah, without coming out, 'I have not seen him. He is far away. He could not come.' So Frith said, 'Then come out of that hole and I will bless you instead of him.' 'No, I cannot,' said El-ahrairah, 'I am busy. The fox and the weasel are coming. If you want to bless me you can bless my bottom, for it is sticking out of the hole.'"

All the rabbits had heard the story before: on winter nights, when the cold draft moved down the warren passages and the icy wet lay in the pits of the runs below their burrows; and on summer evenings, in the grass under the red may and the sweet, carrion-scented elder bloom. Dandelion was telling it well, and even Pipkin forgot his weariness and danger and remembered instead the great indestructibility of the rabbits. Each one of them saw himself as El-ahrairah, who could be impudent to Frith and get away with it.

"Then," said Dandelion, "Frith felt himself in friendship with El-ahrairah, because of his resourcefulness, and because he would not give up even when he thought the fox and the weasel were coming. And he said, 'Very well, I will bless your bottom as it sticks out of the hole. Bottom, be strength and warning and speed forever and save the life of your master. Be it so!' And as he spoke, El-ahrairah's tail grew shining white and flashed like a star: and his back legs grew long and powerful and he thumped the hillside until the very beetles fell off the grass stems. He came out of the hole and tore across the hill faster than any creature in the world. And Frith called after him, 'El-ahrairah, your people cannot rule the world, for I will not have it so. All the world will be your enemy, Prince with a Thousand Enemies, and whenever they catch you, they will kill you. But first they must catch you, digger, listener, runner, prince with the swift warning. Be cunning and full of tricks and your people shall never be destroyed.' And El-ahrairah knew then that although he would not be mocked, yet Frith was his friend. And every evening, when Frith has done his day's work and lies calm and easy in the red sky, El-ahrairah and his children and his children's children come out of their holes and feed and play in his sight, for they are his friends and he has promised them that they can never be destroyed."

More
Magic
Casements

SUGGESTIONS FOR
FURTHER READING

IF you enjoyed the selections in this book and would like to sample the work of all or any of the authors herein represented with further reading, these suggestions may save you considerable time and effort by aiming you directly at the best available novels and stories.

1. WILLIAM BECKFORD   Beckford's only fantasy novel—his only novel of any description, in fact—is the immortal *Vathek*. It is recommended without reservations; a splendid and delicious book! Beckford also wrote three briefer episodes which he meant to be inserted into the text of *Vathek* at the appropriate places; for reasons I can't even guess, no editor of *Vathek* ever put them in until I edited a *Vathek* for the Ballantine Adult Fantasy Series in 1971. This edition is probably out of print by now, but you might try searching for it, anyway. (The easiest way to find out if a book is in print is *not* to ask people in bookstores—they never know anything. Instead, look the title up in a standard reference

work called *Books in Print*. Most libraries and bookstores ought to have a current copy behind the counter for their own use. Ask to see it. There is a supplementary volume called *Paperback Books in Print*.)

With considerable hunting around, and more than a bit of luck, you might be able to find the episodes, anyway. They were published in hardcover under the obvious title *The Episodes of Vathek*. My edition was published in Great Britain by Chapman & Dodd.

2. LIN CARTER　If I had to think of two or three of my books I could most unhesitatingly recommend, I would list *The Wizard of World's End*, a paperback from DAW Books, which is the first in a series of heroic fantasy novels (with a considerable element of humor spooned in for spice); and *The Valley Where Time Stood Still*, a hardcover from Doubleday, which is really a sort of A. Merritt lost-race fantasy disguised as a kind of Leigh Brackett science fiction adventure story set on Mars; or *Under the Green Star*, also a DAW paperback, and the first of a series. But those are just personal choices.

3. L. SPRAGUE DE CAMP　Back in the 1940s, de Camp collaborated with Fletcher Pratt on a series of delightful fantasies in which a couple of modern-day psychologists travel via symbolic logic to fantasy worlds and figure out the laws of magic on a strictly scientific basis. These books were titled *The Incomplete Enchanter, Castle of Iron* and *Wall of Serpents;* they were all in hardcover, and all but the last was in paperback. All are now out of print in any edition, alas, but look for them in secondhand shops and maybe you'll get lucky.

More recently, de Camp has been writing some new fantasy novels for Pyramid Books, a paperback firm. These are called *The Goblin Tower, The Clocks of Iraz,* and *The Feckless Fiend*. They are all marvelously entertaining.

4. E. R. EDDISON　The one thing to read by Eddison, if you read nothing else, is *The Worm Ouroboros,* probably the finest fantasy novel of its type ever written. Dutton did a hardcover edition of the novel most recently in 1952, but the book is currently in print from Ballantine in paperback. The book has three siblings (not quite sequels, or even "prequels"), beginning with *Mistress of Mistresses*. These are richly written but complex, philosophical, and on the whole less fun to read. Go to them *only* if the Worm

absolutely blows your mind. Ballantine has them all in paperback.

5. FRITZ LEIBER His only fantasies are the famous Fafhrd and the
Gray Mouser stories. A paperback firm called Ace Books has
them in print in a number of books with titles like *Swords of
Lankhmar, Swords Against Death,* and so on. You can't miss 'em.
They have never been in hardcover, in this country, at least.
Don't ask me why.

6. C. S. LEWIS A number of his books are fantasies, but in some
(like *Perelandra,* or *The Screwtape Letters,* or *The Great Divorce*) the fantasy element is adulterated with science fiction, or
theological or philosophical speculation, and may not be quite to
your taste. The most reliably entertaining pure fantasies among
Lewis' works are his Narnia books, of which *The Lion, the Witch,
and the Wardrobe* was the first and is the book you should try
first. They are all in print in hardcover from Macmillan and in
paperback from Collier Books. A boxed set is currently available.
And they're scrumptious.

7. GEORGE MACDONALD The two great "faërie romances," *Lilith* and
Phantastes, are available from Ballantine. Most people feel that,
of the two, *Lilith* is superior. MacDonald's children's books, *At
the Back of the North Wind* and *The Princess and the Goblin,*
can be found in a number of editions, as can his rather mystical
and Kafkaesque fairy tales, such as *The Golden Key,* which is
available in a handsome edition from Farrar, Straus & Giroux,
with pictures by Maurice Sendak and an afterword by W. H.
Auden.

8. WILLIAM MORRIS His one, great, indispensable masterpiece is a
gigantic prose romance called *The Well at the World's End,*
which was the most lengthy and ambitious epic fantasy written
before Tolkien. I don't think the book has been published in
hardcover since about 1910, but you can find it in a Ballantine
paperback, or rather in two, since we did it in matching volumes
due to its length. His other romances are simply more of the
same, but on a less ambitious scale.

9. EDGAR ALLAN POE Besides "Silence" and "Shadow," Poe wrote a
third prose poem called "Eleonora." There are a few other works
by Poe which have much to offer the fantasy buff; if you can put
aside your preconceptions about his being simply an author of
horror stories, you will find a strange, haunting, legend-like
beauty in such tales as "Ligeia," "The Masque of the Red

Death," and a very unusual narrative whose style and concept are comparable to Dunsany—"The Domain of Arnheim."

10. FLETCHER PRATT Pratt wrote two of the most brilliant, mature, realistic and thoroughly original fantasy novels ever written. Both are minor masterpieces; one, *The Well of the Unicorn,* may even be a major one. It was published in hardcover in a beautiful edition by William Sloane, and has only recently become hard to find. The paperback edition by Lancer Books must be out of print by now, since the firm is out of business. The second novel, *The Blue Star,* appeared in a hardcover from Twayne called *Witches Three,* with two stories by other authors. The paperback from Ballantine may still be in print. These are the best fantasies Pratt ever wrote, either solo or with de Camp; they are among the best fantasies anybody has ever written.

11. CLARK ASHTON SMITH Smith wrote bejeweled, ornate legends of Hyperborea and Atlantis and Xiccarph and Zothique, as well as modern-scene horror tales in the Cthulhu Mythos, and even some fairly primitive science fiction. A hardcover publisher named Arkham House put together hodgepodge-type collections made up of stories from his different series all jumbled together without rhyme or reason. The first of these collections was *Out of Space and Time* (1942), followed by *Lost Worlds* (1944), *Genius Loci* (1948), *The Abominations of Yondo* (1960), *Tales of Science and Sorcery* (1964), and others. These books had extremely small printings and are almost impossible to find, since Arkham House books become automatic collector's items whose value escalates astronomically as soon as they are out of print. A copy of *Out of Space and Time* might cost you upwards of a hundred dollars—*if* you could find one for sale.

For Ballantine's Adult Fantasy Series, I edited Smith's fantasy series and related tales into individual volumes called *Zothique, Hyperborea, Poseidonis,* and *Xiccarph.* There was to have been a fifth volume called *Malneánt,* but it was canceled. These paperbacks are all out of print by now, and will be hard to find. But Smith is worth hunting for.

12. J. R. R. TOLKIEN *The Lord of the Rings* is the greatest and most successful fantasy novel of our time, but its length (more than a quarter of a million words) makes it rather intimidating to some readers; also it starts very slowly and a lot of readers probably throw in the towel after the first fifty pages. A more accessible entrée into Tolkien is *The Hobbit,* ostensibly a children's book—

but don't let that bother you. Try it first; if you find it to your taste, tackle the trilogy. These are in hardcover from Houghton Mifflin and in paperback from Ballantine.

And don't overlook *Farmer Giles of Ham,* one of the most enjoyable of modern fairy tales.

13. VOLTAIRE   The longer romances of Voltaire are among the most delectable fantasies in all of literature, written in a graceful style, elegant, witty, with a sharp edge to them. Search for *Zadig, The White Bull,* and *The Princess of Babylon,* for they are his finest works in this genre. A one-volume "collected works" is the place to look. Far easier to find and more readily accessible is his *Candide,* but I can't really recommend it since I find it tedious, humorless, and boring.

14. T. H. WHITE   To my taste, White is an infinitely better fantasy author than Tolkien or Lewis. But that's only my taste, so take it for what it's worth. The single indispensable book is *The Sword in the Stone,* still in paperback from Dell. The hardcover edition from Putnam is long out of print, but can still be found in secondhand bookstores, as can the sequel, *The Witch in the Wood,* which is almost but not quite as good.

If you are so unfortunate as to live in environs devoid of secondhand bookstores, you will probably have to settle for *The Once and Future King,* which can be had from Putnam. This is a brilliant and powerful and beautiful and very funny book in its own right, but since White cut down and partially rewrote the first two books for their appearance in the omnibus volume, and in so doing eliminated some of the very best passages and scenes, I recommend the original versions over the rewritten one-volume edition.

Having read these, if you appreciate White's genius for humor and feeling for his period and his people as much as I do, you will want to search out some of his other novels, such as *Mistress Masham's Repose* and *The Master.* They may be tough to find, but the finding of them will be enormously rewarding, I promise you.

IT was not possible to include—even in a book this size—all of the important masters of modern fantasy.

For that reason, I have created another anthology as big as this one, called *Realms of Wizardry.* Therein you will find rare, unusual works by Lord Dunsany, H. P. Lovecraft, Robert Bloch, James Branch Cabell, Donald Corley, H. Rider Haggard, A. Merritt, Hannes Bok, Robert E. Howard, C. L. Moore, Henry Kuttner, Clifford Ball, Jack Vance, Michael Moorcock, and Roger Zelazny.

If *Kingdoms of Sorcery* stimulates your appetite for the fantastic romance, you may wish to explore my *Realms of Wizardry* as well.

The world of modern fantasy is very largely an undiscovered country as far as hardcover publishing goes. This book, for instance, is the first anthology of its kind to appear between hardcovers. I claim no particular credit for being the first editor to create an anthology such as this. It's the sort of book that ought to have been available to libraries and schools a quarter of a century ago, when I was a young reader just setting forth on my own voyage of discovery through these enchanted—and enchanting—realms.

But no such book existed then, and I had to find my way to these "kingdoms of sorcery" without even a map to guide me.

So this book came into being for one of the best reasons in the world: because it was a book I wanted to read and own and learn from, myself. Since no one else had done it, I had to create it.

I suspect that many of the books I love most came into being in that same way, for that same reason.

—*Lin Carter*